# THE CRIMSON TRAVELER

Vol. 1

A Novel

by

MATT STROLLO

LEFT FIELD PUBLISHING
EXPLORING UNCHARTED CREATIVITY
EST 2024
LITTLETON · COLORADO

# COPYRIGHT



First published in the United States of America, September 2026 by

Left Field Publishing.

ISBN: 9781966883098



Library of Congress Control Number: 2026903917

Book Cover by Kristen Gilligan

Printed in the United States of America

# DEDICATION

For my grandmother, Carolyn McGill Almassy.

The woman who showed me the impact a story can have.

May she rest in peace.

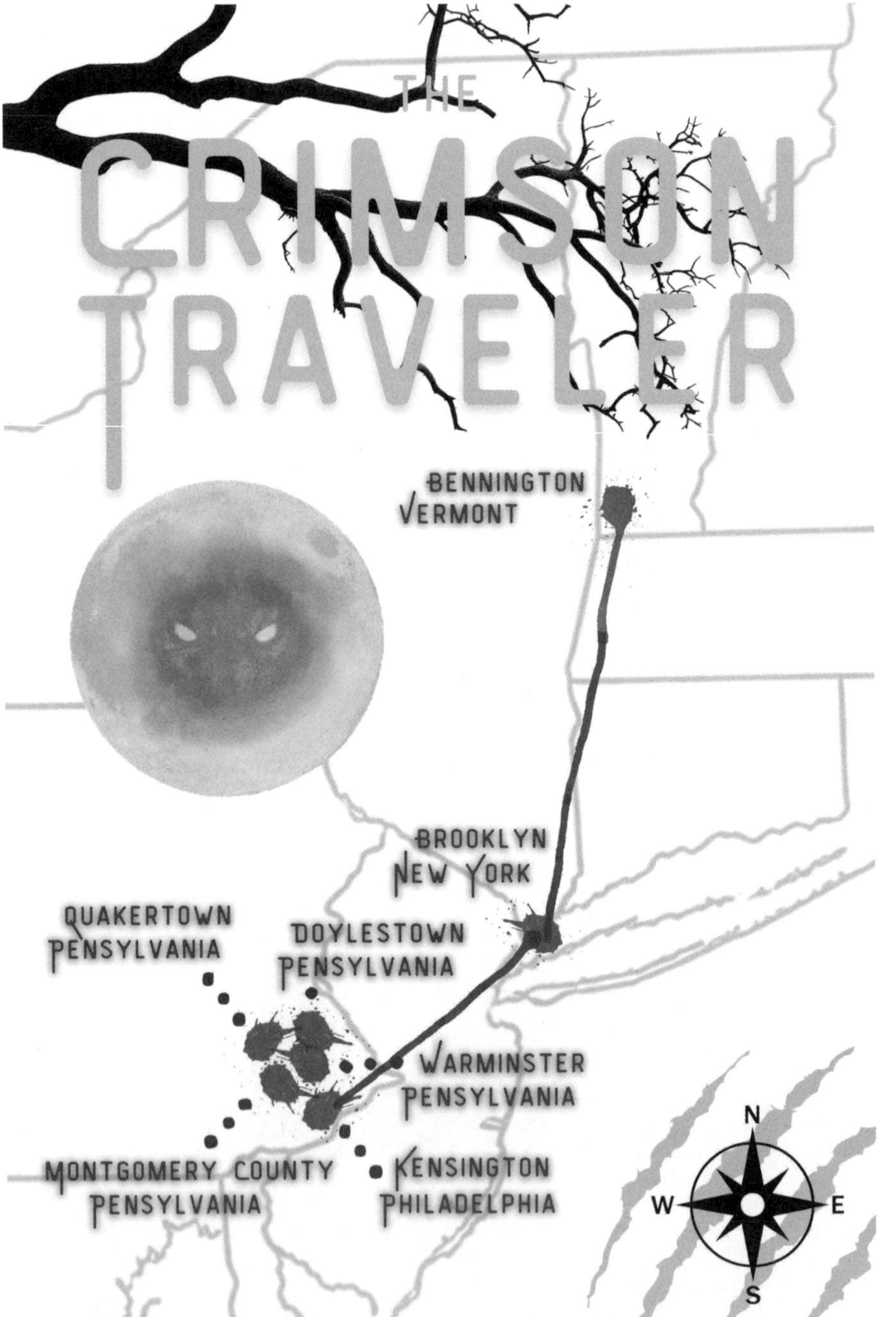
THE
CRIMSON
TRAVELER
BENNINGTON
VERMONT
BROOKLYN
NEW YORK
QUAKERTOWN
PENSYLVANIA
DOYLESTOWN
PENSYLVANIA
WARMINSTER
PENSYLVANIA
MONTGOMERY COUNTY
PENSYLVANIA
KENSINGTON
PHILADELPHIA
N
W
E
S

# DRAMATIS PERSONAE

**Alexandra Elizabeth "Liz" Campbell** – A former Marine Sergeant, now a heroin addict

**Macy Burkhardt** – A mechanic, hauling ghosts from her childhood

**Desmond O'Connell** – A red-eyed Wolf King

**Ben** – Conscience and confidante to the Wolf King

**Cameron Brooks** – A former Marine Corporal, now a drug dealer

**Serita** – Liz's bunkmate, a fellow addict

**Joe Burkhardt** – Macy's father

**Sarah** – One of Macy's ghosts

**Princess Layla** – Brooks' feral fling

**Arthur** – A giant, Brooks' bodyguard

**John Becker Jr.** – An ambitious wolf under Desmond

**John Becker Sr.** – Loyal, but dead

**Young Harry** – A promising pup under Junior

**Ringo** – An oaf

**Pedro** – A dog

# PROLOGUE

*Derbyshire, England*

## 1998

The red-eyed man stood at the precipice of the Shivering Mountain, overlooking Castleton and its winding crannies. It hardly warmed him the way it once had, the crowning chills of the approaching winter shook his bones. Rainwater had seeped into the gritstone beneath his feet, softening the shale, plummeting layers of sod and rock to the valley below.

His skin was the dark gray of chimney soot. The ashes of his family home fastened to him like ink. He dared not remove them. He thought it most apt to carry the remains of his brothers with him to the void.

*Best hurry off now, before the rains wash me of my crime.*

He kicked a pebble from the edge, fixating on it as it chipped and rolled its way to Mam Tor's base. The fall would kill him, he was certain. Behind him, his brothers' souls wept, hissing with dying embers of the fire that had taken their lives. He couldn't stomach it, the anguish in their screams and, perhaps worse, the silence that followed.

*My atonement awaits in hell.*

He stepped from the edge, sure as a man boarding an East Midlands train for his job in London. He thought his breath would leave him with his footing, but the fall was graceful, a feather on an early evening breeze. He thought of King Aegeus of Greek lore, who leapt from Cape Sounion when he mistook his son for dead. If only the deaths of his family were a mistake, some tragic dream from which he'd awaken at the bottom of the mountain.

When the red-eyed man met the Earth below, he did not die, though he longed for it with every blood-curdling wail he sent to the gods. His femurs had broken outward, bowing his legs like hideous malformations. His spine had nearly transected, several vertebrae bulging out of place. Reflex had brought his left arm behind him, where it dislocated and bent ninety degrees in the wrong direction.

He thought of Christ's torment at Golgotha, hauling the cypress and cedar of his execution, whips snapping, stripping him of flesh and sinew.

The red-eyed man righted his arm first, setting the bone with a howl to the heavens. In seconds, it was healed. Next, he pushed his spine into place and the feeling in his legs returned to him. *Moron.* The pain from his broken femurs agonized him. Quickly, he set his left leg, then shifted to his right, tears and snot and saliva dribbling from his face. He was whole again. With cuts, scrapes and bruises gone from him, he stood and stretched, howling once more into the late autumn clouds.

He found a creek nearby and drank from it, shaking all memory of the pain that had just bludgeoned him, of the atrocity he'd committed at his family home. He wondered why he still drew breath, why Hell had spat him from its depths. As he pondered, he spotted a wolf wandering across the moors. The remains of a rabbit dangled from its dripping jaws, twitching with memories of the day's errand. The wolf had been displaced by the fire, yet it didn't wait to hunt anew. It turned and locked a feral stare with the red-eyed man. The man changed his face. His ears morphed to points, eyes glowed, cheeks sprouted with hair, lips parted with fangs. It had been years since he'd been challenged by a pure wolf. *Thank you.* The animal had awakened him, washed him of his self-loathing.

With an icy breeze, the animal turned to go, disappearing over Lose Hill's sprawling peak. The exchange had been profound for the man, more than the animal would ever know. *A lone wolf is only lost if he chooses to be.*

He reckoned he'd have a drink.

He met his right hand, Becker, at Ye Olde Dolphin Inn, sipping stout and stew interchangeably. The barman, Jerry, noticed him first. "Oi, Des!" He pointed. "Hermitage on ice, then?"

Becker's head snapped to him.

"Nah…" Des sat to join his mate, noting his beverage and the faint lingering smell of ash. "Guinness."

"Very well." Jerry hopped to his task.

Becker stayed with his stew as a grin tugged his lips. "Here I sit, preparing a toast in your memory."

Des could only giggle. He'd told his friend to leave him at the hill after the fire. He didn't fancy an audience for his suicide. "Worried you'd have me sounding like a twat. Thought I'd come and supervise."

"What changed your mind?"

The horrid pain of his fall returned to him for a beat. "Nothing. I leapt from the bloody cliff, bent myself in all directions…the void wouldn't take me."

Jerry set Des' ale on the bar for him. "Cheers, mate."

Becker lifted his own. "Well, then…to your passing."

Des clinked his glass. They shared silence to enjoy the hops before Des continued. "You haven't washed. I can smell the flames on ya."

"Thought it better I have a drink first. Draft a proper eulogy."

Des considered the aftermath of the burning. They'd surely left enough signs for the constable to consider arson. "You should wash."

Becker nodded and sipped again. "So, now you've been reborn, what's the move for us?"

"Word'll get to Derby about the fire. Rumors spread 'round this pit like plague." He thought of the big shots around Derby who'd be miffed at his family's demise. "Who do you reckon would stay loyal to me, given my recent actions?"

Becker stirred his spoon in his stew. "The Deacon and his lot are solid. They'll do as they're told." The Deacon was one of the few surviving members of the Buxton Mafia, the gang who owned the Peak Fringe before Des and his family put them out. "Of course, my son will stand by us."

Des thought he might burst with laughter. *The brat who burns ants at the manor? Lights firecrackers in the church confessionals? What an asset.*

"The rest…" Becker shrugged and slurped his brown. "Your family was dear to them."

"And not to *me*?"

"Their shops were protected and their pockets were full."

The man had a fair point. Without the O'Connells running things, the other gangs would fight over scraps, and the commonfolk in Derby would come out worse for wear.

Perhaps a change of scenery was in order. He feared the guilt would swallow him here if he let it. He knew of a few syndicates in America, as much as the idea of that slop hole pained him. He might be able to occupy one, rebuild an operation similar to what the O'Connells had made in Derby.

*One suicide failed. Perhaps I'll try another.*

Des pitched his conclusion to Becker. "So, we comb the city for blokes who'll stand by us…" He truly hoped there'd be more than he feared. "…And make for another shore."

# STAGE I

"I have absolutely no pleasure in the stimulants in which I sometimes so madly indulge. It has not been in the pursuit of pleasure that I have periled life and reputation and reason. It has been in the desperate attempt to escape from torturing memories, from a sense of insupportable loneliness and a dread of some strange impending doom."

-Edgar Allan Poe

# CHAPTER ONE

## Liz

*Philadelphia, Pennsylvania*

**2010 (Present Day)**

In an abscess, deep within the city's colon, sleep found her in erratic bursts. The hall of her nightmare stretched for miles. Its walls sweat blood, creating pools at her feet, and the rumble of artillery shook the overhead lighting. Through the scope of her rifle, she spotted a door with no knob. Light beamed from its outline. Warmth awaited her there. To reach it, she would tread over a mass of graves. She'd fire the weapon again before dropping it for good.

The pitbull brought her back, her fur-coated defibrillator. His nibbling shook the desert from her subconscious. She buried her face in his jowls to shield her eyes from the sun peeking through cracks in the window boards. He nudged in return, drying the cold sweat from her brow.

He'd come to her from a dumpster, an albino pup shivering in the rain. She'd cursed his abandoners half to hell before she knew the gift they'd left. Pedro. Now, she figured the gods had left him.

The room took shape in fragments, decaying wooden floorboards spotted with stains. Her bunkmate, Serita, rested on the couch to her left, striped in fractions with beams of light. The sleeping girl's breathing was a rhythmic hum, hand laying open where she'd dropped the needle.

*No…*

Liz thrust upright and found her footing. Beneath Serita lay shattered glass and empty bags. At these times, she could strangle the girl in her sleep. Without Liz's morning fix, the dope sickness bludgeoned her, thrumming at her stomach, pumping acid to her skull.

She shuffled to the bathroom and soaked her toothbrush with a water bottle. The dust and mouse droppings broke away from the bristles, disappearing into the rusted drain at the center of the rusted sink. She smiled into the mirror when she finished. Her teeth had held up by a fiend's standards, but she was no model for dental hygiene. Tartar stains had formed brown rings around the off-white bone. No matter how she tried, she couldn't scrub them away. She removed her tank top, sweatpants and underwear, showering with the remainder of her seventeen fluid ounces. The house had a stink that seemed to shadow her. *It'll be plumbing and soap again soon, once I get my shit straight.*

She dressed herself, flipping her underwear inside out, and returned to her mattress to feed the dog. She filled his bowl from a height that caused a racket, hoping to rouse Serita as revenge. The girl slept on, undisturbed. Liz pressed two fingers under her jaw until she found a pulse.

She looped her father's dog tags over her head, coupled with her own, and made for the door. She set off to see Brooks, hoping to broker a deal with her fellow desert rat.

Pedro tailed her to the exit and tugged at the seam of her pant leg.

*Fuckin' mutt.*

She opened the door to let him follow.

The El-train rattled overhead. Plastic bags blew like tumbleweed along hills of pavement. The pulse of the city was frantic, yet it seemed something was missing. Liz paled a shade closer to the soulless grays of the urban jungle with every passing night. She wondered if the city hovered over the same abyss as she, afraid to look down and slacken its grip from the shock.

Cameron Brooks, a former Marine Corporal, stood at six foot two, his stellar posture reflecting his time marching in rank. His face was peppered with stubble, eyes bloodshot, the way a fiend's often were. His chest was broad, his arms muscled, though Liz remembered a time before he'd shipped off when they'd been smaller than her own.

On this autumn morning, she found him a block from his stoop, holding court with Princess Layla. Knots of greasy blonde hair spilled from Layla's raw scalp, split ends glistening in the morning sun. Her bitter scent was masked by some sickening sweetness that brought bile to Liz's throat.

Brooks saluted when he spotted Liz and the dog. "Sarge."

Pedro dipped his chest to the pavement and growled. The flaps of his lips unveiled a clenched set of dripping yellow teeth.

"Yo, where's the love, Pedro?"

The dog answered with a rash of echoing barks. Liz held him around the chest and scratched his ears to calm him.

The look on the junkie wench's face tightened Liz's knuckles to a bloodless ball. Princess opened her cracked lips and let her rancid breath billow. "The mutt's got rabies. See his mouth? I know it." She picked at the sores on her neck. "Time to put him down, Liz."

Liz held the dog in place, though she had half a mind to let him rip out the shrew's throat. "Maybe I come by after dark and put *you* down.

I wonder if this strip would even notice, I take a knife to your throat. Won't hurt none... I'll bleed you quick." She motioned to Brooks with her chin. "He knows how I do…"

Brooks turned to the shanty beside him to hide his grin.

In 2004, they'd worked together on a counter-insurgency operation in the mountains of Kandahar. Liz had been part of an engagement team deployed to assist the expeditionary unit with the local population, but ended up fighting off three Taliban ambushes. The Taliban were running scared. With very little to lose, they fought nasty. Their team took heavy losses, and Liz repaid them with her combat knife in the twilight hours.

The junkie's bloodshot eyes glowed with spite. "You people are fucked up…" She wobbled for home. "I'm callin' the fuckin' SPCA."

Liz laughed as she rubbed Pedro's chest.

The Corporal never turned to watch the hag go. He had no love for this woman. "Happy birthday, by the way."

Liz wiped snot from her nose with the back of her hand. "How'd you remember that?" She'd forgotten, herself.

Brooks peered somewhere distant. "I woke up half expectin' to sneak into mess and snatch you up a cake…" His chuckle trailed off when sadness took him. "Different life, huh?"

Liz was hard pressed to remember her life before the needle took over. The days of substance and selflessness seemed impossibly distant. "Ass end of the same one, unfortunately."

When he smiled, Liz caught a glimpse of his teeth. They were alarmingly white for his lifestyle. "Well…hope Serita got somethin' planned for you."

"Ha. Yeah, that's a terrifying thought." The last birthday of any relevance to Liz had been her twenty-first. A year before she'd made Sergeant, she worked as a gunner for an AH-1Z Viper attack chopper. An RPG ripped into the side of the Viper and sent her and her pilot,

Juliana, crashing to the sand. Liz pulled free of the wreck with minor injuries. Juliana caught shrapnel to the chest and choked to death. She hadn't noticed her twenty-first birthday until three hours into the following day.

Liz watched Pedro as he settled to the pavement. "I ain't seen you... thought you might'a found Jesus."

Brooks scanned their block, an armpit. "Be a strange place for him to hide."

"You holdin'?"

"Maybe. Devo's shit ain't doin' it?"

"Serita took it all to the face... bitch needs to cool it. I ain't fit to bury a mom."

Brooks shrugged his broad shoulders. "You got money?"

She spit some minty remnant to the curb. "I was hopin' for a lil' birthday gift." Even with years of street grit, she knew just the face to break him. Her left brow curled upward and a timid grin dimpled her cheeks. She'd used it in the desert to seduce him in her barracks.

He scanned the block to ensure the Princess was out of earshot. "Let's go to your place."

Serita slept on. Liz plopped down on her mattress with a deflating sigh. Brooks sat beside her and fiddled with his equipment. It was always business for the Corporal. He rarely let his breathing stretch long.

She could hear the bedframe song of sex through the ceiling. One of the fiends camped upstairs was laying into a wretch worse than Layla.

Pedro curled in a corner near his bowls and stared at Brooks, exhaling a low, consistent growl.

*The fuck is up with you, boy?* Liz wondered.

Brooks' scent was often ripe, and he wasn't the best-looking fiend on the block, but he'd maintained his Marine Corps correctness through the years. He was a deal more decent than most of the degenerates Liz brought home.

He handed Liz a tourniquet and she choked her bicep, pulling it taut with withering teeth. She noticed her free arm was shaking. This cop was long overdue. Brooks prepped the needle and handed it over.

"Happy birthday, my darling." His ghetto attempt at chivalry made her blush.

"Fuck off."

She set the needle against her bulging vein. The poetry was hardly lost on her. Here they were again, partying with the sauce that bought them each a dishonorable discharge. Liz thought very seldom of reclaiming her honor since she'd left the desert, but she knew that with every plunge of the needle, she strayed a mile further.

She noticed Brooks wasn't shooting. "You don't want none?"

He looked to his arm, pristine, not a track mark in sight.

"I had mine this morning."

*Hmm.* Liz shrugged. *Happy birthday to me.*

She punctured the vein, and the wolf swam through to her heart where it would make a home.

# CHAPTER TWO

## Macy

### *Doylestown, Pennsylvania*

*The traveler's eyes shone crimson bliss, he scrubbed at echoes' dust. Crushed memories in a shaking fist, the wolf cries when he must.* The Scourge lyrics clung to her like a premonition. At ninety miles per hour, a sharp wind found the gaps in her visor, kneading the soft flesh of her cheeks to putty. She ripped the throttle with impunity, hurtling unobstructed along a desolate road. Macy figured she could chase the sun to its roost beyond the tip of the world. Kawasaki Ninja ZX-6R ABS—the bike was her second favorite possession. Her first favorite hung in polished glass on the back wall of her bedroom, a Scourge poster on which Amos Stanfield had scribbled his signature beside a sketch of a satanic alligator.

This plunge through evening was a farewell of sorts. She'd listed the bike on the web. The buyer was a rotund man who might have bent the chassis under his weight. *He'll strip it for parts,* she thought, glancing downward, pondering a eulogy. The man promised eight thousand in cash plus a Honda Civic to cover the remaining five. He seemed perplexed when she demanded a picture of the engine, and near-dumbfounded when she inquired about the timing belt. Replacing it would be a tiresome job–removing engine components, attending to alignment and tension - but she'd suffer it herself at the garage, profiting handsomely when the exchange was through.

The man was understanding, humble, in fact, yet the prospect of her own murder still troubled her as she gunned it for the stranger's house. *He'll strip you for parts.* She'd brought her switchblade along. *Ridiculous, Mace. Paranoia. You embarrass yourself.* She knew full well that, if called upon, she'd be useless with the weapon, but it rested comfortably in the front pocket of her coat. She ran her fingers along the hilt. Something called to her in the tremble of her wrist.

*Keep dreaming, Mace. You're as tough as a daisy.*

## *Warminster, Pennsylvania*

The form of the Ninja's body itched her like a phantom limb. At the Honda's wheel, she settled into her crypt. She rolled in close to sunset. The motor had maintained well. Beside her, the helmet made an imprint in the withering fabric. She wouldn't sell it for any price. It was the only thing keeping her head intact when she'd lost her balance on the expressway two years prior.

She'd been wrong about the buyer—a teddy bear of a man, who planned on surprising his daughter with the Ninja as a graduation present. The switchblade in her pocket felt like a mockery now. Macy had developed a nasty habit of assuming the worst in people, a flaw she'd been struggling to correct. In her experience, assumptions such as these left her feeling alone.

Her father shuffled bills at the kitchen table, one bulb from the overhead illuminating his effort. Macy approached from behind and wrapped her arms around his neck. She felt him jump.

"One day I might just knock your teeth out, girlie."

She reached into her pocket. "Merry Christmas." She set the money down on the table in front of him.

"What're you slingin', dope?" He fanned the bills with his thumb.

"Eight grand. I sold the Ninja to some dude in Doylestown. He gave me that and a Civic for it."

His fingers fumbled as he craned his neck. "You what, now?"

"Throw four grand to the bills and three to my loans. Keep the last one for yourself. Whatever's left can pay the dentist." She brushed a playful fist for his mouth.

"Mace." He spoke to the stack of hundreds. "I don't need you doin' this."

She opened her mouth to speak but thought better of it. It never paid to cut him off.

He motioned to the mountain of debt that towered before him. "It's on me. You understand?"

She didn't. Parting the stack at the approximate center, she pocketed the top half. "Even split, then? I return what you put into it…"

"My half was a gift, Mace."

Reluctantly, she removed a few more bills and folded them into her stack. "A quarter plus interest."

"Yeah…thanks." He rose from his chair at a slug's pace, groaning with the effort. "I'm gonna take a look at the piece of shit." The Honda waited for him in the driveway, dripping oil.

Upstairs, Macy rested her helmet on her bedroom bureau and rubbed her mouse pad to check her other bids. A few nibbles. Nothing substantial.

The episode pounced without warning, a septic avalanche of panic and unnerving dread. *You sold yourself, Mace. Your last memory of her. What are you without it?* In her mind's eye, the Ninja's tail light tapered into thick fog. She fumbled for the Xanax in her nightstand and swallowed one with a single impulsive gulp of day-old tap water. With eyes pinched shut, she imagined the joy she'd given a stranger and the relief on her father's face. *Stay with it, Mace. Don't slip.*

She slipped.

A lifeless purple face came to her, eyes glossed with film. When it spoke, a burst of crustaceans emerged. It belonged to the river now. "What choice did you have?" The voice belched mud-thick aquatic torment, so foreign yet so eerily familiar.

To assist the Xanax, she put on Scourge's *Knee Deep in Bayou Sweat* record. Amos Stanfield's guitar sliced through her episode like a knight's longsword, the grace of his fingers healing her sister's dead purple flesh. Sarah had given her the Ninja. Macy knew parting with it was burying her a foot deeper.

Steve Simpson's bass pounded a steady heartbeat while Parker Fitz's lyrics rode in on Amos' brilliant melody.

*I rest in silence in the throes of bayou muck.*
*I search for guidance from a time I wasn't truly FUCKED!*

Even Parker's switch from melodic singing to screaming wasn't enough to pull Macy from the river. Her mother and father shared a toxic vice. The drink had them. Macy often wondered if they'd enabled each other, if splitting might have been better for the family.

The despicable vice was hereditary, it seemed. On a winter night in 2006, Sarah left Jersey with a load on. She'd managed to get to the bridge before the drink took its debt and sent the car through the railing to the bottom of the river. Her mother couldn't shake the guilt, though she tried her damnedest for a year with therapy and self-help audiobooks. In the end, she left for California to start anew. She called Macy when it was convenient, but it felt like a second loss.

Macy gripped the cross rail of her chair, soaked in icy sweat. She was forgetting something. *What was it? Right... BREATHE IN*...With a powerful intake of air, the images faded. *She hates you, Macy. You backstabber. Disloyal swine.* With every intake, the bite of her thoughts grew duller. The Xanax lifted her from them, from the pit that was death if she made it so. Slowly, dreadfully slowly, she reclaimed control. When her thoughts were her own, she returned to Pennsylvania, to her bedroom, her healing roost, the womb she'd never left.

Her eyes popped open with a slick, wet snap and the attack was nearly through. Drying sweat stuck her hands to the chair when she tried to remove them. *The right choice, Macy. The only choice.*

She moved through a gallery of movie posters and signed t-shirts to sit by the window. Pulling it open a crack, she let the night air dry her doubts.

The woman was there again.

Well-built with wide shoulders, her hair tied up in tight braids. Each one of the past three nights, the woman lingered on a bench in the adjacent field and stared up into the bay window of one of the rich houses across the thoroughfare. *Scouting for a burglary, no doubt.* Again, she assumed the worst, but what else would keep the woman coming back? Macy noticed something new on a second glance.

This time she had a dog with her.

# CHAPTER THREE

## Liz

*Warminster, Pennsylvania*

*"You're a ghost to her now. You come near us again, I make you a ghost for real..."*

The last words she'd heard from Gary, the scum she'd once called her stepfather. She watched him now, his beady eyes fixed on her mother, Monica, across a half-finished meal, the candle flame flashing in red-orange waves. *The dope's done your job for you, motherfucker. Here I sit, a ghost.* She wasn't permitted within a hundred yards of the house, so she watched from a distant bench.

That night had been a festive one for the couple—red wine and a playful waltz across kitchen tiles. The peace her mother had found bruised Liz to her brittle core. *She's forgotten me.*

The tendrils of the sun had receded behind distant trees. The light from her mother's kitchen sliced through dusk to reach her. Liz massaged the pits behind Pedro's ears. An entire day of loathing Brooks had left the dog docile. The hate had fizzled on the commute from Kensington. His tongue dangled from his mouth dripping foamy saliva to the grass.

A hundred yards from her, Liz's stepfather cleaned the dishes and pinched the flames dead with wet fingers. Liz knew what came next. Acid touched the back of her throat and summoned a coughing fit.

Monica fiddled with the flat screen remote while the vulture readied a blanket. He bumped his head into her cheekbone, and she laughed it off, nestling tighter.

Liz's attention fell again to the dog. *That's our cue, boy. Any more and I might lose dinner.*

Suddenly, some otherworldly pain hit her directly in the stomach, sharp and tight like a twisted blade. Dope sickness was always a creeping thrum, but this was something fiercer. *Cramps?* she thought. Her time in the Service had left her cycle in staggered disarray.

Now, the pain doubled her over. Her knuckles brushed the grass and found mud. Pedro unleashed a fit of growling, the same menacing rumble he'd shown Brooks. Before Liz could swat at his snout, the pain passed, and the dog relaxed.

Liz found the window through a salty glaze, but the couple was gone. *Upstairs for a quickie in the dark.* She hooked Pedro's collar and dragged him along.

She trotted four miles back to the city with Pedro trailing. As soon as she hit Philly, she'd catch a bus back to Kensington. Luckily, the Marine Corps gas tank returned after a mile of dusting cobwebs. The woods surrounded her for the first mile, the racket of nature's nightlife bellowing as she pumped her thighs. Miles two and three turned suburban, where every lawn was pristine and every uppity square was inside for *Jeopardy!* before 7pm. She watched as the scenery made a nauseating transformation. For the last mile, she put her guard up. A bum extended a wretched hand to her, stained gloves with snipped fingertips. "You wanna help me out? Just a little sumpn'. God bless ya." Pedro stretched his dripping grin, and the vagrant stumbled back. "Sheeeit! Demon doggy! Hell moon's out tonight! God bless!"

When, after a short bus ride, she arrived at her own pile of bricks, the exhaustion nearly swept her from her feet. She propped a foot on the stoop to catch her breath. Pedro mimicked her. She pondered the most effective obscenities to heave at Serita when a raucous bell sounded in her right ear and her face hit the pavement with a thunk.

The back of her head throbbed as the fuzzy spots crowded her vision. Pedro barked himself hoarse before a thud made him whimper. She twisted her neck and, through the spots, saw him limping down the block.

*Way to have my back, boy.*

"Get the fuck up!"

Two callused hands hooked her armpits and tossed her into the backseat of a black SUV she hadn't seen approach. Heroin had muddled her eagle vision.

The SUV hightailed it back in the direction from where she'd come. Each retracted mile filled her aching thighs with rage. She quelled the dizziness with a violent shake, but the stabbing pain in her stomach was unyielding. The kidnapper in the passenger seat turned to her, puzzled by her discomfort.

"What's wrong wit you, girl?"

"You hit me in the head…fuckin' moron."

She squinted to focus on the loudmouth's face—teardrop tattoos dripping from cheek bones that could slice cheese. Dead eyes the color of ash.

"Why you stealin' from me?"

She retraced the day's steps and came up lost. "You sure you bashed the right bitch?" The pain in her stomach was intensifying, and now it moved to her arms and legs. Her poker face slipped with each throb.

"I'm short three bags, you little cunt. Where you got 'em stuffed?" He reached for her, and she shied away. "I know you ain't shoot 'em already."

Had Brooks set her up? Doubtful. Their history ran blood-deep. She *had* seen the junk do strange things to people. She would have a nice chat with him if she lived long enough. "Got 'em hidden up your mother's ass. I can take you to her. She's trickin' on my block."

He placed a pistol on his arm rest, its barrel staring her in the forehead. He looked like a toddler with his dad's gun.

Liz forced a grin though searing pain. "You a killer then? You the one I've been waiting for?"

He only shrugged.

"Fuck's that mean? You ain't sure?"

"Might spread those legs of yours first..." He cackled to his friend beside him.

Liz smiled as the pain bludgeoned her and ravaged her brain. "I haven't had a good fuck in months…"

His face blurred suddenly, and the noise from his mouth switched off. There was only silence and darkness when the monster took the reins.

## *Montgomery County, Pennsylvania*

Her stepfather's face contorted as he spoke. "You're a ghost to her now... I make you a ghost for real..."

A demon dancer tapped the inner lining of her skull. The waltz drew her through the blood-red hall, its distant door drawing nearer, but still out of reach.

It seemed someone had stapled her eyelids shut. She spent the better part of a minute separating them. The sun peeked through at her first. It was morning. When her vision cleared, an alcove took shape. The sounds of a waterfall followed—delicately splashing against rocks like an orchestra of nature, a wake-up call to a half-dead fiend. Her clothes were torn and her left breast was exposed. She raked her fingers across her scalp, evicting the insects and plunging them helplessly to their grave at her feet.

She propped herself against a rock, massaging a stiffness between her legs. Her kidnapper had probably delivered on his threats of rape, but she couldn't quite tell. *All you had to do was ask, dead-eyes.* She was alive, bad luck for him. She'd turn every stone in Kensington to find him and take a pipe to his kneecaps.

Brooks would answer for this first. While sparring in the desert, she'd often taken hold of the Corporal's throat and choked him to the brink of sleep. She'd choke him purple if he had a hand in the attack.

A slick boulder helped her to her feet, the smell of mud and algae strong with her. A sharp pain jolted up the small of her back, localized between her shoulder blades. This worked nicely with the twisted knife in her stomach, and it was all overseen by the general aches of withdrawal. *My place, shoot up, get dressed, choke Brooks, kill the dealers.* If Serita had tampered with her last gram, the fiend would wander the street for a new bunkmate. *Princess Layla's got room if you chase away the rats.*

Liz tied the remnants of her shirt together to cover her breast, picked a direction and marched. She would hit asphalt within an hour. The woodlands of Philadelphia were all but extinct.

She came to a road snaking its lonely way through brush. Still, the city was nowhere in sight. Liz couldn't figure out the kidnappers' angle, dropping her this far from home. It would have played better if they put one in her head and dumped her in the river. She followed the winding road for a mile before spotting the skyline.

# CHAPTER FOUR

## Macy

*Warminster, Pennsylvania*

*Patience, Mace... One move at a time... Down is death... What choice do you have?* Sarah's voice seemed to find her in times of stress. Macy could almost feel her sister's cold hand squeezing her oil-stained fingers.

Ira was a regular irritant at the shop. He hoarded a small collection of medallion licenses, but was ignorant to the happenings under his fleet's hoods. What really bothered Macy was the way he condescended. Auto advice from a one-hundred-fifteen pound girl never satisfied him.

"You can pass the fucking thing," he said. "I know you can."

Macy propped a hand against her orbital bone. "You're gonna have to put miles on it to clear the codes. I can't run an emissions test until you do. I can give you a temp sticker in case you get pulled over…"

Ira eyed the tattoos on both her arms. "Let me speak to Joe. May I come back?" He reached for the partition between them.

Macy's shrug spoke volumes. *Fuck you* would have been unprofessional.

"He's occupied. You can talk to me."

"You don't understand how business works."

"It's not that. It's…" She shot a quick glance to the front door. "We do things clean. We always have." She had adhered to procedure.

*Don't make waves. Play by the book and you'll never hit trouble.*

Ira chuckled. "How long have we been neighbors? Hmm? How much money have I given you fucking people? Clean?" He showed her his hands. "I'm clean. I wash." He leaned toward her and sniffed the air. "You're clean. I'm not giving you a weapon to hide. Pass the fucking codes."

Macy considered, though it turned her stomach.

"Neighbors take care of each other, yeah? It's clean."

She wished the man would just turn and go. "I'll be right back."

She could hear him muttering to himself on her way to the office. She was embarrassed by her lack of resolve. *Crumbled by Ira's guilt trip. Pathetic.*

She rested a hand on her father's forehead and his eyes popped open.

"Ira..."

"Fuck." He exhaled the word. He marched to the sink, splashed water on his face and stumbled for the front counter.

Her father took one look at the man and rolled his eyes, subtle as a hand grenade. "What's the problem, Ira?"

"Your daughter is incompetent, for one."

Macy and her father furrowed their eyebrows in unison.

Her father pointed to her with his thumb. "This one builds cars from scratch…since she was ten. She's more of a gear head than me."

"I just want you to look—"

"Nah, I don't think so…" His words were sharp, but his tone was meek. "I'm gonna take her word."

Ira stood silent, wearing the expression of an ill-tempered toddler.

Her father opened the partition and put his arm around the man's shoulder, walking him toward the door. They shared a quiet exchange that Macy caught in segments. "You know we take care of you." He patted the man and sent him on his way.

Joe Burkhardt lived a balancing act. He protected his daughter's integrity, but he wouldn't lose Ira's business. He returned to her and brushed her cheek, then made for his cot to catch a few winks before the next whiner came calling.

# CHAPTER FIVE

## Liz

*Kensington, Philadelphia*

A junkie leaned to kiss the curb near her stoop. Liz was always fascinated with the way a dope fiend could sink so far in a state of semi-consciousness without ever falling over. She turned to face her digs with a smile. It felt like ages since she'd last seen home.

Pedro greeted her at the door with a bump of the brow, remorse welled salty in the pits of his eyes. She couldn't help but forgive him, though his days as a guard dog were through. She scratched the fur behind his ears, and all was well between the two.

Serita was awake. This came as a mild shock. "What happened to *you*?"

The prodigal fiend dipped her aching head to the clothes pile by Serita's feet. The colors never seemed to repeat, yet together, they all faded to gray. "Lil' trouble…I can fix it. Let me borrow some of these." She riffled through, ever-changing smells hitting her one by one.

"Mmhmm."

A pair of faded jeans, rips at the knees, and a black hoodie spotted gray. She held them up for Serita's approval. "Cool?"

Serita waved a limp hand, and Liz slid her torn sweatpants to the floor.

"What kind of trouble? Cops?" The tail end of the question was swallowed by a yawn.

"Nope." Liz profiled herself in the mirror. Her hair was a ratty mess and the bags beneath her eyes had taken over her cheeks. She had never considered herself attractive, at least not by mainstream standards, but her reflection was disturbing. *This fucking shit is killin' me.* She wanted more than anything to shake it. *Tomorrow. I start recovery tomorrow.* She'd been repeating this thought for years.

"So what, then?" Serita had flattened out. Her words were always muffled when she did.

"Nothin' heavy. Like I said, I'll fix it." Liz presented herself—the hoodie was a size too small, squeezing her braless breasts in place. The jeans were a size too big, as Liz had always focused on upper body in the gym. Serita had a mother's hips and no tone in her arms to speak of. It wasn't the ideal wardrobe but it would do her better than the rags she'd walked in with.

Serita craned her neck from her flattened state. "Give us a spin."

Liz trudged to her mattress and popped open the false compartment in the floorboards beneath. She pulled out the box, thumbed in the combination, waited for the metallic click and popped the lid. She gathered her syringe, the spoon she would soon need to replace, the cotton ball that needed replacing weeks ago, her lighter that coughed fumes with every strike and the last bit of the gram that had caused her so much grief.

Blue bags, double-wrapped—*the Philly dope way.* She examined the powder and flicked the bag. The darker, the better. This dope was brown sugar. *Mother of Christ, Brooks. You're gonna put me out.*

Serita took a bite of a bagel, and Liz was reminded that she hadn't eaten since the previous afternoon. She rested a hand on her stomach. No hunger pangs. *Hmm.*

She slipped her right arm out of the hoodie, dabbed the bag's contents onto the spoon and boiled it. When it was liquid, she used the cotton to soak it and drew out what she could with the syringe. She wrapped the hoodie's sleeve tightly around her arm, bulging veins in the pit of her elbow, and served herself some breakfast. There wasn't much left after the previous night's score. She'd be sober enough to function.

Suddenly, a surge of pain raced to the tips of her fingers like a thousand jabbing needles. She had partially missed the vein. They called this "muscle popping" on the streets, and it could sober a fiend in an instant.

Serita spotted Liz's folly and giggled. "What, you miss?"

"Fuck you. Fuck. Fuck. Fuck." She smacked her hands together, fingers constricted in spasm. Seconds passed before the pain subsided and the brown sugar was left to take its hold... but, it didn't. While it wasn't her normal volume, she felt next to nothing. It was a disappointment, but her dope sickness had subsided. She would tend to her business with Brooks unhindered.

She left her fixings strewn about and rummaged through the box. She slid the dog tags and cassette tapes aside and withdrew her Walther PPK. She'd managed to put off selling it, as it was her father's last gift to her before he passed, but she feared the junk would have her pawn it soon. She didn't think she'd need it here, but junkies could be unpredictable. She flicked the mag release with her thumb to ensure it was full. If things *did* pop off, she would have six chances to correct them. She racked it and stuffed it behind her into the waist of her jeans.

Before leaving, she passed Serita on the sofa.

"Can you fix my hair?"

With braids gripping her scalp, Liz marched for the Corporal's castle. She hadn't gotten into any fights in a while, nor had she been to the gym, but she could muscle the fiends. She was sure of it. She wouldn't allow Brooks to slip. He hadn't been around often lately, and Liz feared he may have found a new calling. She reached behind her and gripped the handle of the Walther to ensure it was snug.

Princess Layla waited on Brooks' stoop. The maggot raised her brow, confused, but then her jaw parted slowly like the drawstring of some wretched bow. The Princess was terrified. "The fuck you doin' here?" Her shoulder blades bumped the smack den's front door—a quarter-inch piece of plywood covered in graffiti and obscure passages of questionable origin.

"Fetch Brooks before I fuck your face up worse."

Layla's expression was unchanged. "You ain't supposed to…" She searched the street behind Liz, expecting someone.

It took a moment for things to become clear. The Princess put the goons on her trail. Was it at Brooks' behest? She couldn't have known.

Instead of asking, Liz lunged and swung a straight right fist for the girl's jaw. She tripped on a step and caught Layla's shoulder, bouncing the back of the Princess's head against the door. Had this punch found its target, it would have put the hag into a snooze. Her miss was only enough to summon fury.

Layla pulled the hood over Liz's head and spun her sideways into the doorframe. *Dirty bitch.* The pair of them stumbled into the house, onto the filthy hardwood floor. Vile smells. Sickening aromas that burned the eyes. The junkies were scattered in a room without furniture. There were seven, maybe ten. She rode Layla's belt to an upright position before smashing her forehead into the rat's nose. Liz was pleased by the snap of the cartilage. Layla fell to the floor holding her face with blood pumping through the gaps between her fingers.

A large right hand whizzed through fog and stench to meet Liz's jaw. Kitchen tile knocked the wind from her before she'd even known she'd fallen. The Walther burrowed into the meat of her rump. It wasn't time to start shooting, but she reached for her waist to relieve some discomfort. The same thick hand intercepted her wrist, impossibly large with stained yellow fingernails, sprouts of hair lining the knuckles.

She was hoisted from the kitchen tile by a hulking man. Layla cackled to tears beyond his shoulder. Liz heard the Walther clatter against the linoleum, drawing the sentry's glance.

"What, you gon' shoot me, bitch?" He slapped her and sent her reeling into the counter.

Before she could buck, he was on her. He grabbed her arm with both hands and slammed it onto the counter's edge. The way it snapped seemed unnatural, like he'd broken it worse than physics should allow.

Liz heard Layla's hysterical laughter, but the direction was unclear. She tucked her fragmented arm into the hoodie's front pouch as the brute bent for the gun. With her healthy arm, she snatched up the makeshift toaster the junkies had rigged on the counter and clobbered the giant behind the ear. A thin stream of blood burst from the wound and his face met the floor with a *thunk* that shook her footing.

She made for the back door and kicked open the screen. Something sharp bit her right shoulder and a spray of red skimmed her cheek. The Princess cackled and readied a second shot. The Walther was slick, but so was Liz. She fled down the back alley before Layla could finish her.

Though the gunshot wound threatened Liz's life, it was her broken arm that afflicted her most. The bones were bulging against flesh like another elbow. She felt the shattered fragments digging into nerves. She sidestepped into a shed several blocks from Brooks' place with the delusion of mending herself.

The shed was stocked with bags of trash and gasoline-soaked rags, nothing that would function in a medical sense. She fell onto a stool and took a deep breath. She had to look. The heroin was doing nothing, and her adrenaline waned with every jolt of pain. She pulled the arm from her hoodie.

*What…the fuck?*

Her arm was healed. She moved it up and down, massaged it with her left hand, punched the wall with it, even. The pain she'd felt moments ago had washed away. The arm was not broken.

*Some fucking trip.* Perhaps she slept soundly on her mattress, Pedro curled in a ball at her side. But it couldn't have been the junk. Her high had faded away completely. *No…I felt it snap.*

This wasn't right.

She tugged Serita's hoodie over her head. The entire right sleeve of her t-shirt was soaked red. She lifted the sleeve to examine it, found the pencil-sized hole in the fabric. She twisted around. Blood flaked brown on her shoulder, but there was no matching hole in her flesh.

Liz felt faint. She collapsed to her knees on the shed's floor and spewed the contents of her stomach. The vomit was red and fleshy. It tasted of iron. Her mind was a puddle, not unlike the one she'd regurgitated.

There were two explanations for her unhinged afternoon. The first had been fed to her arm thirty minutes before. She was unsure if the confrontation had occurred or if she had dreamt it up in some smack-induced stupor.

The second was that Liz was a superhero. This thought made her laugh aloud as she spit red pulp from between her teeth.

*Tomorrow, I get clean.*

# CHAPTER SIX

## Macy

*Warminster, Pennsylvania*

Macy sucked down a monster of a hit on her back patio.

She shared the blunt with Holly, an old friend from high school who'd returned from Miami for a family reunion.

"Jesus, Mace, could you pass?" Holly ripped the blunt from her hand, nearly tearing it in two.

Macy choked on smoke. "Quit roughin' it."

"Fuck yourself." Trucker's words from a model's mouth.

Holly hit the blunt with finesse, blowing smoke rings and billowing remnants from her nostrils. For a while, neither said a word. The air was crisp, and a sprawling field extended in three directions. The scenery seemed to speak for itself.

The model broke the silence. "Where's the Ninja?"

"Sold it."

Holly let a moment stretch before responding. "What?"

"Half sold it, half traded. Civic's not a bad car. I'm gonna play with it at the garage a little…"

Holly wore the face of a baby with a full diaper. "You had a badass motorcycle that actually made you seem cool, and now you have…a Honda."

"Correct."

The model loosed a guffaw from the bottom of her diaphragm that echoed to the rich houses across the field.

"Cash is cash," sighed Macy. She loathed the way Holly would condescend.

"What'd you use your degree for? A piss pad?"

The blunt was running low. Macy's last hit was weak.

Holly didn't seem to mind. She tended to smoke for the company. "Why don't you come back down to Miami?"

"Be hot for a living? No."

"Cash is cash..." Her mocking tone hit Macy in the nose.

"Think I'd get bored." Macy motioned toward the house. "And I can't leave him."

"He's a big boy, Mace."

Macy smiled as she rubbed her right hand over her left forearm piece—a demon on a motorcycle smashing through the gates of Heaven.

"I'm just saying, it's an option. Beats the life out of Hondas and passing time in that shit garage."

Macy thought rigorously about her next words. The model had a point. It would be the perfect escape. She could send her father money, maybe get him into a better house, pay for his meetings, turn the garage into a chain…

…but her dad would be alone.

"Nah. I'm good."

Hours had passed, but Holly's wildflower scent still lingered on the patio. Macy wasn't sure if she should pat herself on the back for sticking to her morals or punch herself in the face for passing on an exit. The blunt was too weak, regardless.

The stocky girl had returned, no dog this time. She sat on the same bench across the field, staring up at the same window. Macy had her pegged as an angry ex-girlfriend, but perhaps she was just a head case—or a mixture of the two.

She had considered confronting this girl for three nights, but someone this persistent about watching people from a distance was certainly unstable. The girl was built well, so anything physical would be a mismatch.

*Paranoia, Mace... Shelve it... Down is death... What choice do you have?*

She had considered stabbing a man who was trying to do something nice for his daughter. Perhaps the girl was watching over the house for a neighbor, or maybe she just admired the architecture. Not a psycho, a human being.

Now Ira's shrill voice found her. *"Neighbors take care of each other, yeah? It's clean."*

*Okay, Ira. I'll be neighborly.* Macy's legs were moving. The distance between the two girls was closing rapidly. Some strange impulse drove her forward, Sarah's confidence living on.

The girl slid from the bench and clutched her stomach. *I was right...psychotic*, Macy thought. *No. She's in pain.*

She writhed in agony, screaming colorful obscenities at the moon. Macy's tentative walk turned to a sprint. She'd gotten CPR certified after Sarah, and now a test from the gods had fallen into her lap.

When she reached the girl, she heard something frighteningly close to a growl. The girl's gaze snapped to her, eyes glowing yellow. "Fuck off!" Her teeth were pointed, and her voice was guttural and primal.

Then the girl plowed into her. Something sharp caught Macy's shoulder as she brushed by. Her head jerked backward when she hit the grass. Blood trickled through the tears in her sleeve, and a thick fog blotted her vision.

The outline of the moon was the last thing to linger as her lights went out.

Sarah's face was purple when they pulled her from the river. Macy was never meant to see it. Her father struggled to shield her eyes from it, but she saw. For the viewing, they had brought it back to its natural color, but the adjustments they made took away Sarah's true features. Macy remembered the purple.

She hovered over the body while the rank smell of incense caught in her throat. Her sister seemed at rest, but Macy could only think of her final moments, the moments of anguish as she suffocated. The moments that would render a soft pink face to a ghastly purple.

Sarah's eyes flicked open, and Macy jumped.

*Up, Mace. You have to go up.*

Her mouth didn't move, but Macy could hear her just the same.

*Up... up.*

The purple face of death returned and her eyes glossed over white.

*What choice do you have?*

She came to with an icy twitching of her brow. A drizzle of rain slickened her skin, softening the earth beneath her. Her clothes had been torn to rags. In a blink, she'd forgotten her dream. No Sarah. No rotting purple face. Only empty space and the echo of something lost.

*Up, Mace. You have to go up...*

She rolled onto her stomach, and up came the night's meal. Up came the red fleshy pulp that roiled her insides.

Brushing residue from her lips, she scrambled to her feet. She could smell the earthy scent of rain-soaked trees as the wind shook the branches, spraying her with freezing mist.

*I was right to be paranoid…*

Fragments of her dream returned to her. The girl had citrine eyes glowing above a set of dripping fangs.

*You've slipped, young lady. Your mind is gone.*

The encounter seemed impossibly distant, like she'd awakened from a coma to find the world had moved on. She remembered a slashing pain as the girl brushed by. The damp woods came into focus around her and she discovered her wounds had healed. The claw marks that should have been spread across her shoulder were scars that seemed years old. She rubbed a hand over her face. Her septum and eyebrow rings were gone as well, but there were no bumps where the holes should've been.

A blood trail dribbled away from her. She figured she'd follow it. She was in another dream, free of consequence.

Navigating the rain-slick boulders that riddled the hillside, she slipped, scraping both palms to catch herself. Her skin returned to her almost immediately, pristine and fresh like a babe's. *What the fuck?* She sat on a rock and turned her hands in the gloomy morning light. Another remnant from her dream, surely.

She found the corpse at the bottom of the hill.

The buck's skeleton had chunks of meat still attached at the ribs, and what appeared to be teeth or claw marks covered the bones. Her thoughts jumped to *The Strange Case of Dr. Jekyll and Mr. Hyde. "I have been doomed to such a dreadful shipwreck—that man is not truly one, but truly two."* Strands of sinew and torn arteries protruded from the buck's neck. Its left antler had broken at the base.

What troubled Macy was the look in the animal's dead eyes. It was an accusatory look. One that seemed to say, *"I hope you're satisfied."*

She burned her torn clothes in the fire pit out back. *Stretched thin and torn apart. What happened to me?* As they disintegrated, she headed for the bench across the field, where she fished around in the grass and found her phone. The screen was cracked, but she could still make out the web of text messages and missed calls.

"I changed my mind. I might knock your teeth out on purpose." Her father's anger when she called him snapped her back to reality.

"Listen, I got kind of drunk with Holly last night. I didn't wake up until one thirty and my phone was dead. Everything cool over there?"

"Jimmy had to run the counter while I did your alignment...so, we're out at least five customers."

She rubbed circles above her eyebrows. "I can get us more."

"Where'd you go, Mace? Be straight."

*Your puke looked like flesh. No. My own blood from a dry throat.*

"We just hit a bunch of bars. I ended up crashing at Holly's brother's apartment." It pained her to lie this way.

"This cannot happen, Macy. Not without a heads-up."

"I know…I'll come by later to close up. Jimmy can leave early."

"He'll be happy to hear it."

She could still see the deer's carcass. *Claw and fang marks in the bone.* The smoke from her clothes had gotten out of hand. "I've got to go. I'll see you." She hung up and clumsily doused the flames, smoke swelling further skyward into her mouth and eyes. *So much blood. You woke up covered in it.*

She slipped into the shower to wash it away along with the smoke stench. She swallowed an Excedrin to combat the headaches. Slipping on fresh underwear, she finally had time to put things in perspective. She first had to accept she was awake, a chore in its own right. She had seen enough movies to understand the signs, but it still seemed so ridiculous.

She booted up her computer and started typing. "Cannabis-induced psychosis." Auditory hallucinations, derealization, anxiety. *Clothes torn to pieces.* She searched again. "Commonly laced substances with Marijuana." LSD, coke and heroin. *That's it. Fucking Holly. What are you trying to do to me? But the blood, you can still taste it.*

New search, "Schizophrenia." Detachment from reality. Hallucinations. Developing in late adolescence or early twenties. *There it is. You're no wolf, you head case. A padded room is what you need. Weeks of observation in a hospital.* She always worried she hadn't given herself enough time to mourn.

She waited, touched her face and then her shoulder. *Wounds already healed.*

*Fuck it.* Her fingers brushed the keys as if frightened of what they might conjure. "Werewolves."

She found loads of fan fiction and some interesting artwork, along with forums riddled with misspellings discussing rituals to turn a man into a wolf. There were a few rumors about a drug trafficking ring filled with men who could shapeshift. The sources were all questionable. One headline read, "Magician Becomes Wolf Before Live Audience." *Another crock, for sure.*

A legend from England popped up when she scrolled a bit further. "The Derbyshire Incident." Man-wolves running England in the nineties. Even if the rumors had merit, it seemed unlikely anything that far away would find her here in a Pennsylvania suburb, tucked away from the world.

She had a set of chains gathering dust at the garage. She'd used them for towing cars years before, but she had a mind to lock herself to a tree tonight as a precaution. She'd risk looking foolish to protect her father. She'd bury the keys to the padlocks near enough to reach the next morning. *Will this thing know where to dig them up? Do we share thoughts?* Her fingers hovered over the keyboard. *Who would know the answer to that question?* The woman with the yellow eyes. She needed to speak with her before it happened again.

# CHAPTER SEVEN

## Ben

*Bennington, Vermont*

The Wolf King's advisor sat bent forward, hovering a quarter inch above the ceramic toilet seat. *Regal Oak,* he mused, assessing the cabinets with a soft caress. The hand towels were an understated gray. The lilac scent from the candles covered his sickness well. This privy dripped class. Ben wondered if the halfwits he'd passed on his way in were the true owners. Beneath his boots, arabesque baroque mosaic tile. *Thirty dollars a sheet. It sings. Every choice belts a symphony.*

Ben had no interest in coming to this party. He'd been traveling South with Desmond, the red-eyed wolf god who'd turned him, to investigate an anomaly. This god of his had an otherworldly bond with the man-wolves he created. Some strange magic from the shaman who made his family human. Whenever one died, Desmond would become sick until the body was burned. This illness would worsen over time, he'd said, to the point of insentience. Ben remembered him burning Dennings when he'd died up at the lake. When he'd been *killed.* He'd made an embarrassing attempt to usurp Des and lost the top half of his head for it. Ben figured the burning of the corpses severed their connection somehow.

A few days back, Desmond felt the familiar ailment, though faint, that signaled the death of one of his own. It had only worsened since.

The wolves of Lake Derby, Vermont were all accounted for. Desmond had another pack in New York running drugs through a strip club and one dealing heroin in Philadelphia. The corpse had to be one of them. All the wolves knew the rules. And yet the body remained unburned.

Des was adamant about seeing to it himself. He'd chosen Ben to come along and take the reins if he grew too sick to function.

Three years ago, Ben had been a real estate agent who dabbled in a bit of money laundering. Now, he searched for a wolf's corpse. *Funny life.*

The bathroom's clock made a metallic clicking sound to mark passing seconds.

*Tick. Tick. Tick.*

Some poor girl, worryingly young, who'd crossed paths with them on their trip, had convinced Ben's charming British leader to take this detour. He was now surely fucking her witless in the next room, losing sight of the urgency of the trip's purpose. *A passing broad gives him the eyes, and suddenly the mission falls to ash.*

He flushed again, embarrassed of the mess beneath him. A foul omen. His body hadn't been afflicted with illness in years. Leaning on his left buttock, he noticed the dark spot on the inside of his right thigh, about the size of a quarter. A brush of his thumb and blood seeped through coarse hairs. It was just as he'd feared.

*Tick. Tick. Tick.*

This patching sickness had emerged among the lakeside wolves in the last three months. Des was baffled as to what caused it, but so far, it had been a death sentence.

*That's how it started for Dennings.* A legend among wolves until the patches took his sense. He'd made his move on Des and lost his head before the illness had a chance to end him... a mercy. *Did the poor prick think becoming the alpha could save him? Or did he just want it over with?*

Ben thought of his own experience back when Desmond had passed the wolf to him. Stage One was rocky. He had no control. The thing would rend flesh and prowl by the lake, ripping the throats from game, stripping each to bone. Come Stage Two, while he still had no say in the time of his transformations, he made his own decisions as a wolf. He could see through its yellow eyes, feel its feral impulses. Stage Three was complete control. This was the high point. No longer did he become quadrupedal when he transformed. Instead, his eyes changed to yellow and fur sprouted on his cheeks and chest. He grew claws that could shred flesh, but he remained mostly man.

This patch was a rotten bastard, a wallop of reality. "Stage Four"—the name the lakeside wolves had given the condition—would begin with an itch and end with an agonizing death as an abomination. An end like that wasn't what Desmond had promised any of them. Ben scratched at his patch roughly. Black flakes of blood welled under his nails, but the patch remained.

*Tick. Tick. Tick.*

His phone rattled against his ankle from inside the pocket of his bunched-up jeans. He fished it out and opened the screen.

The King was calling.

Ben finished up and went out into the hall. He inched away from the sounds of the party, thumps of the EDM bass mixed with bursts of laughter. He moved toward the bedroom, where the noise abated to a worrying quiet.

The color left Ben's face when he set eyes on the dead girl. She lay face down on the bed with her back torn to ribbons, eyes set on sorrow beyond the reach of man. Ben could not avert his eyes, not even through fits of gagging.

"I didn't mean to, mate." Desmond's demeanor was boyish. A clueless child standing before a spill. He paced the room with a hand against his forehead, naked as his birth.

The poor girl's neck had been snapped, head bent at an impossible angle. Ben turned to his friend and sighed. "You're a fuckin' trip, you know that?"

“We’re closer to the body now. I got overwhelmed.” Des removed his hand from his temple and opened his eyes. “Before the lecture, I’ll concede…I might have done better to avoid this stop.”

“Why are we here? Why risk it?”

“Thought a shag might ease this fuckin’ ache. Anyway, I brought you South for your wits, mate. How do we tend to this?”

Ben searched the room. The Wolf King had always valued his intellect. He thought of the bobbing heads he'd passed on his way to the toilet, college kids racked by coke and ecstasy. The smart move may have been to slaughter the party to a man and set the house ablaze. But had they really seen him? Would they remember anything from the last twenty-four hours? Ben turned to his King.

“We’ll leave through the window.”

# CHAPTER EIGHT
## Liz

*Warminster, Pennsylvania*

*What's this bitch, a statue?*

The tattooed rodent sat fixed to the bench. Liz knelt behind a tree with Pedro at her side. She couldn't observe her mother's evening from this distance.

After the mess at Brooks' place, she figured it best to steer clear of Kensington for the day. She copped in the Northeast and shot it in a homeless shelter but felt no effects. She was fine with it, as long as the sickness stayed away. She came to her mother's early, while her stepfather was still at work, thinking it may have finally been time to have the discussion she'd been rehearsing in the mirror for years.

This girl threw a wrench in her plan. Remnants of the previous night returned to her. The girl was familiar. The events were fuzzy, but their exchange could not have been pleasant. She'd been waiting there for over an hour.

The sun was setting, staining the clouds with fleeing alizarin. Liz hadn't been able to pinpoint the exact time her new condition took hold, but it seemed to wait for dark. She scratched Pedro's head. She wouldn't have him near when her consciousness slipped. She'd never forgive herself if any harm came to him.

Peeking around the tree trunk, she could see the girl finally trotting across the field into the back door of one of the adjacent houses. Her focus lifted skyward. Dark was danger-close.

*Cocksucker…*

She nudged Pedro toward home. The conversation with her mother would wait, but Liz had found a new enemy in the scrawny mass of ink.

Pedro kept pace for half a mile, ambling between Liz and the guardrail. Her thighs were no longer sore. This thing, whatever it was, seemed to heal all her physical ailments, track marks in the pits of her elbows included.

Her mental ailments were a different story. *"The fuck are you doin' here?"* She couldn't shake Layla's toothless face. It was a valid question, all the more cumbersome to carry. Liz thought of an even better one. *What am I? What is it that's taken me?*

She remembered when Brooks had shown her the needle for the first time, on the floor of her barracks, her back against the icy steel of her bunk. Inside was the cure for the desert. All her pain and her fallen friends would be carried off.

*Brooks…what did any of it mean?* They had shared things she'd take to her grave. Now he'd fed her to the wolves. *No…I don't buy it.* The Corporal was many things, but he wasn't a liar. He was a man who'd shown all his cards on day one. Deception simply wasn't in him.

Without invitation, the twisted knife returned.

It plunged into her stomach with even more ferocity than before. She dropped to a knee, leaving denim and skin on the asphalt.

It was too soon. The sun wouldn't go down for another hour. *Too soon. Too sssss—*

All blurs and iron smells. Claws. Shredding.

She went over the guardrail.

Falling. Rolling. Landing. Bleeding.

She coughed up dirt. Damp leaves itched at her back.

The dog. *Don't follow, you dumb shit.*

A kick to the ribs, and he stumbled for the trees.

Before logic or guilt could set in, the fur came calling, and the evening sun was snuffed out like a candle flame.

# CHAPTER NINE
## Desmond

*On the road out of Bennington, Vermont*

Ben cruised the truck into a chill evening. He hadn't spoken a word since they left. Something had changed about him on the trip from the lake. There, he'd been brimming with advice and colorful commentary. Now he seemed to have become a mute.

A memory from the lake hit the Wolf King as he watched the trees buzzing by his window, snow dressing their branches—the memory of shortening the head of his would-be usurper up North. Dennings was a Vermont boy, not an Englishman. Derby folk knew far better. His patches must've given him funny notions. They left him in a hurry, spilled red on the snow when Des was through with him. Ben had advised him then, as well, about how to keep the rest of the pack calm.

When Dennings fell, Des made sure to burn him. Falling weak when one of his own died was one of the few embarrassments the Wolf King still had to suffer.

"So wut, now we ain't talkin'?" He wouldn't endure dead air a moment longer.

Ben seemed entranced by the repetition of white lines disappearing beneath the truck's hood. "*You're* talkin'."

Ben's demeanor on this drive had Des wondering if he should've brought the Deacon—a mute, one of the few wolves loyal enough to follow Desmond across the sea. "If I admit again that I was wrong to pull off for a shag, might you quit acting like my fuckin' wife?"

Ben adjusted in his seat. "This trip's got me stressin'." He searched for gum in the glove box and popped a piece into his mouth. "Jackson's sittin' on a lot of sugar up there. Kid's strong, got a good head, but I don't know. Stage Four is hittin' hard lately and I don't like leaving things at the lake."

Jackson was one of his other Vermont hounds with a head on his shoulders. *The Older Brother.* He'd earned the moniker tending to the needs of Desmond's litter. *Strong bloke.* He'd honed his wolf skills—movement speed and close combat tactics—on straw men in the field by the lakeside warehouse, as well as on the occasional defector. Des wondered if he should have brought *him* South.

"Jackson's proven himself. I've no worries."

The roads in Vermont were what Des thought purgatory must be like. Torturous repetition, a tedious journey through nothingness until you forgot everything you ever were. He stared into the void as the truck's headlights burrowed into the dark, Ben gone silent again.

"Been thinking of Esme…" Desmond said.

"Who?"

"It's a story. Salinger."

Ben pointed when the memory found him. *"With Love and Squalor."*

"Right. Enlisted man encounters an orphan choir girl before the D-Day landings…she sends him a gift that mends his mind after the war."

"Rings a bell."

"So where's mine?"

"Your…orphan girl?"

"My Esme. A pleasant bird to ease my troubles…thought I might have found her back there."

Ben grinned for the first time in ages. "You ain't ever been to war."

"Not for my *country*..."

Ben chewed his bottom lip. Something troubled him. Despite his gifts for rationality, he never did well at masking a dangling detail. It leapt from him, then, his words blasting forth like vomit. "I found a patch."

Des went slack-jawed and remained that way for miles of persistent night. Suddenly, the silence made sense. "Where?"

"Inside of my right thigh."

He leered at Ben's infected leg. "Let me see it."

"I'm drivin'."

"Pull over."

With a sigh, Ben did as he was told. He put the truck in park, flicked on the hazard lights and unhooked his belt. With his jeans below his knees, he cupped his testicles to the side and showed the King the first sign of his inevitable end.

"Fuck."

"May I pull 'em up now? This may look curious outta context."

Des popped his door and stomped into the black. He paced the roadside, sporadically searching for answers over the dark field. Now, in addition to his own illness from his fallen soldier, his most trusted wolf was beginning to rot. *The patching...is it my own error? My punishment for rejecting the shaman's rituals?*

Ben leaned over the shift. "We can turn back...I'll switch with Jackson."

Des weighed his options, but he knew Jackson was best suited to keep the lake in check and Ben was the superior advisor. And how long before Jackson suffered the same illness? "No...he's good where he is."

Staring out into the dark, Des saw flashes of another life. Fire and ash. The Mother Hill loomed large in the distance with ruby eyes surrounding it. Slowly, they lost their luster until smoke swallowed them whole.

He said nothing more on the drive. Whichever of Desmond's Southern wolves had fallen had caused a rippling ruckus with his death. Had they been responsible, the King would never have left Vermont, never have crossed paths with the poor doomed slut, never have been overwhelmed and overreacted. He'd been clear to his men about burning the dead, drilled it to every man-wolf from the Northern tips of Vermont to the Pennsylvania plains. This was irregular. No wolf had forgotten this act since Des had crossed the Atlantic eleven years ago. At most, the King felt a fleeting brush of nausea, soon relieved when the body was burned. Something was off about this. He feared he had an enemy he hadn't accounted for. He prayed he truly was the only red-eyed beast still living.

# CHAPTER TEN

## Macy

*Warminster, Pennsylvania*

The chains she'd used to restrain herself to a tree had failed. She'd awakened to splintered steel in her teeth and the gamey taste of venison on her tongue. This time, she'd prepared a change of clothes in the brook where she'd parked the Honda. The vomit leapt from her. She barely kicked the door open in time to let it spew to the mud below. She blasted Scourge to the limits of the Honda's busted speaker. Parker spoke to her again. *This face is one of a collection, scars in places I can't feel. I'm bleeding in a foreign tongue, could it be THE FACE IS REAL?! I'M SPENT! I'VE HAD ENOUGH OF ME! I COULDN'T TASTE IT UNTIL IT SNATCHED MY THROAT! I swim in fog through the Ouachita, BOUND BY BLOOD AND CREOSOTE!*

When she returned to her yard, she found the girl's dog beneath the bench, paws tucked under his chin, shivering away the bloodless fingers of death. His fur was still damp from the storm.

"Hey there..."

She scratched his head and he let out a whimper, his eyes sunken deep. It took some coaxing and a few strips of bacon to guide him across the thoroughfare and into the kitchen where she patted him with a towel.

He warmed to her quickly, or perhaps he'd warmed to the bacon.

He appeared to be a purebred pit bull, white as snow save for a patch of brown over his right eye. She spun his collar to have a look at the tags. The writing was worn. She rubbed a thumb against the metal, drying residual rain.

Pedro. His name was Pedro.

Below the name, the faint scribbling of an address.

# CHAPTER ELEVEN

## Liz

*Kensington, Philadelphia*

Liz contemplated on her mattress while Serita fed her baby at the breast. The kid's father had left him while he went to score. *Model parenting.*

Liz had slipped in at dawn to change her shredded rags. She wondered where Pedro had run to, but she wouldn't blame him if he'd found greener pastures. Now that her mind was somewhat clear, she would try to find a better system for this thing, whatever it was. Maybe try and figure out where it came from.

She focused on Serita and the feeding. "Your titty ever get sore? I always wondered."

With eyes pinched shut, the child looked to be asleep, but his lips drew milk with such ceaseless pumps.

"After a while. This one's got motors in his lips... finna take my nipple if I let him."

Liz had never felt this type of connection to anything. She doubted she would ever have a child. Her hormones were erratic from the physical stress she'd endured in the Corps. She figured she was about as nurturing as the desert that corrupted her.

"Cunt. Bite it. Chew on the cunt." Marcus had returned from his bit in the psych hospital, and already he was off his meds. He wobbled in the corner, chatting gibberish to his shadow, burying rotten fingernails half an inch into his forearm. “I’m gonna find the cunt! I’m gonna dig it out!”

“Marcus! I’m gonna fuckin’ smack you!” Liz was always blunt with him.

When he looked her way she could see the absent, vacant eyes of a man lost to his song. She cocked her fist, and he folded in the corner, muttering quietly to his demons. With assistance from her pocket mirror, Liz fed the needle to her neck and held court with her own.

*One more—a goodbye shot.*

She waited. Nothing.

Even through the neck, her high was a dull memory of what it used to be.

“Yo, I think you got ripped off, girl.”

Serita’s brow furrowed, but her attention stayed with the baby. “Did the trick for *me*.”

Liz gave the smack a chance to set in. She’d never known heroin to have a delayed fuse.

“Devo said it was hammer. Look how dark it is.”

It *was* dark. It must have been her new friend ruining her swan song.

Serita shrugged and the baby’s head lifted with her shoulders. Liz shoved her gear aside and approached the pair. She rubbed the back of the kid’s head as he suckled away, his innocence a stark contrast to his surroundings. “Let’s hope he ain’t making memories yet…”

“Tell that to CPS.” The smirk that followed showed her crooked teeth.

There was a brisk knock at the door, the stiff cadence of police. Liz’s heart began to pound heavier than it had in years. She would’ve handled it better high. “Who the fuck’s that?”

“It’s Freddie Krueger, Liz.”

*Wouldn’t surprise me, lately.* Liz lifted her mattress, propped up the floorboard and slid her implements underneath. “You ain’t expecting no one?” She moved for the door slowly.

"Just check through the fuckin' hole."

She took Serita's advice and peeked through the jury-rigged peephole they had poked in the door.

It wasn't the cops, nor was it Freddy Krueger. It was worse.

The girl stood at about five foot two. She wore a tight black Scourge t-shirt, and both of her arms were covered with tattoos from wrist to elbow. There was a shaved segment of hair above her right ear, the rest was tied up with a strand draped over an eye.

Liz hated this girl. She came from a different species, plain and simple. Her mother's neighborhood spawned a certain type. The type to linger on a bench for an hour to inject herself into a problem. The type to hunt down a residence and crowd the peephole with her sniveling face. Liz had every intention of ignoring the freak until the dog caught her eye. Pedro panted beside her attached to a leash she didn't recognize. It was Serita's idea to write their address on his tags, and now Liz thought she might choke her bunkmate again. She scoffed and pulled open the door.

"The fuck you doin' with my dog?"

The girl seemed confused. Her words lodged in her throat. "I, um…"

"Come here..."

She unclipped him, and he ran to Liz, licking violently at her face. His tail wagged the way it did when they'd first met.

"Found him in my yard."

"The fuck was he doin' *there*?" Liz was prodding her. She knew exactly what Pedro was doing there.

"Not sure." The girl stared at Liz like nothing else existed. Everything she wanted to say was trapped on her tongue.

Liz didn't need her to say anything. She knew why this rodent had come knocking. The dog was just lubricant. "Okay…fuck off."

She didn't. "I need to talk to you."

"You sure don't."

The girl didn't move, Chuck Taylors locked to concrete. "I think this would be better in private." Tats looked past Liz, at Serita and the baby. Then her eyes shifted to Marcus, now in the fetal position in his corner. "And I think you know why."

Liz caught something that might have been determination in the girl's voice. "I don't know what you're talkin' about, but you got five seconds to get outta my sight before I hurt you."

Tats didn't react. She seemed to be processing the threat. "I'll be waiting in the blue Honda across the street... we only have a few hours of sunlight left."

Liz kicked the door shut. Something lingered. A troubling feeling. *The little bitch is absolutely right.* The girl said we. "*We* only have a few hours of sunlight left." Liz must have passed the condition to her. That was the run-in she recalled in fragments.

"What was that about?" Serita rocked the baby into a trance.

Liz scratched Pedro behind the ears the way he liked. "Don't know. Lil' bitch is weird."

It took Liz half an hour to come around. The blue Honda waited patiently, baking in the sun. Tats turned her half-shaven head toward Liz as she crossed the street. She leaned over and flicked up the passenger-side lock.

"Glad you came to your senses."

"Shut the fuck up."

Suddenly Tats found her courage. "Do you think I would have come to this neighborhood if I had a choice?" She scanned the street, noting the smack heads wobbling in and out of consciousness. "Look, we've obviously got a problem. I need your help fixing it." The girl had the nagging voice of a rodent to match her appearance.

"Why?"

"For starters, you're the one who turned me into a wolf."

Liz let out a cackle she couldn't restrain.

"You don't think that's what this is?"

"I don't know what shit you're on, but let me know where you got it." Liz opened her door.

"Just tell me who turned you. Give me that, at least."

Liz found the girl's beady eyes for the first time. "Nobody turned me. I turned me. Don't let me see you on that fuckin' bench no more."

Before Liz could escape, the rat piped up once more. "You must be making somebody proud."

Liz paused a moment and returned to her seat. "'Scuse me?"

"You need *that* to get by…" She pointed to a leaning dreg on the sidewalk. "You must be someone's shining star."

Before Liz could process, her hand was around the girl's throat. She slammed her head into the driver's side window, sending cracks across the glass in four directions.

"Listen to me, you tatted-up scrawny bitch. I don't *need* anything. Whatever I do, I do 'cause I *like* it. Now disappear from my life before I snap off your pigeon head."

Liz released the slender throat and stepped into the sun. The Honda barreled up the road, trailing the scent of burning rubber.

# CHAPTER TWELVE

## Ben

*Brooklyn, New York*

Ben had the same dream again. The great wolf leading hundreds of lesser hounds like an army, charging through the woods, a thunderous roar in his midst. He exhausted all four of his legs to maintain pace in the ranks.

He saw the great wolf split in two. Now, both led the pack, plundering through foliage that cowered in their wake. They brought the pack to a clearing and turned to face their brethren, eyes ruby red—a stark contrast to the yellow eyes of the wolves who followed them. One of the red-eyes howled loud and true, and soon a contagious howl grew until it thickened the air.

They bellowed on until one of the lesser wolves slew one of the greater, decapitating it with a lethally swift claw strike. The howl deadened, and the night was still. The murderous lesser wolf's yellow eyes turned red, and it grew in size, taking its place beside the other.

Ben felt a sharp pain. Through the fur coating his chest, he could see red. Rivulets of blood sprouted from his torso, and the taste of iron erupted from his tightening throat. Through clouded vision, he could see the lesser wolves charging at the red-eyed beasts. The racket faded to a whistling air conditioner as he died.

He awakened in a sweat, despite the whistler spraying ice to his left.

The King must have tried freezing him as a remedy. He slid out of bed and gathered his thoughts on the hotel carpet with the smells of stale beer and cigarettes for company.

He had heard of a similar dream up North at the lake. Jackson mentioned it, Dennings wouldn't shut up about it, but no one had died at the end. Half of them were likely keeping it quiet, afraid of blistering their tender egos, or perhaps they were waiting to take a swipe at the King's head themselves, as Dennings had unsuccessfully tried.

The sun cloaked Ben in warmth from the hotel balcony. He'd slept later than he'd planned, but figured he needed the extra rest. Des was sitting cross-legged on the banister, staring over Brooklyn like its liege lord. *The Great Wolf,* Ben thought. *But there's only one of him.* Des had a mess of abilities, but multiplying was a stretch.

He couldn't shake what Des had done to the girl. Ben had seen enough death up North since Des and his pack took over that it didn't faze him much anymore, but he had a teenaged daughter from whom he'd been estranged. He couldn't help but think of her when he saw the brutal end the girl had suffered.

He slid open the balcony door and joined Des. The King stared straight ahead at the skyline of Manhattan. Something troubled him. Des didn't meditate this way unless a notion itched at him. It happened a handful of times in Vermont, mostly when someone brought up England. *What is it, Des? What happened to you across the water?*

"Dream must've been delightful keeping you out near noon," the King remarked without turning.

Ben approached the railing and braced against it. "Not the word I'd use." He scratched his thigh, and a searing pain replaced the itch.

Des smiled, gaze locked forward on some unseen complication.

"The Great Wolf again?"

"Of course. I pray the Lord might strike me stupid in my sleep…have me dreamin' of puppies and tits."

Des sniggered like a child would.

Ben omitted the part about his death. He wouldn't upset his friend any further.

Des waited a beat. "What I did to the girl…was unbecoming. I lost my composure for a spell."

Ben didn't often see Des troubled by his actions. He appreciated the humanity from the King, knowing how embarrassed it made him. Ben wouldn't rub his nose in it.

"The dream…it was a little different this time."

"How so?"

"Looked like there were two of 'em leadin' us."

"Hmm."

"That mean somethin' to ya?"

"Dreams mean fuck-all to *me*, Ben."

Ben shrugged. He scanned the buildings and distant traffic to see if he could find the secret truth to the universe Desmond wouldn't share. "You got any enemies I don't know about?"

Des stayed with the slaps of the East River.

"The mess in Derbyshire…whatever that was…it's finished, yeah?"

"Why d'you ask?"

"I dreamed about two kings…and I know I ain't the first. That fucker Dennings wouldn't shut up about it."

"He shut it," Des said. "Eventually."

"And you come South to deal with this personally. We've got a mess of wolves we could send down, but you take the risk. I just wanna make sure there ain't some other King Wolf walkin' around droppin' your boys to draw you out."

Now the King was silent. Ben worried he was onto something.

"Who'd have reason to take out Carter? Could he have pissed someone off? Or might this be your past creeping up to bite you?" Carter was the irritating British twit Des had left in charge of his

Pennsylvania wolves. He was the only one not answering the King's phone calls.

Desmond's exhale joined the wind in a heavy rush. "I'm certain I tended to my baggage long before I left home. I'd like if you didn't press me about it further. I've got aches enough as it is. Carter could have been struck by a fuckin' milk truck for all I know. If he's snuffed it, he ain't been burned. That's what's troublin' me. Could be someone we don't know about. Someone else got…carried away."

Ben had always lectured Des about the making of new wolves. Population control could quickly become an issue if any howler could just make another. Des half-listened. He wanted an army, so he welcomed the numbers.

Des slushed saliva between cheeks, inflating one side of his face and then the other. "I should'a kept him up North…sent Jackson to run things down there."

Bad numbers on the ledger could only be moved around so much. Send Jackson to Pennsylvania and Carter brings his problems to Vermont. There weren't enough reliable wolves. Ben picked at his thigh some more. *And fewer every day.*

Des noticed the discomfort. "You don't have to tiptoe 'round your condition like I'm some Mary who might burst into tears."

Ben checked his nails for blood. "I figured you had enough on your plate." Desmond's expression showed he'd grown tired of Ben's elusiveness. He decided to spill his guts. "I saw my own death…in the dream."

"How'd it happen?"

"I don't know…just bled out. One of the red-eyes died, too."

This got the King's attention.

"Killed by a yellow, then *that* one's eyes turned red."

Desmond processed the new details. "Your mind's startin' to go. I've seen it before."

"Dennings?"

Des nodded. "And others. He was havin' all sorts of delusions. Then his words stopped makin' sense."

"I don't think so. Plenty of the lakeside wolves have had the dream. The ones who haven't are probably hiding it."

Des hopped from the railing and approached him. "They may be slippin' as well. Anyway, don't trouble yourself with them. When we burn the body, I'll start thinking clear again. We'll figure a way around all this mess."

Ben wasn't sure why, but he slumped against Des' shoulder.

Des hugged him back. "No need to be a poof about it."

Ben laughed for the first time since they'd left Vermont.

# CHAPTER THIRTEEN

## Liz

*Kensington, Philadelphia*

*They wouldn't have lasted five minutes in the Corps. They would have washed out in basic.* Two cops had come for them shortly after noon—one rotund, the other scrawny. Liz flexed bulging triceps and thrust forward, breaking loose from the skinny cop's grasp. He stumbled in his effort to reclaim her.

"You pull away from me again, you get maced."

Liz obliged him. She'd prefer to keep her eyesight for the trials ahead.

Marcus was less graceful in his walk to the wagon. The cops sweated streams to restrain him while he shouted obscenities in three languages. Liz could see them cringe when his breath hit them. A mixture of cigarettes and rotting corpses. She remembered it well.

They tossed both fiends into the van like luggage, Marcus howling and wheezing when the wind left his lungs. "I'll eat your children, you hunchback Nazi pig!"

Liz wiggled to her feet and claimed the bench, cuffs digging into her sciatic nerve.

Marcus made no effort to improve his position. He lay with vacant eyes, rambling in a language he'd invented.

"Marcus…"

He muttered on. Liz was lost to him.

"Relax, Marcus. Shut up."

Now the moans began. He rolled to one side, pressing his face against the grating, then onto his back, whispering to the ceiling, red imprints crisscrossing his cheek. This became a cycle.

"Marcus, you fuck! Shut your mouth!"

Finally, he stopped rolling, and the gibberish faded to a mumble. Liz lowered her voice when she spoke to him, afraid of sending him into another spasm. "You with me?"

No response.

"Why'd they scoop us, Marcus?"

He stared at nothing, tongue clasped between teeth. Liz was sure he'd found a hidden truth there, her question lost in some thick pulp.

"I was bad." His voice startled her, faint as it was. Whether he was answering her or the ten demons in the van with them, Liz didn't know.

"You were bad after they got there. Why'd they come for *me*?"

The short-lived peace had a violent death. Marcus gyrated his hips and slammed his head against the metal floor. "I was bad! I was bad! I was baaaaaaaaad!"

The skinny cop screamed through the cage. Liz waited for him to turn his back, tucked her feet past her cuffs and slipped her arms to the front. She caressed Marcus' forehead. He was leaking sweat and panting a cloud of death. It reminded her of a young girl from the desert.

Juliana. A nineteen-year-old kid from Brooklyn. A piece of the wrecked Viper protruded from her chest, and she was choking on blood. All the caressing in the world couldn't mend her.

"Easy," she said now, atoning for her silence on the battlefield. "It's cool, yeah? It's all cool."

Nothing was cool.

If she stayed in the van, the cops would die. They were a nuisance, but she wouldn't have their deaths on her conscience.

"Get your cuffs back where I put 'em or I will."

She hadn't noticed the scrawny one's glare.

She slipped her feet through and put his mind at ease.

Liz cooked up two explanations for the arrest. The first involved the tattooed brat ratting on her for bashing her head. The second involved her unhinged episode at Brooks' place, though she couldn't imagine fiends calling the cops.

Either way, it seemed she would meet her end here. They'd put it on the news that a rabid dog got loose and keep her name out of the papers. Her mother would never even know she'd punched out.

That was the narrative she had accepted before she found her strength.

She pulled her wrists apart, and the cuffs snapped like a child's toy. She broke the metal rings off each wrist without a strain. The loudmouth in front didn't seem to hear. *Where the fuck was this against the toothless princess?* This thing, whatever it was, must have had progressive symptoms. She set the broken cuffs gently on the seat beside her and returned her hands to the small of her back.

Marcus had seen what she'd done, and even a Schizo as lost as him knew to be afraid. For an instant, Marcus seemed sane. His eyes were saucers as he shuffled away from Liz and tucked into the corner of the van. She started to reach for him, but he kicked at her hands. She returned to her place before the cop could notice her.

"Be nice back there, okay? Let's have a quiet ride to the station."

Liz was leaving the van. Marcus was staying. She hadn't had a situation so clear-cut in years. She found his eyes through rapid twitches. "Behave yourself. I'll come visit you if I can."

Marcus was a good kid when he took his meds. He deserved better than an eastern district lockup.

Liz pressed her feet to the grating and planted a front kick on the van's back door. It dislodged and skittered onto the asphalt behind them, shooting sparks like geysers. She could hear yelling as she tumbled to the street, tucking and rolling to absorb the impact. The van screeched to a halt, but Liz kept moving.

She'd have a serious discussion with the tatted girl before she fled the state and became a myth.

# CHAPTER FOURTEEN
## Ben

*Brooklyn, New York*

The bones in Becker Jr.'s hand popped in Desmond's grip. *That's the way, Wolf King. Mask your weakness to the pups.* Junior was another hanger-on from Derbyshire—British to his bones, the brat son of some long-lost family friend. Des had mentioned he was in his late twenties, but he looked younger. Despite his boyish appearance, if the stories were to be believed, the man was a holy terror. No pain read on Junior's face. His smile never faltered. The King could rip his hand off at the wrist, and he'd be grateful.

Junior spoke with whistling arrogance when Desmond released him. "What's the issue with Carter's boys? Kindlin' run low?"

The club was dark, rank with the smell of stale beer, much like New York itself. If Ben could design his own hell, this wasn't a far cry. He played billiards against Becker's giant of a crony in the room connected to the brat's office. He sank the five into the side pocket, and his opponent sighed through a thick beard.

The brat rambled on. "Shoulda sent *me* down there. I'da kicked 'em in their knickers 'til they could rub two bloody sticks together."

Ben loathed him already. He couldn't gather Desmond's feelings on him. He couldn't read the King much at all of late.

"Just something I'd rather tend to personally." Des scanned the club through the office window. "You've done well here. Your old man would be proud."

The kid's eyes lit up. "I reckon so—I mean, I hope so, yeah." Junior handed Desmond a golden shot of brandy and scooped up one of his own. "To the old man."

Des nodded and downed his toast.

"May he hunt forever with the almighty." More of the booze dribbled from the chump's lips than made it into his mouth. "So, who's this bollock you come South with?"

Ben sank the three-ball. *Sniveling little shit.* He focused on the muffled thunks as the three made its descent to the return. Causing a scene would be careless, though he wondered about the sound the kid would make should his guts spill to the carpet.

"Easy. Ben's a good lad." Ben pretended not to hear. "He just *dresses* like a bollock."

Junior shot spit strands with his laugh.

"So, listen. When we get to Carter's, we could be walkin' into a do. I may need to ring ya."

"You think it's somethin' down there?"

"Don't matter what I think. Would you answer the call?"

Doubt choked the pup's words for the briefest of moments. It may have slipped by Desmond's ear, but Ben heard it clear. He smirked to himself. "Anything you need."

"Good lad." He gave the kid a tap on the cheek. "That said, I don't want to let New York slip, so that's a last resort scenario, you understand? I need you to move some extra powder to atone for the sloppy doings down there. Keep Travis and the cunt with the eye busy. I know they like to sit on their asses."

Becker nodded.

"Can I trust you to keep things chipper?"

"Great deal better than the geezers down South, I know that

much."

"And your boys, they know the drill?"

Junior glanced at his bearded comrade, the one Ben had been hustling all afternoon. "Ringo! I go down, what do you do?"

"Have myself a barbecue."

Junior smiled boyishly in the King's face. Des patted his shoulder, and Ben squeezed his pool cue until a crack ran to its tip.

# CHAPTER FIFTEEN

## Macy

*Warminster, Pennsylvania*

"You got some fuckin' balls sitting right where I told you not to be." Her voice was fainter than Macy remembered, and it looked as though the woman had run a relay through hell.

Macy stood away from the bench and brandished her switchblade.

Its glisten caught the woman's eye, and she repaid it with a smile.

"You know I could take that from you and stuff it up your ass."

Macy feigned confidence, though she knew the woman was right. "Probably…but I wouldn't make it easy." She was sure the woman could hear the gaps in her vocal rhythm. Her John Wayne façade was paper-thin.

"You rat me out?"

Now she was unsure how to react. "To who?"

"The KGB…the fuckin' cops. How hard I bust your head?"

The back of Macy's skull pulsated with the reminder, though the wound had healed within seconds of impact. "I didn't talk to anyone about you."

"You sure? Think on it."

Macy didn't have to think at all. "It's worry enough keeping *myself* under the radar."

The woman read Macy's face carefully. Her eyes sharpened as she studied. Macy wondered what she did for a living if it wasn't shooting dope. She watched the woman's broad shoulders ease, and she slackened her grip on the blade.

"Yeah…" Her chestnut eyes locked on the weapon. "So, you gonna stab me, or what?"

Macy flipped the knife closed and returned it to her pocket. "I get worried. Thought you might have come to finish what you started." She tapped her index finger on the back of her head.

"You got a hard fuckin' nut..." She giggled. "Break a nose or two with that."

Macy couldn't help her smile. "Look, what I said…I needed your attention." She expected an apology in return, but it never came. Her own words shattered the awkward silence that followed. "So, someone snitched?"

"Cops are on me. I had to get out of the city."

"Why'd you come *here*?"

"To fuck you up for snitching…but I actually almost believe you."

"Alright." Macy was baffled.

"I can help you if you can give me somewhere to stay. Can't show my face nowhere else."

"So, I harbor a fugitive?"

"Don't be dramatic. I just need a place to keep out of the fuckin' rain 'til we can fix this."

Macy gave her house a longing look. *Someone like this only folds out of desperation.* "I've got a shed. I can make it cozy for a time... I can't keep you in the house. My dad would ask questions."

"Good enough."

"But you have to swear you'll see this through and not bail on me if something better comes along."

The woman's gaze hit the clouds as she discharged a laborious breath. "Yeah, whatever."

Macy remained silent. She had to hear it, even if she couldn't quite trust the woman's word.

"On my honor as a street rat…" She held a calloused right hand in the wind. "It ain't been easy for me either."

Macy nodded and made for the house.

"Yo…"

She listened as she walked.

"You got a shower I could use?"

"Follow me."

The woman followed. "I got another question."

"Yeah?"

"How come you didn't turn yourself in? You seem like…kind of a pussy. No offense. People like you run to cops when trouble comes."

Macy rubbed her tattoos. *Do I look like some square?* "Last night I chained myself with steel. The *thing* ate right through. I get put in a rusty cell, I'll end up hurting people. Maybe killing them."

"Hmm."

Before they made it to the door, Macy had to ask. "Why didn't *you*?"

Her grin was anything but warm.

"'Cause fuck them."

Macy could hear the woman singing. *Fleetwood Mac? Possibly.* Her voice was surprisingly soothing. She'd been in the shower for thirty minutes, but Macy didn't have the heart to boot her. She'd seen where the woman was living and figured showers hadn't come along often.

She gathered what blankets she could from the linen closet, carefully choosing the ones her father wouldn't miss. The shed in her yard was hardly hospitable, but the blankets would make it passable for a night.

When the woman finished her shower, Macy brought her out to her new bunk, a puddle of blankets nestled beside the snow shovels. She was expecting a 'thank you.'

"It'll do," was all the woman could manage. She fell to the pile of bedding and propped her back against the shed's wall.

"I never got your name."

"I never got yours either."

"Macy." She held out her hand.

"Liz." She kept hers right where it was.

Macy dropped her hand, and Liz sniggered at the discomfort.

"Okay. Let's talk about who bit you." Macy's courtesy had run dry.

Liz's brows curled upward. "You think I'd let a motherfucker bite me?"

"So, what, you were born like this?"

"Started a few days back."

"That doesn't make sense."

Liz cracked another condescending grin and cleared snot from her face. "This shit with us starts to make sense to you…you should worry."

"Look, it had to be something." Macy grabbed a cushion. "You scratched me, I turned. It's gotta be a transfer-of-fluids type deal, no?"

"Like the movies?" Liz's eyes widened.

"Not exactly. I found a few things on the internet. Some online cult claiming their leader was half wolf. Something about a wolf-run drug ring. A magician who can turn people to animals. Some other even more ridiculous crap about England."

Liz waved a hand dismissively. "Goofy shit on there."

Macy fluttered a sigh past her lips. "I know it's flimsy, but I would have thought our thing was ridiculous a week ago."

Liz chewed the inside of her cheek. "I got in a fight the other day. Some big asshole broke my arm." She clicked her tongue to simulate the snap. "Nah but that was afterwards. I changed the night before."

"What happened the day before that?"

"I didn't exchange no fluids…" The words stuck to her tongue, and she went mute. In a flash, she was on her feet pacing the shed from wall to wall.

"What? You got something?" Macy stood as well in an effort to balance out the universe.

"You gotta drive me somewhere."

"Where?"

"Back to my hood. Lemme borrow a hoodie, I gotta hide my face."

# CHAPTER SIXTEEN

## Ben

*Brooklyn, New York*

Ben buried his face between the stripper's breasts. He felt her nipples stiffen on his cheeks. She gyrated her hips and bumped her pelvis against his, but he couldn't shake the taste of betrayal from his pallet. For the first time since he'd met Desmond, he felt used. He'd never considered himself an insecure man. At thirty-nine, he'd just about rid himself of ego, but his patch had him feeling old and worn.

His thigh was itching.

Peeking past the stripper's shoulder, Ben could see Junior emerging from the fog of the club. The kid parked his presumptuous hind three feet from him. A glass of whiskey clinked icily in hand.

"Oi!" He motioned to another girl. "Me mate, here, is making me jealous." She swayed over to him and plopped in his lap. Junior barely managed to keep his whiskey upright.

For a while, the shallow tones of the club's music were the only sounds. Then Junior piped up again. "You're holdin' somethin back, mate."

Ben wasn't sure if the kid was speaking to him or the stripper. "What's that?"

"You've got this fold in your face when you look at me…like you caught some stench."

Ben kept his eyes on the girl's stomach. "Observant."

The kid chuckled. "So, what is it, mate? We're not school girls, are we?"

Now Ben looked Junior in his snot-nosed face. "You want honesty?"

"Christ's truth."

"I think you're a sycophant."

Junior's eyes went blank. "You're gonna have to forgive me. I chased skirt through grammar school."

"You're sucking up to Des for attention. Like he'll anoint you if you try hard enough. It's embarrassing, if you wanna know... Christ's truth."

Junior loaded a response as fast as his thick head would allow. "Shame." He rubbed the contours of the girl's hips. "But while we're on the topic of embarrassing, Des told me about your problem."

Ben's heart dropped to his stomach.

"Been a bit itchy, yeah?"

He'd been fighting fiercely to cope with impending doom, and he'd trusted his friend to keep it between them. Instead, Desmond spilled the beans to the first overconfident drone they crossed on their trip South.

"You needn't worry, guv. My old man went the same way."

Ben moved the stripper aside to ensure he'd heard correctly. "What?"

"You're in good company. No need to be ashamed."

Yet another thing Des had kept from him. He was sure Stage Four had only affected the lakeside wolves, but a Derbyshire man?

"I'll be sure to cook you all the way through when you finally go."

Ben tossed the stripper from his lap, and she cursed him halfway to hell. He beelined for the exit door.

Junior bellowed a satanic cackle that tortured him long after he'd left.

# CHAPTER SEVENTEEN

## Macy

*Kensington, Philadelphia*

The police cruiser skulked in the shadow of a willow oak, leviathan arms swaying with an early autumn breeze. An ancient tree, older than the dilapidation surrounding it. The god of this lamplit strip. Macy spotted subtle movements—the silhouettes of two officers. The train rumbled above them, rattling her to the bone. The Honda's A/C pumped warm air. Liz switched it off and cracked her window. "You try'na fuckin' melt me?"

"What's *this* about?" Macy tipped her chin to the scouts in blue.

"They got a hard-on. I need you to fetch somethin'."

"And if they spot *me*?"

"They're lookin' for a doped-up bruiser, not a pigeon with tats."

Macy struggled to keep the muscles of her face taut and ambiguous. "You don't think they'll stop anyone goin' in there?"

Liz balled up a fist and pounded it onto her forehead, punctuating words with the smacking of flesh. "They might have people watchin' the back…" She set eyes on the sunroof and slid open the partition, unveiling the tracks overhead. There was something foreboding about the twisted mass of metal and the grin that tugged gently at Liz's lips. "How are you with heights?"

Macy remembered climbing trees as a child. Sarah showed her the way. “Heights, I don’t mind. Trains could be a problem.”

With her chin, Liz motioned to the gap between the tracks and her roof. “Can you make that jump?”

The space between metal and shingles was five feet…maybe six. “I don’t know…”

“Well…flap the wings God gave you.”

Liz hadn’t given her a choice. She would stick the landing or shatter her legs. This was the price for partnership. “What am I fetching?”

The room was dark save for the setting sunlight she’d let in. She sidestepped piles of clothes and broken bottles on her way to the hall. The rhythmic thrum of hip hop blared from a room at the end of the corridor. She made for the stairs in a hurry. The staircase spilled into the kitchen where filthy dishes covered a roach-riddled counter, and a foul smell curled her stomach. Something had surely died in this house.

Covering her nose and mouth with the sleeve of her jacket, she stumbled for the living room. Here, the smells were urine and rotting wood. The fecal scent of human neglect. Liz’s friend was slumped on the couch like she said she’d be. She stifled a sob at the sound of Macy’s footsteps.

“Hey.”

The girl found her through a glaze of tears.

“I’m a friend of Liz’s.” The word ‘friend’ felt odd. “She sent me to grab some things.”

The girl nodded and wiped her face. “Under the mattress.” She pointed across the room to Liz’s bed where Pedro slept soundly.

A scratch from Macy startled the pup from a dream. He nestled against her leg and showed his belly for her to rub. "'Scuse me, boy." She nudged him, and he moved from the bed. The floorboards came up easily, where she found the box she'd been risking her skin for. A heavy case for its size, two clips fastened with a combination lock.

The girl on the couch wiped her face. "Tell Liz I'll feed her dog."

Macy had every intention of leaving, but something about the weeping girl kept her. "You okay?"

Her jade eyes caught Macy unaware. There was beauty here in this nest of excrement. It took several hard swallows before the girl could speak. "They took my baby."

Macy wasn't sure how to respond.

"I didn't do nothing wrong..."

She let the moment linger, ill-equipped to offer any type of relief to a grieving mother. She wondered if her own mother cried this way, dwelling on the life she'd fled. *Should I have run with you, mom? Spared myself from this?* She clutched the case tightly and turned for the kitchen.

When she emerged from the alleyway, a rhythmic pulse found her. Liz waited in the driver's seat, grinning and bobbing her head, mouthing rapid lyrics. She rolled her window down, and the rhythms took form. "Hop in, Minnie Mouse."

Macy squeezed the case, chucking worried glances to the police car. "Slide over…"

"I'm good where I am."

"Liz…"

"You wanna do this here? Put on a show for the boys?"

Riding passenger in her own car felt degrading, like she'd been stripped nude and tied to the hood.

A few blocks from the cruiser, Liz pulled the Honda to the side of the road. Macy handed her the case, and she checked the lock for misplaced digits. "Good." She set it on the back seat. "Pedro okay?"

Macy nodded. "He's taken care of."

"Serita?"

*Missing a child, distraught.* "She's fine."

"Good, good. Let's head to my friend's spot. It's close."

"Wait." Macy looked to the sky. "Sun's almost down."

Liz looked past the squalor at the horizon. She looked at the clock. 6:52. "Fuck."

Liz parked the Honda in the dead-end Macy showed her. Macy stepped out, pulled her shirt over her head and slipped out of her shorts.

Liz scrunched up her face. "The fuck are you doin'?"

"I don't wanna rip my clothes."

Liz pondered that for a moment, shrugged and stepped out to start stripping. Macy struggled not to notice Liz's body. It didn't arouse her—she wasn't into women—but she found it interesting. Her arms and legs were muscled, as was her midsection, but her hips were padded with fat. Where Macy's breasts were small but firm, Liz's drooped.

It wasn't long before Liz clocked her. "Don't get excited, now."

Macy looked to the dirt while Liz slid her panties to her feet and tossed them into the back of the Honda. "That's it. Keep your eyes down there. You'll be doin' enough droolin' tonight, you need to pace yourself."

Macy longed for better company on this uncomfortable foray, but instead, she got a bully. She grabbed a bottle of glass cleaner from the back seat and started covering the windows with it.

Liz jumped at the squirting sound. "The fuck?"

Macy explained as she worked. "I've been thinking. I don't know how it's been for you, but my senses have been sharp. Taste, smell, everything heightened." She moved to the windshield and poured out the remainder of the bottle. "I don't know how far this thing takes us when it hunts, but…" She chucked the empty container. "If we're anywhere close, we'll smell the ammonia…find our way back."

"All right, Martha Stewart," Liz muttered.

It was near dark when both women entered the brush. Macy gave parting instructions. "We'd better put some distance between us so we don't kill each other. We'll meet here in the morning."

Liz marched for the woods without another word.

That night Macy dreamt of chewing. Tendons. Bone. Everything broke between her jaws. The body beneath her twitched, and then it didn't. Something was sated—something beyond hunger for which she couldn't find the word.

# CHAPTER EIGHTEEN

## Brooks

*Quakertown, Pennsylvania*

**Two Days Ago**

The cabin where he cut his drugs was a quiet refuge, miles from the stench of his concrete sprawl. Brooks tried to find comfort in the vacancy, but it left room for his ghosts to traipse in unannounced.

This one's hair fell to her shoulders in chestnut curls. The contours of her frame were lost beneath her tunic. She stared at Brooks from across the cabin, her good eye brimming with accusatory fire.

Half her face was missing. The Corporal's bullet had laid waste to her features, and yolky bits of her destroyed eye still clung to her cheek. She stared until the silence grew too thick to swallow.

"What?" He waited while the girl sulked. "You know, my privacy is precious to me. I don't come by it often."

The girl didn't react. Brooks was growing impatient.

"What about the ones who strapped it to you? Why don't you go bother them?"

She stared for a bitter stretch before disappearing into the next room. He listened to receding footsteps. *Ghouls*, he thought. *The damned take no vacations.* This one-eyed devil came from a group of phantoms Brooks had brought with him from Afghanistan. She'd become the most persistent by far.

He swallowed hard in an effort to set aside his grief while the pungent stench of death nipped at his nostrils.

He lifted the trap door in the cabin's living room floor, and an army of flies took to the air. The body was tightly wrapped in a white trash bag. Blood pooled around the face, leaving damp red stains. He'd been living with the smell for days. The necrotic stink had become a form of torture.

He slipped on a pair of plastic gloves and gripped the body by the shoulders. He hoisted it onto the wooden floor, and its head made a resounding *thump* when he lost his grip. Dragging the body into the woods took every muscle in Brooks' back. The sun beat on him mercilessly.

The soil was loose, giving way for the shovel without argument. Brooks burrowed two feet into the ground by the time his arms gave in. Any deeper and he would pass out from exhaustion. He gave the body a sturdy kick, and it rolled into the hole, landing facedown in the soil.

He'd make a formal apology in the afterlife. Facedown burials had been used in certain cultures to humiliate the dead. *That one was an accident, friend. Don't* you *come back and haunt me, too.*

He jammed the shovel's head into the pile of loose soil and covered the body bit by bit. When the trash bag disappeared beneath the dirt, he tamped it down and kicked leaves and twigs over top.

The blood that Brooks trailed through the cabin came up easily when he put a mop to it. The smell took some doing. He bombed the living room with Febreze, but the combination of rotten flesh and apple pie was somehow worse. He fished around in the kitchen drawers and found a dusty roll of duct tape. Crouched near the trap door, he taped back the trigger on the canister and dropped it in like a gas grenade, slamming the door shut to trap the scent.

Killing was easier in the desert. You could leave the bodies where they dropped.

Brooks beat into the soaking earth with his paws. The trees took on phantom shapes as they buzzed past, and his fur kissed the bark, chipping pieces of it here and there.

He had the buck's scent. The oils of its skin and the iron in its blood left a trail for him to chase. With each stride, he whittled down the distance until the frightened animal caught his eye. He could see it skittering through the brush, its front legs struggling to keep pace with its hind. It tripped over tree roots, just barely maintaining balance.

*Give it up, friend. I'll snuff you out quick. I promise.*

The buck seemed to have heard his thoughts. It slowed to catch its breath for just a moment. Brooks lunged. He clasped his jaw around the back of the buck's neck, and its spine made a sickening *crunch* when he twisted. Suddenly, the night was still.

Brooks stared into the dead buck's eyes. The animal hadn't noticed his own death, like a lackwit late to a punchline.

He sank his fangs into the stomach and pulled its entrails through the fleshy ruin. The metallic taste whet his appetite. He buried his jaw deeper into the animal's core for a second go. He stripped his meal to the bone and cleaned the skeleton of cartilage. When he was through, he snapped its ribs with his teeth and sucked out the marrow.

With his stomach filled, he scanned the surrounding woods. He caught something bright in his peripheral. A yellow strand of caution tape danced in the wind. Brooks had tied several of them to trees, marking a boundary he couldn't pass.

A few weeks before, he'd considered his condition a curse. The taste of iron from his pistol danced tauntingly on his tongue.

Now, he had adjusted well. The rush of his prowling nights dwarfed anything he'd experienced in the desert. His phantoms receded when the wolf took charge and he had given all of himself to the beast.

But beyond the rush, beyond his ghosts abandoning their haunt, Cameron Brooks was finally in control.

# STAGE 2

"Trauma destroys the fabric of time. In normal time you move from one moment to the next, sunrise to sunset, birth to death. After trauma, you may move in circles, find yourself being sucked backwards into an eddy or bouncing like a rubber ball from now to then to back again. ...In the traumatic universe, the basic laws of matter are suspended: ceiling fans can be helicopters, car exhaust can be mustard gas."

-David J. Morris, *The Evil Hours: A Biography of Post Traumatic Stress Disorder*

# CHAPTER NINETEEN

## Desmond

*Brooklyn, New York*

The crack in the club's restroom mirror separated Desmond's face at the nose. To its left was the Des of old—a scamp that hauled his roots by chains through the dust of time, a hellraiser of a hound who shattered hearts and heads. To its right was someone new—an empty shell, a monarch with a stain he couldn't scrub. The aches in the Wolf King's head grew with each Southward mile, and nausea washed in like a wave of sewage. *A shag'll help.* Time and again his mantra had proven false. A shag hadn't helped in Bennington, it wouldn't help here.

The loo's door screeched when it swung open, preceding the pitter-patter of boots through a lake of urine. A man with a grasshopper's face bellied up to a urinal. His mandibles clicked together, echoing something regal in this pit of human waste. The bug was hardly majestic, but the surrounding stink made him seem like a prince. Its front legs poked through a checkered button-down, its hind split the cloth of khaki pants. Des had been staring too long, and the bug took notice.

"The fuck's your problem?" It mimicked a human voice masterfully, a middle-aged rasp that reminded the Wolf King of his father's.

Des could only manage a twitch of his jaw.

The bug flushed and washed its front legs in a sink stained with rust. Desmond had burning questions, though his brush with the insect was brief. He chose the most pertinent. "How far can you jump?" He focused on the bug's hind legs—bulbous, jagged, powerful.

The bug killed the faucet and left Des' inquiry wallowing in the stench. The establishments in the States were likely to spread disease. Desmond longed for the pubs of Derbyshire. To enter one was to enter a home.

He knew the bug was another figment, but still wondered if the club's patrons would notice an insect of its size.

Suddenly, his consciousness wavered. He saw visions from the Mother Hill—a burning barn, blood dressing the snow-dusted courtyard of his father's estate. He stumbled to a stall and braced himself against it.

The door opened again, and in stepped his younger brother Daniel. *Blood of Christ.* His red eyes had a slick sheen to them still, though he'd died twelve years ago. "Looks like stress is takin' the piss from ya."

"Fuck off. I've paid my dues." With thoughts of his family came thoughts of the end. The agonizing screams of their deaths. The Mother Hill aflame.

"Desmond…"

If he kept from looking again, the vision would surely fade.

"Des!"

He turned to see Ben waiting by the door with a curl in his brow. "Yeah?"

"You all right?"

Des found his breath and made for the sink to wash his face. "Yeah."

"Good…come out to the truck, I need a word."

In the truck, Ben rubbed his eyes to ward off sleep. "Two developments, one minor and one major. The minor—what the fuck are you doing telling Junior my private business?"

This development, Desmond had to ponder. "Ah, fuck off. The patch?"

Ben nodded.

Des wondered when he'd become so sensitive.

"I mentioned it in passing so the little cunt would go easy."

"It affects me."

"Mate, you're not unique. Half the bloody Lake is hacking blood. And anyway, who cares what the brat thinks? He's got tit milk on the breath. His old man was something, but…" Des glanced back to the club's entrance.

"Well, you see, this brings me to the major. How exactly did Junior's father pass?"

The King looked to his hands. "He, uh…

Ben leaned in close. "Don't fuck with me."

Des smiled at the wolf beside him. "Who's this, now? You find your balls?"

"I'm supposed to be here for guidance, hmm? You want me to be your fuckin' life coach? How long you been bullshittin' me?"

At times, Des thought Ben was too inquisitive for his own good. He'd never let a dangling detail go. Des gave him a pat on the cheek. "I didn't want to hurt morale, cause panic up North. The wolves I've turned in the States haven't held the same as the ones in Derby. Weak American blood, I thought. But now, my Derby boys I've brought over have been fallin' off as well. I'm fucked as to why."

"How the fuck am I supposed to advise you if I can't trust what you've told me? How long have you known about this illness, really?"

"It hit Becker a few weeks after it kicked off at the Lake. I've never known it before then." Des knew Ben would stay skeptical, but he needed to keep things tranquil until they burned this body. "Sorry, mate. You've been good for us. I should've been completely open with you."

Ben rolled his eyes, unmoved by the King's sentiment. "I need more sleep before we hunt this corpse."

Dawn was approaching. Ben chunked his truck to life and made for the hotel.

# CHAPTER TWENTY

## Macy

*Warminster, Pennsylvania*

She awakened to sticky blood on her breasts. She washed herself in a nearby creek, the frigid water tightening her skin. When she was clean, she closed her eyes and concentrated on the surrounding scents. Pine, cedar, soil, blood and faintly…ever so faintly, ammonia.

Liz waited at the car, pacing like she'd stopped for coffee. She spotted Macy and smiled. "I was this close to leaving your ass in the jungle." She held her thumb and forefinger millimeters apart. "Get dressed, bitch, we got a big day."

Macy pulled her clothes from the Honda and stepped into her underwear. "Where are we headed?"

Liz sighed like a pierced balloon. "The Land of Oz."

The complex they watched now made Liz and Serita's place look luxurious. Its front door was a warping piece of plywood, corners bending to allow the rats easy passage. The stoop was a mass of cracked cement, crevices filled with paper cups and napkins. Every window had been broken.

Liz tipped her chin. “Guy I know lives here.”

“He the one who turned you?”

“He’s worth talkin’ to. Let’s leave it at that.”

Macy figured it would be easier to extract teeth from Liz than information. “Any idea when he might be around?”

“He’s always out front checkin’ on his people. We’ll see him.”

Macy eased into her seat, and the muscles in her back thanked her. Her fingers twitched, desperate to reclaim the wheel.

“So what’s *your* deal?” Liz’s stab at small talk caught Macy off guard.

“Sorry?”

“You seem to like prying in my shit, I figured I’d pry back.”

*Hmm. Could be baiting me, but I’ll bite.* “I work on cars at my dad’s shop. I got a side thing going too, but it’s been slow.”

Liz gave her a look like a child would, forced to eat broccoli. “They got little twiggy goth bitches twisting wrenches?”

“I built a supercharged 5.2 liter V-8 from scratch.”

Liz revved the Honda. “Yeah. That sounds like your work.”

Macy could only giggle. “I wouldn’t put a V-8 in here.”

“You should put one up your ass.” This girl was fragile for how strong she looked. A tender ego bound in muscle.

The plywood front door blew open. A filthy girl with a stained T-shirt and greasy straw hair stepped into the sun. Liz stared her down, knuckles clenching white.

“You know her?”

She hesitated. “Nah. Ass-ugly though, right?”

Macy found it difficult to disagree. “What’s this guy look like?”

“Black. Short beard. Big-ass nose.”

They watched the girl on the stoop as she scratched her face and picked at scabs in the crook of her arm. If Liz had been an average dope addict, this girl was a Crown Princess. Macy couldn’t find a single complete tooth between her lips. *This is where your habit leads, Liz. Consider it a toothless omen.*

With substance abuse in abundance, her father came to mind. "I've gotta make a call." She popped her door and stepped onto the concrete.

Liz caught her wrist in a vise-grip and yanked her back. "The fuck you do. Why don't you get a megaphone... tell her you found her teeth?"

"You said yourself, doped-up bruiser. No one's lookin' at me."

"Shut the door…and shut your fuckin' mouth."

Macy did as she was told. The look in Liz's eyes raised the hair on her neck. The whistle of the wind carried a strange serenity through the sordid strip. Perhaps the girl on the stoop really *was* a princess and Macy lacked the vision to admire her castle. Whatever the case, this was a place filled with ghosts. She reckoned Liz had died here some time ago and the person beside her was, in truth, a revenant. The same could be said about her counterpart across the street. Macy followed her instincts, the way she always had when trouble found her. She went elsewhere.

In *this* place, Sarah had never died, her mother had never left, her father's smile had never faded. The smell was barbecue and the hemlock trees Sarah made her climb. The sounds were birds and the buzz from cicadas and Sarah's voice. *"Pinch with your thighs."* The hemlock's skin had torn hers to ribbons. *"That's it…now swing."* She moved from limb to limb, shaking needles free and bending branches like living arms. *Sarah, the acrobat. Sarah, the orangutan. Sarah, the ghost.*

"Yo, Punky Brewster." Liz's voice pulled her from the tree. "Game face."

A silver Toyota sputtered across from them, kicking up a smoke screen at the castle's gate.

"I don't know whose shit-ass ride that is, but that's him."

The driver stepped out. A black guy with a beard, but his nose wasn't near as big as Liz described. He kissed the dope princess on the cheek, twisting Macy's stomach, and the two of them stepped inside.

"Should we talk to him?"

Liz gazed at the plywood door as if to start a fire. "Not here. I wanna see where he goes."

She struggled to stay several car lengths behind the Toyota as it bolted from the city. Macy knew it wouldn't be a struggle if *she* were behind the wheel. "Ease up a little."

"I know how to fuckin' tail someone. Shut up."

*If only that were true. He's blind if he hasn't made us.* "This car's got sensitive pedals. You're not used to them."

Liz squeezed the life from the wheel as a trickle of sweat traced her jawline.

"You hear? You can't ride him this hard…"

"It don't help I got a little gerbil poppin' off in my ear."

Macy slumped against her seat. "You should've just let me drive."

"Alright, here…" Liz grabbed Macy's hand and placed it on the steering wheel.

"What are you doing?"

"Get your scrawny ass…" She grabbed Macy's hips and lifted her up, sliding her own body underneath. They wrestled to claim new seats.

"Are you crazy?" The car slowed and swerved as soon as Liz removed her foot from the gas. Macy pumped the brakes to regain control. "What the hell is wrong with you?"

"Loaded question, sister."

Macy backed off until she tailed the Toyota at a manageable distance. “Do you *want* to fix this? I’m startin’ to wonder.”

“Right now, I kind of wanna choke you, but I’ll do like my therapist said and restrain myself.”

Macy was losing count of Liz’s physical threats but was starting to realize most of them weren’t credible. She also knew, if Liz did in fact have a therapist, they certainly wouldn’t be making house calls. “Who is this guy? Is he the one that turned you? ‘Cause, if not, this is time we can’t afford.”

Liz pointed to the Toyota, her index finger gyrating. “This big nose fuck is the only guy I exchanged fluids with in the past month. He let me use his needle. I didn’t get bit, I didn’t get scratched, and I didn’t fuck nobody, so it had to be that. That’s if we’re going by your flimsy ass rules…okay?” She took a breath, and her shaking finger went still. “Good enough?”

Macy kept a consistent pace as she stared into the gleam of the Toyota’s taillights. “Yeah…” She looked at Liz who was still pointing. “Yeah, okay.”

The Toyota turned off the road and ventured a half mile into the woods. It stopped at a cabin. Liz’s friend with the moderately-sized nose left his vehicle and went inside.

Liz glared at the white pine before stepping out.

Macy followed close. “What are you doing?”

Liz kept walking as she answered. “We go back years…nothin’ to fear from him.”

“Liz, hold on.” Macy shut her door and struggled to catch up. The hemlocks around them brought her to a different time. “How do you know he's alone? Are you sure—?"

"Jesus Christ. I had to scratch a fuckin' windbag." She stepped onto the porch and opened the cabin door.

The blast of the shotgun left a high-pitched ringing in both of Macy's ears. Liz left her feet and the porch and her windbag of a partner.

# CHAPTER TWENTY-ONE

## Ben

*Philadelphia, Pennsylvania*

"Des…" Ben shook his red-eyed comrade, and he slumped into the door, his head belting the glass. They entered Pennsylvania, and the *great wolf* had gone comatose. *There you go. Some fuckin' Wolf King, huh? Droolin' on my upholstery.*

He shifted focus between the road and his friend's throat. He wondered if a man who fancied himself a lupine demigod would die like a frightened child should his jugular come open. He hated himself for the macabre thinking. He had considered Desmond a friend, but he had a feeling the King was omitting more details about the patches. Des lied with such ease, it unnerved him.

His thigh was itching.

Carter lived in a Philly suburb, and the path through the city was unavoidable. Dread seeped into his pores. The city stank of piss. There was roadwork where it needn't be, and the drivers were reckless.

Ben prayed to the God he'd abandoned that it would be a simple burn job, no backup required. Junior would only make matters worse. The kid was everything he couldn't stand about youth. He spoke with confidence beyond his years but cared very little about the quality of his words. His generation seemed to simply speak to be heard, siphoning attention with empty noise. Somehow, Desmond saw potential in him. Perhaps it was the British roots or his history with the kid's father. It mattered little to Ben.

He pulled over next to a mural to gather his thoughts. Some deep impulse told him to dump Desmond on the side of the road and steer the truck home.

The King slept on, moaning incoherently in shuttered intervals. "Daniel…"

*Who?* Another secret he kept or just rambling? He'd ask if Des ever recovered consciousness.

The current state of things was a far cry from what Des had promised any of them. He mentioned power unparalleled. He'd make them all gods. Ben felt like a burden now, though in truth, Des had become one just the same.

A portrait of Bob Marley loomed outside Ben's window. Next to his face were the words, "Wake up and live."

He was unsure how best to heed Bob's advice. After all, Des was the one wallowing in some dream half a world away. *Open your eyes and read, Des. What would Junior think of the state you're in?* It would have been worth the kid tagging along so he could see how far his idol had fallen.

*He ain't here...and I am.* Perhaps it was that simple. Maybe Ben *was* the one sleeping, stewing in self-pity, itching his thigh like a flea-ridden dog. He had become bitter, something he'd promised himself he wouldn't do. When he was laundering money, he at least felt useful. He often struggled with the morality of it, but he knew his purpose. Perhaps this was still the case. His responsibility lay before him—help the King solve the mystery of the unburned goon and keep his royal head on his shoulders. He may have been more of a lackey to Des than a true friend, but he would be the best lackey since Tonto or the Boy Wonder.

Now Marley's half-smile seemed condescending. Ben studied his paint-chipped eyes. "Don't tell me what to do."

He peeled out with the red-eyed burden in tow.

## *Montgomery County, Pennsylvania*

Ben idled on the cobblestone driveway while Des wobbled and moaned in the passenger seat. Adorned in natural granite cladding, the house suggested something rustic, but its picture windows and vinyl shutters set a place for it in the twenty-first century. The jet-black awning above each window furrowed like eyebrows would. Ben caught a damning glare from the design that made him feel unwelcome.

"The fuck did Carter do to this place?"

Desmond's chin dipped toward hell as strands of drool dangled and leapt for his lap.

"Hold tight." Ben stepped out, followed the walkway and rang the bell.

A red-headed girl who looked just shy of twenty pulled open the massive oak door. The innocence of her face caught Ben off his guard. He stretched his salesman's smile.

"Hi, there."

"What's up?"

"I'm lookin' for Damien Carter."

"He doesn't live here anymore."

"Hmm. He sell it to ya?" Ben straightened the cast iron lamp light and tightened its bulb.

"Who are you?"

"I come from Vermont. Lake Derby."

She waited a beat. "You a wolf, then?"

"You know it."

"Prove it."

Ben changed his face, his yellow eyes reflecting in the lantern's glass cover. "So, Carter?"

"He went to his cabin to cut the drugs and hand 'em off. Said he'd be there for a while."

"Who's in charge here in the meantime?"

"Eduardo."

"Who the fuck—?" He noticed the girl blush. "Look, my buddy's in the truck, but he's in bad shape. I'll grab him, then we're gonna speak to your guy."

"What's his deal?"

Ben marched for his truck. "He's havin' a day. You Southern wolves are sloppy. There's someone down close by, and no one bothered torchin' him."

The girl shook her head with a bend in her brow. "Wasn't us. We know how things go. Got a fire pit out back."

"Well..." He draped Desmond's arm over his shoulder. "Someone slipped up."

"Why would it affect *him*?"

He brought Des to the door. "He's got a connection with the ones he turned. Anyone in his bloodline."

She stared him down with a slackened lower jaw. She didn't buy a word of it.

Ben grew impatient as the midday chill grew crisp. "Jesus. Des...show her some tit."

Des bore his true face for the red-haired wolf girl. The upper cartilage of his ears gathered into points, fur sprouted along his cheek bones, his incisors grew into fangs and his eyes glowed like rubies. Ben could see their reflection beaming in hers. It swiped her breath from the air.

"Pretty, right?"

"You're the one." She hadn't blinked and tears coated her freckled cheeks. "Saw you in my dreams."

Des retracted his fangs and slumped deeper into Ben's side.

"We'll talk about that. Take me to Eduardo."

The red-headed girl led the two men through a nest of howlers. They gawked and taunted as Ben dragged his friend along the hardwood. "Who's this crippled fag?" "New recruits, Cat? You might find some that can fuckin' walk." The girl waved them off, afraid of the consequences that would surely follow.

They passed rooms of howlers cutting drugs, rooms of howlers sorting cash, and rooms of howlers fucking each other senseless.

A pair of double doors opened into a large room where more overzealous wolves sat at tables and laughed over their meals. In the back, beyond the piano and cocktail bar, was a wooden throne, and the "master" was warming it with his fraudulent rump. Eduardo was done up like a punk rocker—the spike-studded jacket, the eye shadow, the swish in his hair.

Ben was embarrassed for him. He took in the tableau and laughed aloud.

Eduardo smiled at his guests. "Who's this, Cat?"

Ben felt the burns from several pairs of eyes, but he wasn't worried. He was fairly certain only one pair in this room burned red. He answered for the girl. "This is the guy whose seat you're warming. If he could speak, I'm sure he'd tell ya how charmed he was. That or open your throat and feed ya to the pit."

"How do you figure?"

Ben scanned the crowd. "Got a bunch 'a fresh ones, huh? Most of the old crew are probably cooked... Stage Four hittin' you down here too?"

"The fuck is Stage Four?" He looked around at his crew to see if anyone recognized the term.

"Oh, you know…patches and sores, occasional bloody coughs…transforming to a wet rat."

The light left Eduardo's eyes and his chin tipped for the floor. "We've had a few." It pained him. He must have been close to someone.

"Yeah…" Ben knew all too well what it was to watch the patches take a person. "Little slice of hell."

Eduardo tried his best to straighten up, maintain his stature. "You're wrong…about your friend. Damien Carter started this pack. He values his privacy. Likes to shove off to his cabin to work for a few days here and there."

"Do ya think that's wise, knowing what we know?"

"I think it was Carter's call."

Ben pressed a soaking palm to his forehead. This was the ache that struck him in New York. A searing aggravation. The new wave of wolves would likely kill him before the patching. He sauntered for the throne. "Get down from there."

Eduardo stood abruptly. Some of the greenhorns followed his lead.

Ben kept coming. "Let's see those red eyes, then, if you're what you say you are."

"There's only one wolf with red eyes. Carter had his blessing, and I have Carter's."

Cat swallowed and studied the floorboards.

Ben reached the foot of the throne and craned his neck to lock eyes with the pretender. "I don't know if this is what he had in mind…but you're welcome to ask him." He motioned to Des.

Eduardo spit his gum to the foot of his throne. "Bullshit."

"Des. You got one more in ya?" Ben didn't need to turn. Gasps and whispers fluttered through the room, and the defeated look in the phony's eyes washed over him with a sudden sweetness. "Come on, then. Don't make me climb this…old knees."

A wolf from the crowd moved toward Des. Ben grabbed him by the throat and changed his face, prepared to remove the chump's head.

"Hold it!" Eduardo held a hand in the air. "This is the one who made us…anyone touches him, I'll put you in the pit."

Ben laughed again and released the curious wolf. "I promise I'll put you there sooner." He changed his face back.

Eduardo's descent from the throne was wobbly. He came to rest a foot from Ben's face, choking him with his cologne. The pretender's gaze moved from Ben's eyes to his throat. "You've got something on your neck, friend."

Ben cracked him one on the jaw and sent him reeling to the throne's wooden steps. The hum of his unconscious wheezing floated gently in the silence. The false king had found the sleep of babes, there at the base of his obnoxious throne. Ben envied him.

He lifted fingers to the side of his neck and found the fool wasn't lying. A second patch. Its timing couldn't have been worse. With a swipe of his claw, he tore a piece of the pretender's jacket away from its stitching. He wrapped it around his neck to mask his shame. "Alright, then." He addressed the room. "Who knows where I can find Carter?" He searched the silent, sullen faces for an answer. "Don't be shy, now. I'm exhausted from my travels. I might take silence for an insult."

"I know where he is." A raspy voice slithered through the crowd. Then, a short man with a scruffy beard stepped forward to give it a face.

Ben smiled and held his hands out. "*It is said that the skill of the Dwarves is in their hands rather than their tongues…yet that is not true of Gimli!*" He stepped toward the short man. "Talk to me, dear friend."

A sour grimace cut through shrubbery. "Me and Carter spoke a few times."

"Carter and I, but…continue."

"He didn't want people to see him all patched up, so he's been spending more of his time at the cabin. Didn't want any of us there. Like my man said…" He motioned to Eduardo. "He values his privacy."

"Well, that was mighty careless."

"None of us ever seen eyes like that in person. We started to think it was made up."

"Carter knew better. That's what hurts me." Ben bunched a fist over his heart.

The short man shrugged. "Patches do strange things to the brain, I guess."

"Don't I know it? Can you show me this cabin?"

"Yeah. You got a ride?"

"Out front. Help me with my friend? Like I said, old knees." He snuck a glance at the sleeping fraud.

Ben's new piss boy approached Des and lifted him from the hardwood.

"Okay, folks. We will return, so don't get too comfortable. Des is gonna have some words for sleepin' beauty over there when he recovers. You try and hide him…well…" He chuckled at the thought. "My friend's got an anger problem." Ben gave them a bow. *"Parting is such sweet sorrow."* He lifted Des' other arm and, together, he and the short man carried the King out to the truck. "What's your name, friend? Or would *Gimli* suit you?"

"They call me Short Steve."

"Is there a Tall Steve?"

"There was. We burned him."

"So, just Steve, then."

Steve wrinkled his nose as he pondered this. "I guess so."

"Okay, Just Steve." Ben settled into the driver's seat with Steve beside him, the Wolf King moaning sporadically in back. "Point the place out to me."

# CHAPTER TWENTY-TWO

## Liz

*Quakertown, Pennsylvania*

*"I'm cold, Mommy."*

She'd returned to the hall of her nightmares. The little girl's voice was an echo in her psyche, one she'd once known well but tried fervently to muffle. With step after apprehensive step, its volume grew. Beyond the walls, shells exploded and the rapid, repeating sound of automatic gun fire trickled over top like a sharp rain.

The knobless door appeared through her rifle's scope again. She blinked, and it rushed to meet her. She pressed an ear to the wood, sounds painting a vivid picture. A little girl and her mother cocooned in a blanket. A quarter-inch thick piece of fabric, yet a shield from a world of pain. And the mother's song filled the air.

Her voice soothed the girl into a half-sleep, twisting through the hall like a healing breeze, silencing the sounds of war. Before long, it was the only sound. Liz decided she wouldn't mind dying here. With her ear pressed to the knobless door, she mumbled the lyrics that had been with her so long.

It had been years since Liz felt this sort of warmth, but like all things warm in her life, it went cold in an instant, before she could take time to appreciate it. Behind her, something thick and dark consumed the hallway. It snuffed out the mother's voice, and the door became a wall.

Its eyes were blinding yellow, its shadow nipped at her toes and coarse hairs tickled her skin. The beast was quick, and it was true, and there was nowhere for Liz to run.

When the contours of Brooks' throat came into focus, Liz squeezed his larynx and sprang to her feet, pinning him to the cabin wall.

"You try'na blow my tits off, Brooks?"

The absence of alarm in the Corporal's face was puzzling. "No, Sarge, I was not. But I will spill your guts to the floor."

It was only then she felt the prick of his knife against her abdomen. She'd known Cameron Brooks since before they'd shipped off and she'd seen him at his worst. He was not a man to retreat from a threat. She released his throat, and he sheathed the knife, both motions fluid as one.

Macy piped up from across the room. "Are we okay?" Liz had forgotten about the girl, her squeaky voice an unwelcome reminder.

Brooks was stern with his response. "That's up to Sarge."

Liz shrugged.

"Next time you wanna choke me, though, you best finish it."

*There you are, killer.* This was the Brooks she remembered sparring with for hours on end. "How long was I out?"

He sat down at a wooden table and propped his feet up. "Almost two hours. Spotted your tail on the way over. You're gettin' sloppy." He massaged his throat with thumb and forefinger. "Thought you might be out for blood, but I went with the stun rounds anyway. I knew I could talk you out of it."

Liz slowed her breathing. "Why would I wanna kill *you*?" She slid a wooden chair between her legs. Her chest throbbed.

"Layla told me about your visit. Wasn't sure what I did to get you gunnin' for me…then your friend here explained things."

Macy leafed through a book, her attention miles away.

Liz retorted, "She ain't my friend."

Brooks pressed feet to the floor and shrugged his chair forward. "Sarge, you gotta know…I had no idea it could spread that way. I thought I was doin' you a solid with that needle."

The laughter spilled from Liz's lips like drool. "Well, I'm as fucked as you now." She followed the joists in the ceiling with her eyes. "Guess it was always s'posed to be this way."

The muscles in Brooks' face contorted. He was battling the urge to smile. "Macy tells me you're looking to put a stop to it."

"What? You ain't?"

He removed his hand from his throat, the abrasions now a memory. "It's not so bad."

"Shut the fuck—"

"Hear me out." Liz let him speak. "I got control. Took some time, but... when I turn, it's still me."

"Congratulations."

"Sarge." He leaned forward and dropped a bomb. "I don't get high no more…"

Liz stared into his eyes, their pupils the proper size.

"I don't need it," he said.

Liz looked down to the pit of her elbow where her track marks had once been. "Yeah." She hadn't been high or dope sick in days.

"Who was it turned you?" Turned out, Macy *was* paying attention. "I'd like a word with *him*."

"That's gonna be a little tough."

"Hey, gang." The voice spun Liz to the door as if she'd been struck. The man was middle-aged, maybe late thirties, with gray at the temples. He wore a scarf around his neck in seventy-degree weather.

But he had a ninja's creep to him. No one had heard him enter.

Brooks dislodged a shotgun from two hooks on the wall and lined up the barrel with the mystery guest's head.

The man didn't flinch. "Whoa, now. Who practices hospitality entertains God himself."

Brooks' finger twitched. "Who *are* you, friend?"

"Just that. A friend." The cabin's wall caught the man's eye. He brushed fingers against it, conjuring memories inch by inch. "Wow. This takes me back." His smile was infectious. "This white pine or…eastern white cedar?"

Brooks stared like the man had spoken Japanese.

The man waited for an answer that never came, nodded and picked splinters from the wall. "Looks like pine." He closed his eyes and sniffed the air. "Smells like my childhood. Used to hole up in one of these fishin' for perch and carp up North. Ate us a ton of canned beans." He evaluated the cabin's interior while Brooks' shotgun threatened to speak. "Got a nice finish to the place too. But then, I never much had a taste for furniture. It was always structure for me…" He knocked his fist against the wood. "Not so much the tits and lipstick."

"Yo…" Liz clapped for his attention. "The fuck you doin' here?"

His eyes squeezed the muscles in her shoulders. "You're a bruiser, huh?"

Liz considered strangling him with his scarf.

"Lookin' for Damien Carter. You know him?"

Liz looked to Brooks for an answer. Macy did the same.

Brooks had nothing. "Never heard of him."

The guest's lower lip folded over the upper in what might have passed as a frown. "Interesting. Heard this cabin was his, but... I guess the truth must've fled this crew."

Liz spoke for her Corporal, afraid he might flinch and discharge a round. "Must have. Now fuck off."

The man's eyes turned poisonous. Liz saw something primal in his stare. She wondered why a man like this would be so comfortable with a gun on him. *You a wolf, too, Mr. Canned Beans?* The shotgun was no threat to him. He would have Brooks' head if he chose. She considered her options if Brooks' weapon was as useless as it seemed. She wondered how quickly she could reach his throat. It looked like the man was ready to pounce. Liz planted her feet to counter, as sweat dripped between her shoulder blades.

The man threw up his hands. "My mistake." He backed out, onto the porch. "You folks have a nice evenin', yah?" He brushed his hand along the frame as he left. Liz peeked outside and caught a glimpse of a red truck before it disappeared up the road.

Macy marked her place in her book and stood. "Any idea?" She motioned to the trail their guest had left. There was a presence in the air Liz didn't like.

Brooks finally lowered his weapon. "No." He took grateful breaths.

Liz closed the door, latched the lock and rejoined the conversation. "Alright, Brooks. Start spillin' it. Who's Carter? You bullshit me, I'll beat you 'til your nose looks normal."

He fell back into his chair with his weapon glued to his chest. With Liz and Macy hovering over him, it had the feel of a deposition.

# CHAPTER TWENTY-THREE

## Brooks

*Quakertown, Pennsylvania*

**One Month Ago**

He'd gone to the cabin to see Carter for his supply like any other week. Carter sorted and bagged his dope like an artist, perfectly symmetrical squares of brown sugar tucked neatly into a black duffel. Brooks almost felt bad when he sliced it open at his place, like he was defacing something beautiful.

On this day, he knew things were different before he even noticed the closed drapes and broken glass. It must have been battlefield instincts he'd retained from the desert. "Yo, Carter, it's Brooks!" He circled to the front porch and found that the door had come open a few inches. He felt for his hip and pulled his .45 into the mid-afternoon sun.

Slowly, he stepped for the open door, scanning for movement, periodically checking his six. On the balls of his feet, he climbed the porch steps and pushed the door inward. The furniture was torn and shifted out of place, papers were strewn across the floor and a strange smell hit him that he couldn't quite compare to anything he'd known.

In the back corner, he saw a trembling mass of fur. At first, he thought a black bear might have come looking for treats, but when the creature stepped into the sunlight, Brooks saw something that brought him near sick. Its face wasn't far from a sewer rat's, damp hair and saliva dripping gray to the floorboards. Its ribcage was compressed and emaciated, covered in spots with the same greasy gray-black hair. The hands and feet were what troubled Brooks the most. Sharp claws protruded from the tips of its fingers and toes, but aside from the matted hair sprouting from the knuckles, this thing's hands and feet were human.

"The fuck…?"

The monster pounced with blinding speed and buried claws in Brooks' chest, knocking him onto his back. He drew his .45 out of reflex. A stabbing pain followed the motion of his shoulders. The back of the creature's head came apart when he fired, but its claws had dug deep wells into Brooks' pectorals. He kicked to dislodge the beast. When he sat up, two crimson waterfalls ran straight to his waist, forming a reservoir on his jeans.

The dead creature's eyes were unsettling. With moisture at the ends of their almond shape, it appeared the thing had been crying.

# CHAPTER TWENTY-FOUR

## Liz

*Quakertown, Pennsylvania*

She admired Brooks' reversion to his training, even amidst a dope haze. "Semper Fi, huh?"

Brooks' lips were locked in a flat line. "My wounds healed. That took a while to get past. I put him under the floor, but he started to stink, so I buried him outside."

Macy interjected. "So Carter is a corpse."

He nodded.

She returned to the journals she'd been flipping through, disappointed.

Liz waved her hand in Brooks' face. "What you were sayin'…about not gettin' high…"

The wavering orange glow of a flame caught her eye through the cabin's back window.

Macy and Brooks turned toward the fire when they noticed her expression. For a slow stretch, no one reacted. The flames danced in the window, pulsating like something living. They would take the woods with them if she stared too long. And so what if they did? Liz had had her fill of wilderness.

Brooks ran to the sink and opened the faucet over a plastic bucket. The rushing water woke Liz's adrenaline ducts. She darted outside with Macy trailing.

The flames licked the air, and smoke stung Liz's eyes. The repugnant scent of charred flesh abounded. Liz and Macy kicked damp leaves onto the burning corpse, but it was Brooks' bucket that doused the flames for good and sent a curl of black smoke billowing to the heavens. They backed away from the scene to keep from gulping down ash.

Liz was the first to speak. "Yeah..." She coughed, and her mouth filled with the taste of smoke. "Our man with the scarf. We're gonna have words."

While Macy studied Carter's diary and whatever else the recluse had been reading, the soldiers pulled assorted traps from the crawlspace. Liz assumed the larger were for bears and the smaller were for wolves, but they'd both crush a leg pretty easily. They set them in a staggered grid around the perimeter, leaving one small path of safety that they showed to Macy when they were through. The time was 4:48 p.m..

Liz grabbed s shotgun of her own and joined the armed Corporal on the porch to keep watch.

"I marked some trees with yellow tape where the roads are. If you're in control tonight, keep an eye out." Brooks kicked back and sipped a glass of ice water with his hand on the butt of his weapon.

"I turned early the other day. That ever happen to you?"

He considered for a moment. "Few times. It was the smack I think...weakens the body... harder to hold it off." Beads of sweat raced along the contours of Brooks' forehead. He gritted teeth and stared into the woods, his breathing staggered.

"What, you scared of that 'perch and carp' pussy?" Liz knew full well Brooks had seen much harder things in the desert.

"Nah, it's this f—fuckin'…" His eyelashes fluttered like a butterfly's wings.

Liz looked to the tree line and found nothing.

Now his molars clattered against each other. "You remember that girl?"

*Juliana? No. He wasn't there.* "Little haji girl?"

He nodded.

"The one with the vest?"

"Yeah." She'd charged his battalion with enough C4 strapped to her to chip a crater in the earth. He stopped her with a bullet through the face. "She won't fuckin' leave me be…hasn't missed a day since I slept her."

Liz looked to the trees again, like she might be able to share his hallucination.

"I thought the wolf would send her packin'…but there she is. Wearin' that fuckin' look."

Liz picked up his water from the table between them and handed it to him. "Fuck her. She'd have smoked all of you."

His shaking hand rattled the ice as he sipped. "Maybe…maybe."

While Brooks blinked the images away, Liz thought about her own misgivings in the sand. With the Viper's guns at her fingertips, she'd leveled camps in an instant. Juliana had been a wiz at strafing maneuvers. She'd put the targets right in line for Liz to erase. Later, in the mountain raids in Kandahar, she'd blasted a Taliban rifleman though the lung with her M4. She would've put another through his head, but the ambush had taken two of the translators she'd been protecting. She watched him wheeze until he died.

The dead had crossed her mind minimally since her return to the States. As far as she was concerned, it was all part of a simulation. But now, years after leaving it behind, God knows how many would meet their end by her hand. Her nightmare had followed her home after all.

"The fuck are we still doin' here, Brooks?"

He gathered control of his breathing—a steady intake through the nose, a steady exhale past his lips. "What do you mean?"

What *did* she mean? What had she ever meant to the fabric of humanity? "Juliana…she woulda …" Her gaze fell to the nook of her arm.

Brooks turned to his Sergeant and passed his water to her.

"I gotta think that rocket was for me. I mean, how far you think that haji was? Hundred yards? Two hundred? Wasn't cake. When I crawled free…I thought I was dead." She'd felt the desert wind near after and knew hell couldn't have been that hot. "The girl got shrapnel, and I got this life." She traced fingertips where the needle had kissed her.

"You give her too much credit."

"Maybe…but I know she wouldn't 'a turned to dope…burned everyone close to her."

Brooks considered things again. His tongue always pushed the back of his teeth when he was lost in thought. "You're lookin' at it through a dark lens."

"Huh?"

"Moms used to say that whenever I got moody. A dark lens. Like you got sunglasses on. Make a sunny day look like rain." Sometimes the Corporal's musings weren't as profound as he thought. "Think of it like this—when's the last time you doped up?"

*Yesterday…in the neck. Weak garbage.*

"Better yet, you wanna get high right now?"

For the first time in years, Liz realized the urge was dead. "Nah. Not even a little." Had the wolf saved her life? No chance. Liz struggled with the idea that a beast renting her flesh may well have been the answer she sought from the start.

"There you go. See? You're no fiend."

She dug for comfort in the notion but found a brick wall. "Just a wolf."

His nostrils flared, and his Adam's apple made harsh, jagged movements. "I'm sorry I got you mixed up in this."

It was the first time she remembered Brooks apologizing. She slid fingers into his clammy hand as he shook phantoms from his vision. "I blame the haji that missed."

Her thoughts returned to Juliana. Liz yanked at the Viper shard in the girl's chest as she died. The scar had crossed her right palm until the wolf healed it.

She bobbed her head at the door. Inside, Macy raided Carter's reading material. "She reminds me of her, you know." The girl did share features with her former pilot, but she also shared a neighborhood with Liz's mother. She must have come from a similar ilk. "I think God sent this one to torment me." She smiled at the implication.

"Maybe you should be nicer to her, then."

The thought made her wince.

# CHAPTER TWENTY-FIVE

## Ben

*Quakertown, Pennsylvania*

A grunt sputtered from the Wolf King as he broke from Ben's grasp. The side of his face hit the loose patch of soil when he fell.

Ben understood his meaning. "Right here. Where the dirt's all uneven," he said.

Steve started digging and before long, a filthy white trash bag emerged. He tore it open and the stench had both men covering their faces. Steve spoke through his hand as he examined the rat creature's face. "Jesus, I can't even tell if it's him."

"Who the fuck else would it be?" Ben bathed the corpse in gasoline. This rancid bag of flesh had been his bane since he left the lake. He wanted to raise Carter from the dead so he could pay him back properly for the trouble he'd caused.

Steve motioned to the cabin in the distance. "Who did this to him?"

"We'll figure that out later…" Ben struck the lighter's flint wheel with his thumb. *Farewell, fuck face.* He dropped it onto the corpse, and it went up. He would have loved to watch every atom of this nuisance fall to ash, but the fire would be noticeable from the cabin. They scooped up the Wolf King and made for the truck.

The smell of charred flesh adhered to their clothes and followed them back to Carter's house.

Ben rolled his truck into the drive at dusk and hopped out to assist his groggy commandant. Before he could reach for the back door, Desmond emerged, sprightly as a child at a carnival.

"Jesus. Ya with us again?"

The Wolf King's fangs shined. *"Now go and tell his disciples, he is going ahead to Galilee!"*

"Gettin' quicker at it, huh?"

He closed his lips as Steve stepped into the porch light. "Who's the dwarf?"

"Steve. He's all right."

Steve pressed his knee to the pavement and bowed to his master. "Anything you need…I'm yours." *You'd better fetch a bib, then.*

Desmond's laughter shook the cobwebs from his vocal chords. "Get off your bloody knees, mate. You'll dust up your trousers." He pulled Steve to his feet with such force that Ben thought he might toss him to space. "Who was it went down?"

Ben answered. "Carter."

"Fuck."

"He went to live in a cabin like some recluse…had some company."

"Who?"

"I didn't know 'em. Didn't seem like they knew what was goin' on."

"You spoke to them?"

"I spoke. They pointed guns at me. Seemed scared."

"We'll revisit that." Des jabbed his finger in Ben's face. "The fuck is that on your neck?"

Ben brushed his fingers against the strip of fabric from the pretender's shirt. "What do ya think?"

"Another?"

"You think it was gonna stop?"

The King's face drooped. He was bothered by Ben's degradation, whether he wanted to admit it or not. "What's the deal *here*?" He motioned to the oaken front door.

"They had a guy, called himself their leader 'til I fixed his jaw for 'im. The patching has hit them as well. Carter included."

Des snapped to him. "Carter was patching?"

"Oh, he was well beyond that. We dug up a fucking rodent. They might not have *needed* to kill him."

Des considered this for a moment. "Point the twat out, yeah? The one made himself king."

Inside, Eduardo propped himself against the bar with an elbow, gulping some golden spirit. Des sauntered to him, and he shrunk like a punished dog. "You done yourself up, huh?" He spoke two inches from the sham's face, and for a moment, Ben thought they might kiss. "Put on a show so everyone thinks your cock's big…and beneath it all, there you sit, common as muck, the stink of man on ya."

It was the icy shine of fear that had replaced the arrogance in Eduardo's eyes. Ben had seen something similar on the black kid with the shotgun, a glaze you might catch on a gazelle the moment before a lion makes a meal of his sweetmeats.

Des unbuckled his belt, zipped down his pants and pulled out his cock. He let go a stream of urine on the pretender's boots. The hiss could be heard above the seventies soft rock. When he finished, he buckled himself. "I'll consider it squashed if you will."

Eduardo nodded as the sour stench touched his nose.

"You knew Carter?"

Again, a nod.

"He lose his marbles? What business he got in some fuckin' cabin?"

The interrogation went on while the howlers in attendance reveled at the red-eyed beast. It seemed they'd forgotten Ben had delivered their god to them on his knees. He slipped out to escape the ammonia scent of royal piss.

# CHAPTER TWENTY-SIX

## Macy

*Quakertown, Pennsylvania*

Macy read Carter's findings vigorously. It seemed the man had done his research. His collection of books was riddled with colored post-its, and their spines had worn to the lace. From what she'd read, Carter spent more time discounting the material than acquiring new knowledge.

He'd been searching for ways to rid himself of his curse. Folklore, herbal supplements, occult incantations. He'd come up short from every angle.

She came upon a small leather-bound journal. In it, Carter tracked his experience. It was broken into four stages. In the first, he seemed fearful, but his fear became excitement as the pages progressed. He'd been a smalltime gangster in England before a family of wolves had given him a choice. He mentioned a man named Desmond, the eldest brother, how this man had 'yanked him from obscurity' and 'blessed him with a gift.'

The second section rambled about gaining control. Carter was able to make his own decisions once turned, much like what Cameron had described. He spent this section cataloging the meals he chased down and the rush he felt.

In the third, Carter wrote about his new ability to turn whenever he chose, how Desmond had crowned him a prince. This segment was dated April 1999. He wrote about his time in Derbyshire, serving under Desmond in his efforts to 'repair things.' *Christ, could the internet have it right?* After they migrated to the States, it seemed Desmond had put him in charge of a pack of wolves in Pennsylvania before 'returning home up North.' Macy remembered that the man with the scarf had mentioned 'up North' as well. She assumed he was Desmond, though he didn't seem like much at a glance, and he certainly wasn't from England.

In the final section, things became opaque. It was clear Carter had lost interest in the writing. His sentences were short and far less revealing. 'The itching is what's worst,' he wrote. 'A constant reminder how I've failed the King.' After that, the writing became nonsensical. Whatever followed Stage Three was dark. It sucked the life from Carter and made him bitter...before Brooks made him a corpse.

Macy set her findings down and took a breath. Even Carter, as close as he was with the supposed Wolf King, couldn't find a way out. Would she be cursed to become the same pathetic creature Brooks had encountered? She thought of her father, how much he'd lost. Was she lining him up to lose more?

She felt an episode coming on again. She dug her feet into the throw rug to hold it off. *No...Carter wasn't asking the right questions. He didn't try hard enough.*

Sarah's face found her again.

*Up, Mace. You have to go up. What choice do you have?*

# CHAPTER TWENTY-SEVEN
## Ben

*Montgomery County, Pennsylvania*

Sporadic moans. The soft, staggered rasps beckoned to him through the shed's gate. A Stage Four lingered in the shadows. It might have been snoring. It might have been a death rattle. Whatever the case, Ben knew he was listening to his fate.

The girl was silent on approach. Her name was Cat. *Fitting*...Her voice shook him. "Depressing, right?"

He was inclined to agree. "Why do ya keep 'em? Why not feed the pit?"

"This one was Eduardo's girlfriend..."

Now the kid's morose expression made sense. He touched the fabric at his neck, the gesture instinctual. "I'm gonna join 'em soon. Well on my way."

She studied her feet. "Sorry."

Ben looked at the girl's small, pale face, the innocence of her words giving it a childlike glow. "Eh...I've about had it with this wolf shit, anyway. It's a haven for egomania. That's the kind it takes to want this life...like your former boss in there. You give people a taste of this, and it blackens the soul."

Cat shrugged. "What about you? What color's *your* soul?"

She was pretty, but young. She might not have broken twenty. Her red hair was tied in a bun, but a few strands spilled loose, kissing each dimpled cheek. The waitress from Bennington returned to his thoughts—what Des had done to her. "You said you saw Des in a dream. How'd that go?"

"Two master wolves leading a pack. Then one of them gets killed and another takes its place."

Ben had often wondered if the dream was a delusion, but every howler that confirmed it brought a second red-eye closer to reality. "Yeah, that sounds about right. Did you die at the end?"

"I don't think so…but I have this pain in my chest when I wake from it. A sharp burn."

"Benjamin!" Desmond's voice had become less and less welcome. Ben was still bitter at the Wolf King's dishonesty about the patches. He wondered what else Des might have lied about, if his baggage from back home had truly been sorted. "We've got work…hold on." He froze when he noticed the girl. "What's *your* name, luv?"

"Cat." She didn't seem nervous. Ben admired that.

Des rolled his lips and showed her his fangs. "A cat amongst wolves, eh?"

"Des…" *Not this one, amigo.* He guided his friend toward the house. "What are you talkin' about 'work'? I thought we were through here."

"Not just yet. We're takin' a trip to Carter's cabin."

"Fine. I've got some questions for his friends." He thought of the girl in the back of the cabin reading at the table, how different she seemed from the other two. *The guy with the shotgun and the bruiser had murder in their eyes, but the other…*

"Friends? They killed the bastard."

"All the more important I get answers from 'em." They may have been able to shed some light on this second red-eye, if he existed. "We should know why they dropped Carter, no?"

"Right, good." Des pointed in Ben's face. "I'll kill 'em after."

"Calm down for a second." Ben sat on a wicker bench beside the garden. He scratched his thigh with his thumbnail, then his neck with the opposite hand. "I'm gonna say some things that might upset you, but you brought me South for guidance, so here it is."

Des nodded and started pacing the walkway slowly as he listened.

"It should be clear to you now that expanding South was a mistake."

Des rubbed his stubbled chin as he pondered this.

"Philly brings in a lot of cash, but population control is no longer manageable. This sickness is droppin' too many reliable people. That's not even considering the sloppy job they've been doing of burning the dead."

"What's the move, then?" Des never liked being lectured. He would always interject to trim the fat.

"I'm concerned about Carter's killers same as you, so let's get to the bottom of it. Then I say we round up those willing and bring 'em all North."

"And the unwilling?" Des smiled. He knew what ought to be done with them.

"You can see to that."

Des entered the house and marched to the imposter with piss-covered boots. "Eduardo…" They had gotten acquainted while Ben was away. "You've wronged me. Dressin' like a King and that…no good."

Eduardo bowed his head, a puppy that had rummaged through the trash.

"Redeem yourself, yeh? Help me avenge my mate."

The vassal perked up, sniffing opportunity in the King's decree. "Anything you need."

"Right…you." He pointed to Short Steve. "Ben says you're alright. You'll tag along. We'll shove off after dark. You're both stage three, correct? I shouldn't worry?"

Short Steve answered, "We're threes."

"Lovely. We make for the cabin at nightfall."

Ben picked Cat's brain at Carter's bar, sipping bourbon and munching on snack nuts. For a young girl, she was well-versed in the arts. She rattled off facts from works well before her time.

"Where'd they grow you?"

The way she giggled was the only indication of her youth.

"I'm serious. You mention free verse to kids these days, they'll spit some Scourge lyrics at you and call you a queer."

"I read a lot. Keeps me sane…now more than ever."

Ben's daughter had been a bookworm.

"I hear ya. How'd you come by *this* mess?"

"Steve." She motioned to where the imp was sitting.

Ben detected bitterness in her voice. "He rub you wrong?"

"He's…a lot to deal with."

Ben studied the shrimp, his physical defects shining from tip to tip. "Guy's five-four."

"Doesn't seem it sometimes."

"How'd he turn you?"

"Uh…" She blushed and crossed her legs.

"Mmm. Yeah, that'll do it." Ben would wager sex had turned half the howlers in this house. "What about *him*? How'd *he* come by Carter's crew?"

The girl struggled to find words. She seemed uncomfortable with Ben's prodding.

"Never mind." There was darkness between the two that Ben decided to leave alone. The house had endured enough strife for one day. He wouldn't stir the pot.

Ben took in the atmosphere. Carter had wrangled a halfway decent crew, but they lacked direction—amoebas floating through space. Des would use them any way he could, but in the end, they would be worse for wear. Numbers were critical to the Wolf King. It was always quantity over quality. If they could muscle for him, he didn't give a blessed glance at the content of their character. Some, like Cat, Ben knew would play ball and head for the lake when called upon, but it wouldn't be a bloodless process. They had built a throne, after all.

"Are you scared?" The girl's concern read genuine.

"What? This?" He pointed to his neck, and she nodded. "I would have died if Des hadn't come to the States. Financial crisis hit me hard. I got mixed up laundering money for *this* crew up North before Des took over. They had a rat, and the previous owners weren't taking any chances, but Des came in before they could grease me. Gave me a promotion, in a way. So here we are. Sometimes I feel this was borrowed time anyway." He let the last sip of bourbon linger on his tongue before sucking it down. "I worry about what happens after I'm gone, though. Sometimes I feel like a giant hand over a leaking hull."

She had no answer for him. From what Ben had seen in the South, it seemed wolf-men would herd to the first one ballsy enough to step up, even if it was a post-punk reject with a studded jacket. Ben wasn't around for the Derbyshire days, but he'd once thought the Brits had more substance. Junior had disavowed him of that notion. Over a long enough timeline, it was always some alpha male bullshit. No way to run a business. But what would this kid know about any of that?

Steve hobbled to them. He braced his tiny mitt against the back of Cat's arm. "I need to talk to you."

The girl looked to Ben and Ben to his empty glass. "We can talk here."

"What did I just say?"

Ben responded for her. "Ease up, Napoleon. *Glory is fleeting, but obscurity is forever.*"

Now Steve acknowledged him. "What?"

"There are better ways to compensate for…" He scanned Steve from his bulbous head to his elfin boots. "…inadequacies…than pickin' on little girls, yah?"

"You got a King speakin' for you, but you ain't one…so butt the fuck out." He grappled for Cat's attention again. "Move your ass."

"I might bark on occasion, but I'm not your fucking dog."

Ben struggled to keep from laughing aloud.

Steve brought his hand up to clout the girl, but Ben caught him at the wrist. "That's enough, friend. Have a drink. Build some stilts. Whatever gets your blood up…but leave her out of it."

Steve stared for an eon before shaking loose.

Cat stayed put. "You didn't have to do that." The girl's blush matched her ginger hair.

Ben poured himself a second round.

# CHAPTER TWENTY-EIGHT

## Liz

*Quakertown, Pennsylvania*

Brooks noticed the piles of paper that Macy had spread across the table. "What'd you find?"

She rattled off facts like a computer. "Confirmed a lot of what I already knew, but I found some interesting things. They have the wolf broken up into stages. Stage one is feral, no control over timing. Stage two is when awareness sets in. Can't choose when you turn, but you have the wheel when you do. How long it lasts is different for everyone. Carter seemed to think it depended on will. Some wolves with strong enough willpower have been able to advance to Stage Three—complete control. You can change at will. After that…Carter seemed to have transformed into that sewer rat creature because of some illness. He kept notes. The details are a little fuzzy, but I'll keep reading tomorrow."

The kid was proving useful for reconnaissance.

Liz found the new discoveries amusing. "Shit. Two motherfuckers with the strongest will on the planet—marines and dope fiends." She glanced at her Corporal. "Will had us duckin' haji bullets in the desert…goin to sleep every night on Kensington Avenue fed and high." She bumped fists with Brooks.

His expression remained flat. "And what comes after?"

"Dark lens, motherfucker. We ain't turnin' into no rats." Liz fluttered her lips and beckoned to Macy. "Come on, librarian. It's getting dark."

They left Brooks in the cabin to get undressed.

Liz stretched all four of her legs. The moon's reflection was slick against the trees, and the scent of flesh crept through her snout, summoning saliva. She followed it through the brush, kicking stiffly with hind legs and navigating with the front.

The fleshy scent became a fleshy taste as she ran. A few paces more and she would have her meal. She brushed a fallen tree and crept over a hill. When she found the carcass, she stood face-to-face with her competition.

Another wolf chewed away at the doe's midsection, its yellow eyes beaming murderous bliss. Liz let out a howl. She wanted to test the wolf, see if it would defend its food. It propped front legs on the dead doe's rib cage and howled back, this one louder and more menacing. Birds left their roosts in its wake. The wolf's jaw dripped with slobber and strands of meat.

This would be a fight to the death if Liz chose to make it so. She wasn't sure if it was Macy, Brooks or a stranger that returned her challenge, but she knew that a fight would be more grief than a half-eaten doe was worth.

She stepped away, surrendering her meal, and took to the woods to hunt another.

# CHAPTER TWENTY-NINE

## Ben

*Quakertown, Pennsylvania*

The trees were faint under the dimness of the cabin's porch light, an impressionist piece dusted over. The four wolf-men cast demon shadows over the pine. He would have his answers from the cabin dwellers, even if it required blood.

Two cars were parked in the leaves beside the cabin. Des peeked into the windows, tapping the claw of his index finger on the glass. The woods were still, and Ben was certain the tap had echoed for miles.

Des glided swiftly to the cabin's front door, avoiding staggered bear and wolf traps.

*Feeling cautious, are we?* He must have really shaken Carter's killers to get them decorating the lawn.

Desmond's hand twitched as he prepped for entry. "Little pig, little pig…"

Ben's patience had worn paper-thin. "For fuck's sake..."

Des turned the knob, and the door swung open with a creak that sounded like a crone in labor. The cabin was silent. The four of them moved on the balls of their feet as they searched its interior, loosening up when they found they were alone. Eduardo pulled open a trap door in the living room floor and peeked around in the crawl space beneath.

When he pulled his head out, he shook it "no."

Ben wasn't surprised. He remembered the look in the black kid's eyes as the shotgun rattled in his hands. "I wouldn'a hung around either."

Desmond fished around in a pile of books and papers. "These are Carter's. Someone's been diggin'." He turned to face his comrades. "Why would they leave it?"

Steve and Eduardo wore the blank-slate faces of toddlers.

"They were spooked. I put a scare to 'em. The fire, too." Ben wondered if the three he'd seen were the unknown enemy he was worried about, or if perhaps this was a crisis of circumstance.

"This is extensive, mate. Unfinished."

Ben sifted through a logbook that charted Carter's lupine activity. "Christ, this fucker was verbose."

Desmond stood in the doorway, examining the still night and the woods. "They left their motors…probably wolves as well?"

"Wolves? Maybe. If they went to the woods to turn, they aren't Stage Three." *An enemy that drew us South, but only Stage Two? Fat chance.*

Des looked to the left of the porch. "Here we are."

Ben stepped out to see a pile of folded clothes waiting in the lamp light. "Doesn't make any fucking sense."

"We'll wait here 'til morning and see what's what."

In the yard, a bear trap closed around Short Steve's calf. Ben covered the chump's mouth to cut short a shriek that would have brought the woods down around them. After a fit of laughter, Ben spoke in the snared punk's ear. "Keep it down. Don't get hysterical, now." Ben got a read on the trap—an easy enough mechanism. "I'm gonna get it off you, but don't go pitchin' a fit when I take my hand away." Beads of Steve's sweat rolled over Ben's hand. The short man nodded.

Desmond approached them, avoiding more traps. "Are you fucking kidding?"

Ben knelt for the trap, and Steve broke his promise. "I'll kill 'em! I'll fuckin' kill 'em! Get it the fuck off!"

Ben shushed him. "Shut yer yap. Gimme a second." He released the trap slower than he could have, and the elf was free.

He hopped around as his leg righted itself. "They're dead. I swear, they're fuckin' dead."

Des slugged him in the jaw and dropped him. "Next one takes your head if you don't stuff it."

Steve struggled to his feet as his jaw realigned.

Ben pressed the trap to the ground, putting it back the way it had been, with a little extra hair and blood.

"Now that you may have fucked us out of an ambush, we'll wait down the road." The King made for Eduardo's Chevy.

Steve hobbled for the truck, while Ben stuffed Carter's journal into his jacket pocket.

They waited at an old roadside stand where they had a clear view of the cabin's driveway. Des and Eduardo watched from the Chevy beside them. Ben leafed through Carter's ramblings to the tune of Steve's snoring.

It was a chronicling of sorts. At least it started that way. He spoke of his time in Derbyshire, muscling for the Draper Mafia. After Des recruited him, he tracked his progress with the wolf. *"I've been called by a god to reap vengeance."*

*What a fucking loon.* Ben skipped ahead to the patching.

*"The itching is what's worst. A constant reminder how I've failed the King."*

*You failed him long before that, you fucking hermit.*

The next line stopped Ben in his tracks.

*"My only comfort is the fact the King's mother passed the same way. I'll show her my gratitude on high."*

Ben read it several times to be sure he was comprehending. He thought of the sincerity in Des' voice when he told him about his ignorance of the illness. He glanced at the Chevy. Inside was a liar who'd played him from the start. Promised him the life of a god when he knew where it could lead.

Ben felt sick. He wanted to kill the sleeping man beside him, take the throats of the two men in the Chevy and hang himself.

Sleep never found him that night. Only more itching.

# CHAPTER THIRTY
## Macy

*Quakertown, Pennsylvania*

She crawled from the brush with faint images of the night past. Blood had dried on her breasts and neck again—a deer's, she hoped. The spigot outside rattled an icy chill, but the blood flaked away to the dirt like red-brown snow. She found her clothes on the cabin's porch and dressed herself, then entered to find her veteran counterparts laughing up a storm.

Liz noticed her first. "We thought you might'a chased an ice cream truck…"

"Ha." Macy sat down at the table to return to Carter's papers.

"I had control last night." Liz's comment stopped her. "Most of it, anyway. You?"

"I'm more aware every time." What first seemed like a dream had become more real, the flashes of lucidity, like climbing out of a panic attack.

Liz nodded.

Macy would've been more excited with their progress if she didn't know where it ended. She searched for the journal but couldn't find it. "Did you guys move this stuff?"

Liz loaded shells into a shotgun. "What do we want with some dead rat's diary?"

Macy sifted some more and found nothing. "Someone was here."

Both marines snapped to attention.

"You sure?" Brooks peeked out the window.

Macy closed her eyes and focused on the scents. There were at least two she didn't recognize. "Positive." She wanted to look into the mystery man that came calling, see if she could press him about Desmond, but if he was springing a trap, she'd rather get as far from the cabin as possible and search for another lead.

"What's the play, Brooks?" Liz asked.

He stepped back from the window. "We ain't safe here."

"We haven't been since we came out." Liz racked the shotgun, her face as blank as a house cat. "What's the difference?"

"I gotta keep up appearances with my people. I don't need more problems, lemme put it that way."

"I'm kinda in the same boat there." Macy had almost run dry of excuses to text her father. "We can search for a cure someplace else."

Liz and Brooks looked at each other, then back at Macy. Liz spoke for the pair of them. "We discussed it. We're not that interested in a cure."

"What?" Macy was sure she'd misheard.

Liz let out a deep sigh. "This shit's been good to us. I'm aware now when it takes me. If all that shit you've been reading is true, soon I can turn when I choose. The fuck am I doin' trying to cure that?"

"And what happened to Carter? You good with that?" Macy remembered how Brooks had described the sewer rat creature, how Carter had described his *own* degeneration. How anyone could accept that as their fate was completely baffling.

Liz stood and approached slowly. "You don't know where we come from. The shit we've seen. That thing Brooks put in the ground…if that's how we go…" She looked at Brooks again. "We're good with it."

Macy felt sick. "What about me?"

Liz thought a moment. "I owe you for putting me up."

*Not to mention you turned me.* She could feel the itch of her dormant claws threatening to emerge from the tips of her fingers.

"I'll go with you today. Make sure you're sorted. They don't like me much in the hood no more."

*What does that do for me?* Macy wondered. She opened her mouth, but Liz had already moved on.

"Yo, who's that giant you got at your place?" she asked Brooks.

He sniggered. "Arthur. He's a fiend like the rest, but he puts the fear in people. Need that these days... savages in the mix."

"He's got my Walther. Can you get it back for me?"

He stared at her while she itched at the pit of her elbow. "I'll see what I can do."

Macy gathered a few of Carter's notes that she hadn't yet gone over. The rest was kindling as far as she was concerned. She'd learned all she could from them, though she would've liked a second read of his journal. "Cameron, could you put your number in my phone?" She tossed it to Brooks, the screen still cracked from her first encounter with Liz.

Brooks entered his digits and tossed it back. Liz smiled and stepped into the windy morning. "Cameron…"

The veterans posed as allies, but in truth, they'd abandoned her.

# CHAPTER THIRTY-ONE

## Ben

*Quakertown, Pennsylvania*

Steve roused from sleep when Ben rapped his fist against his window. "Got a question for you. Hypothetical scenario."

He shook a dream from his head. "Go on."

"Say we were to pull you and the crew from that house, bring you up to the lake…you think there'd be a fuss?"

Steve flipped through radio stations. "Can I be honest with you?"

"That's what I want."

"Be a whole lot more than a fuss."

Just as Ben had feared. It would come to bloodshed getting this den of morons to play ball. "This is you speaking or the consensus?"

"Both." Steve found the Allman Brothers on the radio and let it play. "We got a good thing goin'. Money in our pockets, power like none of us ever seen before."

"You'd have the same up North."

"Nah." He tapped his knee to the music. "It ain't home. It's fuckin' *Vermont*."

Ben wondered how much of the crew shared Steve's feelings. Des had sold them all a false bill of goods, but he didn't think they should suffer for it. "When Stage Four hits, home's gonna look like a fuckin' vet quarantine. Your next stop will be the fire pit."

Steve shrugged. "It's only been a few of us turned into those rats. Carter and the boys he started out with. Hasn't hit the rest of us."

*Oh, good Christ.* "You think you're special? Des turned the lakeside wolves first, and a wave just hit up there. You think it's not comin' for you?"

Steve hardly reacted. He was oddly nonchalant for a man facing unavoidable death. "If it does, we'd rather die somewhere we know."

Ben found it hard to believe a wolf like Cat would share this fatalistic outlook. Eduardo, maybe, but it was unlikely Steve was speaking for the group. Ben thought about how he might determine who was stubborn and who was rational, how he might manage putting down the problems, including the red-eyed backstabber he'd almost considered a friend.

While he juggled plans, the two cars previously parked at the cabin pulled out of the woods. "Motherfucker." His cellphone rumbled in his pocket, and he fished it out.

Des spit orders from the Chevy. "Stay on 'em but keep some distance. I want to see where they go."

"If we're doing 'em, we should keep it quiet, yeah? And we gotta burn 'em too."

"Right. If they split, we'll take the Toyota."

It was about twenty minutes before the cars finally diverged. Ben stayed with the Honda, pondering his options. Away from his Wolf King, new possibilities suddenly presented themselves.

# CHAPTER THIRTY-TWO

## Macy

*Warminster, Pennsylvania*

She paced herself as she rolled toward home.

Liz grinned as she surveyed the cracks Macy's head had left in the driver's side. She'd brought her shotgun along and wedged it in the nook below the glove compartment.

Macy adjusted in her seat. Driving on four wheels still felt strange to her.

Liz looked at her and snapped. "The fuck are you doin'? Sit still."

"I used to have a bike. Kawasaki Ninja. Six hundred CCs, four stroke, liquid-cooled, clutch—butter smooth. That thing tore ass." She could still see it clearly. The road flying by her in a blur, weaving through cars like wind. "Never really felt comfortable in a cage."

Liz canvassed the Honda's interior. "Where'd this hunk of shit come from?"

"Bad decisions."

Liz gripped her shotgun and racked it.

"What's wrong?"

She fixed eyes on the rearview mirror. "Fucker's tailin' us."

"Who?" Macy craned her neck and found a devilish red truck a few car lengths behind.

"I can blast him from here if you keep this shit straight." She cranked the window down, her bicep rippling with the motion.

"No."

"What?"

Macy touched the shotgun's barrel and guided it down. She'd find a cure. If the marines didn't want to help her, she'd need someone else. *Paranoia, Mace. Shelf it.*

"I want to talk to them."

Liz shook her head. "What makes you think they're talking types?"

Macy pulled the Honda into a small field, and the truck followed. Its size was monstrous in comparison.

"Let's see if he'll listen to reason."

"You fuckin' serious?"

The girls stepped out. Liz aimed at the driver. He stopped in the field, fabric still tight around his neck. From the passenger side, a shorter man with a neat beard emerged.

The man with the scarf was a snarky one. "Why are folks always itchin' to shoot me? Is it my face?" He smiled wider than the grill at his back.

Macy got to the point. "Are you Desmond?"

He tilted his head, the shotgun's presence as menacing as a cloud in the sky. "No. How did you—?"

The short man piped up. "We dustin' 'em, or what?"

Scarf sneered at his partner. There was no love between these men. "Will you calm down? Let's all curb the theatrics please."

Macy continued. "Carter left some information behind."

"Yeah…" He pulled Carter's journal from his jacket. "Quite the read. What say we lower the weapon and discuss a few things?"

The bearded man scoffed. "Are you shittin' me?" In an instant, his face transformed. His eyes went yellow, fangs poked through his lips, and claws shot through his nails. He hunched his back, prepared to pounce. *Stage Three. We're dead.*

The other rushed to him with blinding speed and removed his head with one swipe of his claw. The bearded man's body dropped to its knees while his head spun through the air and landed with a soft *thud* at Macy's feet.

She bent over and spewed chunks of last night's deer into the grass.

"There. Now you're Shorter Steve." He gripped the headless body by the shirt. "I'm sick of this shit."

Liz spoke up for the first time, shotgun still locked on the man's head. "Damn. You gotta teach me that."

He flicked out a lighter but hesitated before returning it to his pocket. "If you lower the shotty. Unless you want some of what *he* got."

She did as he requested.

"How did you two know Carter?"

Liz spoke for them, as Macy was still wiping vomit from her lips. "We didn't."

The man smiled. He seemed genuine, similar to Macy's father. He looked close in age, as well, graying slightly at the temples. "I can appreciate the lack of trust. You hold that weapon like it's natural. You a hunter?"

"Somethin' like that."

"How did *you* know him?" Macy asked. "Carter, I mean."

He looked at Macy, who had almost rid herself of the acid taste. "Look, he was part of my outfit. I wasn't fond of the man. I won't miss him. I just need to know what happened."

"It's almost funny." She thought of the strange few days she'd had. "We came on this wolf thing by accident."

"Well…some rotten luck you have. Carter get you?"

"Carter got her friend. They shared a needle. She got me."

Liz snarled and twitched the gun toward Macy. "Girl, shut your fuckin' mouth."

In the moment she was focused on Macy, the man zipped to Liz and leveled her with a blow to the jaw. Macy stumbled backward, but the man steadied her.

"It's okay." The man's tone was calm and reassuring. "Let's just keep talking while she rests, you and me."

Macy spoke through frantic breaths. "Yeah, okay."

"I'm gonna be as honest as I can, and I'll ask for the same. Cool?"

Macy glanced at Liz. Her head was still attached, which was better than the man had done for his colleague. "Yeah, okay."

"Tell it true, now. Did you know Carter?"

Macy's knees began to tremble. "No…it's like I said. He was her friend's supplier."

"The black kid."

Macy nodded. "He came for the drugs, and Carter attacked him. He spread it to her accidentally when he shared his needle. She spread it to me when we crossed paths."

The man scratched his neck. "Just a big fuckin' mix-up." He looked Macy over. Not in a way that made her uncomfortable, but like a father concerned with his daughter's well-being. "Anyone else involved? Have you made other wolves? Met any?"

She shook her head 'no.'

"All right." He thought for a moment, pacing the field and itching his neck incessantly.

Macy cut in. "How do we get rid of it?"

"Hmm?"

"Carter was looking for ways to lift the curse, but…that didn't pan out. I just want it gone."

The man smiled as if she'd told a joke. "You find the answer to that, I hope you'll let me know."

If Macy was reading him right, he didn't seem like the Wolf King Carter had raved about. He was soft-spoken, oddly rational.

"Do you mind if I ask your name?"

"Macy."

"Macy. Hmm." He looked like he was doing math in his head. "I don't want to worry you, Macy, but it's probably best I kill you both."

The blood fled from her face.

The man must have noticed the color leave her. "Relax. Relax." He reached for her but caught himself. "I'm not…I wanna find another way. Just let me think."

Macy was racked by brain fog. She'd never been threatened so politely.

"What are you, Stage Two now?"

Macy shook her head. "Not yet."

"Hmm."

"How long do I have?" She thought of the rat creature Brooks had described.

"It's different for everyone. Not all of us even hit Stage Three. Not sure what determines that. Strength? Insanity? I don't know."

Macy remembered Carter's journal. He seemed to think it was willpower, but he also seemed to be losing his mind.

It was a good stretch before the man spoke again. When he did, his voice was faint. "Stay out of this. Keep clear of the cabin." He fetched his partner's corpse and dragged it, leaving bloody tracks in the dirt. Before he reached the truck's bed, he turned and pointed to the head. "Pass me that, please?"

"Uhh…" Macy threw her hands up, unwilling to chuck a freshly severed head to a stranger.

He trudged for it and lifted it by an ear. With one hand, he dropped the body into the truck bed. The head followed, and he covered it over with a tarp.

Macy found some semblance of courage. "What am I supposed to do?"

"Just keep away for now. Come by the cabin in a week or so. If I can settle things, I'll find you there." He started the truck and backed out from the field, taking off down the road.

It took a few hard smacks to wake Liz. She shot up like from a nightmare. "Fuckin' shit!"

"Easy. He's gone."

She struggled to her feet, lifted the shotgun and scanned the woods. "Text Brooks," Liz said. "Tell him he might have a tail."

# CHAPTER THIRTY-THREE

## Brooks

*Kensington, Philadelphia*

Stevie Wonder bellowed from his speakers as Brooks rolled onto his sun-soaked block.

Layla waited for him on the stoop, balancing a cigarette between chapped lips. She'd been looking exceptionally decadent as of late, and her scent had grown exceptionally foul. "The fuck? You don't love me no more?" She pursed lips for a kiss. Brooks planted one on her cheek, breathing only through his mouth.

"Arthur around?"

"Inside. You kiss *him* on the lips?"

His attention was pulled to the *clop-clop* of hooves against concrete. Halfway down the block, Brooks could see an Afghan Arabi sheep galloping along the pavement and disappearing into an alleyway. The things were everywhere in the desert. They had fat hind parts, and their ears swung and slapped like pendulums. How this one had forded the Atlantic was a mystery.

"Fuck you starin' at?"

He pushed past the squalid wench and bumped his face into Arthur's chest. The giant's pecks had been reduced to heaping mounds of fat that would have smothered Brooks if he hadn't braced himself.

"Where you rushin' to, little man?"

"Nowhere…checkin' in." He scanned the boarded-up dope den, junkies in states of half-sleep along the walls.

"Right as rain here." His voice boomed like a thunder god's. Even the most mundane of statements seemed profound from Arthur's mouth.

"Good."

Arthur itched at the pit of his arm where a lake of sweat had soaked through the fabric of his tank top.

"You come across a piece recently? Little Walther PPK?"

He tilted his giant head. "Why?"

"Belonged to a friend of mine."

"Shit." Arthur's laugh set off a hurricane on the other side of the world. "That scrappy bitch was your friend?"

"She wants me to get it back for her. You got it?"

"Pawned it already. I didn't know you spoke for her. Lil' firecracker bopped me upside the head." He tilted his face forward to show Brooks the scab behind his ear.

The buzz of his phone against his thigh startled him. He opened it to a text message from a number he didn't recognize. *"Watch your back. You might have a tail."* He could smell sand. The iron taste of blood hit him in the throat.

Arthur's face contorted, and a *shemagh* wrapped itself around his head. With his forefinger, Brooks pulled back the plywood covering the front window. A pickup with a 30-cal mounted in its bed loomed at the curb. An insurgent spoke to Layla with an AK slung over his back. He quick-stepped for the back door.

"Little man! Why so antsy?"

Arthur's words were lost behind him in a thick desert fog.

# CHAPTER THIRTY-FOUR

## Macy

*Warminster, Pennsylvania*

Macy rolled the Honda into her driveway and saw her father's Range Rover. She should have stayed at the cabin. His presence here at noon meant bad news.

She found him on the kitchen floor, tear tracks still wet on his cheeks. His eyes were raw, and he'd been sweating. Macy knew the deal. When their eyes met, he broke.

"Where is it?"

"...Sink."

There, she found a near-empty bottle of Johnny Walker. "The whole thing?"

A dip of the head was his response.

She emptied the residue, the opaque sludge at the bottle's base. She knew Sarah would have done a better job, kept him from slipping. Her sister would have busted the bottle over his head.

He panted before a sob took him. "I can't shake it, Mace." His face was a dripping mess, snot and saliva mixing on his chin. "I can't shake it..."

*You and me both.* The purple face found her. Another attack was near.

She tore a paper towel from the roll and handed it to him. He wiped away the dribble as more fell from his eyes and nose to replace it.

"You don't need to." She found his eyes through a river, a beautiful blue. She remembered staring into them as he swung her and Sarah around on the beach. "Come on…" She hooked him under an arm. "We're takin' a ride."

She laid him in the back seat of the Honda. The look on Liz's face could have soured cheese.

"Who's she?" Nobody answered. Her dad closed his eyes and interlocked his fingers over his chest.

Liz didn't speak a word. She'd run out of quips. Macy didn't mind. She was getting sick of that song, anyway. She decided silence was the best soundtrack for their ride to rehab.

Liz perched cross-legged on the Honda's hood when Macy returned to the parking lot. She tapped fingers on her kneecap, and Macy took the gesture for impatience.

"Go ahead." She waited for the insult. "I needed to handle this."

Liz fixed on the entrance to the detox center. Something stirred in her. It might have been gas as far as Macy could tell. Liz had proven professionally difficult to read. *Go for it, Mace. Tell her about Sarah.* Her lips wouldn't allow it.

They each found their place in the Honda. Liz's silence offered Macy space to gather her thoughts. If she hadn't been tied up with the wolf business, she'd have been there to slap the Johnny Walker from her father's grip.

Despite the scarfed man's paternal efforts to dissuade her, she would keep steadfast in her search for a cure. She had faith pursuing Desmond would shed some light, fill in for a God that had been silent to her.

*Up, Mace. You have to go up. What choice do you have?*

# CHAPTER THIRTY-FIVE

## Desmond

*Kensington, Philadelphia*

The bird's teeth would put the worst hag in Britain to shame. Her breath summoned a cloud of rank mist. "I don't know nothin' 'bout him. Ain't seen him in days."

"Save it, luv. We saw the bloke walk in."

A puff of her cigarette was her answer.

"What about two girls? A half-shaved midget and a brutish bird with braids."

Something lit up in the hag's eyes when he mentioned the latter, but it was quickly overtaken by confusion. "I already gave her up. Cops scooped her the other day."

"We must be thinkin' of a different bird."

"No…I mean, I don't know. They said they would. She lives a few blocks away. Under the tracks…"

Desmond followed her finger. "Can you show me?"

The hag laughed and flashed the broken brown disasters that chewed her food. "How much you got?"

He looked back at Eduardo, whose eyes widened. "Got a twenty on me, I think."

"Nah, not enough."

Des found the hag's bargaining instincts oddly charming. "Come now. Take us on faith, yeah? We'll pay you on the back end."

"Now or never, baby." She placed her cigarette between lips and puffed hard.

Desmond gripped her by the throat, and she spit it to the pavement. "What? My time's not precious to you?" Only whimpers escaped from the girl's windpipe. "Eduardo, we're takin' the princess with us." He passed her back as she coughed up a storm.

Desmond made for the piece of plywood that someone fancied a door, when a hulking man filled its frame. "The fuck's all this?" His voice was deep and dark. It made Des feel like a child in the arms of Zeus.

"Apologies, mate. I've gotta speak with someone inside." When he tried to push past, the brute propped his hand in the center of Des' chest.

"What you doin' with my girl?"

Des turned to see Eduardo wrestling the wench into submission. "Just borrowing her for a time."

"Yo, get your funny-talkin' ass over there and get her." He gave Des a shove that felt like a truck.

The King bowed to the pavement below. Negotiation had failed. He almost felt sorry for the oaf. "I've been called a violent bloke. Irrational." He pointed at the giant's face. "But I tried my utmost to be proper today. It's a process, yeah? Small steps."

The brute deciphered little of Desmond's musings. "The fuck you say?"

He rushed to the big man and reached into his gut. The oaf responded with a choking gurgle. He found the spinal cord with his fingers and snapped it in two. The big man crumbled to the porch, and Des half-expected a resulting earthquake. The hag belted a muffled scream through Eduardo's hand. Desmond felt nothing. No nausea, no headaches. The man was either human or a wolf from a different line.

He stepped over the fallen giant and met a circle of junkies, some with needles protruding from their arms. They certainly weren't howlers. Des was puzzled as to why the man he'd followed would frequent a place like this.

He approached the only one of the bunch that seemed sober, and the junkie edged away from him, shaking. "Relax, mate. Let's 'ave a look at your arm." The frightened man obliged. Desmond opened his forearm with a swipe of his claw. The blood ran and ran, the man whimpered, and the wound stayed open. *The fuck is the do here?*

He left the frightened man to tend to his wound and checked the kitchen for his target. The back door had been left open a crack, so he popped his head through and canvassed the alleyway. Perhaps his man had spotted the tail, or perhaps he was tipped. It made little difference. Des walked back through the circle of smackheads. He had a date with a snaggletooth hag.

The shanty the hag showed them wasn't a great deal nicer than the smack den they'd just left. The car reeked worse the more she blathered. "This is where the bitch lives, but I'm tellin' you, they scooped her."

"What's that copper doin' watchin' the place, then?"

"I have no fuckin' clue. I look like a badge to you?" *Far from it, luv.* A flurry of tears erupted from the hag's eyes as she glared at Desmond's arms, stained red with the giant's blood. "You didn't have to do Arthur that way…you could'a just hit him. He would'a got the message." Now the bird let loose a sob.

"Would you spare me the hysterics? I'm in a mood."

"Fuck you! I'll call my cousin, and we'll go to work on your bitch ass! Fuck—"

Desmond twisted her head until her neck snapped and then continued until it faced Eduardo. "There. Maybe *he'll* listen to your drivel."

Eduardo looked like he might spew. "Didn't we need her?"

"I need a fuckin' Aspirin after that shite." The hag's body slumped between the seats with her head torqued a hundred-eighty degrees. Desmond considered the cop cruiser. "The question now—do I carve up these coppers like Christmas hams, or do I play it like Ben would?" He clicked his tongue against the roof of his mouth as he swapped focus between the cruiser and the alleyway beside the house. "Wait here."

Desmond found another dumpy fiend on the living room couch. It seemed the city had an infestation. Next to her, a dog roused from slumber. It bore its teeth and greeted him with a hostile growl. "Cheers, mate."

The girl looked up at him, her eyes glistening with salt.

He held out his hand for the mutt. "It's all right…we're related." The dog submitted to him the way man and wolf had always done in his presence. "There's a good geez, huh?"

Finally, the girl piped up. "Can I help you?"

Desmond lingered on her question. She'd been unintentionally profound. "You know something, luv? I'm not sure *anyone* can help me."

She scoped him the best she could manage in her state. "You a cop?"

He couldn't help but smile. "Not exactly. I'm lookin' for someone. Black fellow, goatee, mates with a musclebound girl."

Her bottom lip retreated behind her top row of teeth. She knew them. "What do you want with them?"

"Discuss a few things. Friendly chat."

Her breathing hastened. His inclinations unsettled her. "I'm not too sharp, but…I can see that's code for somethin' worse."

Desmond smiled as the girl wiped tears from her face. "What troubles you?" He scratched the dog's head, and it curled into a submissive ball.

The girl swallowed. "They took my kid away from me."

"They?"

"CPS."

"Cunts."

She managed a smile. She might have been pretty before smack sucked the life from her. "Now I'm just tryin' to find the right dose so I can die."

None of this made sense. This girl was no more a howler than the hag with the cranked neck. The three wolves that snuffed Carter were only associated with drug addicts and pond scum. "You've given up, then?"

She searched for a response in the coating of soot that dressed the floor.

"I had my family taken from me back in England." The girl brought out the truth in him—a portion of it, at least. "My home burned. My father, my brothers, they all cooked black." It came back to him then, clear as a photograph—smashing the Molotov cocktail onto his bedridden father, watching the flames take him. The old fool had only been laid up because he'd spent so long praying before the corpse of the shaman who made him. He'd forgone food, sleep and all else. *Pathetic.*

"I'm sorry."

Des held a hand in the air, unwilling to accept her sympathy. "I'm not sure what kept me upright, heavy as the guilt was, but here I stand. Perhaps a bit less, but the same bloke."

They shared a delicious silence. Even without words, the girl spoke to him. When the snores of the dog grew tiresome, she spoke for real. "I don't know what my friends have gotten into. Whatever they did…whatever trouble they're in…it's not my business."

The King nodded as he stood. The girl had gotten his message, maintained her integrity even in her last moments. "Wish my mates were as loyal as you. I mean that. It's a rare thing." Loyalty among wolves was bought and sold, red eyes or no. "I apologize for what I have to do now." His father needed putting down—an evil wretch, he'd have spoiled the world with his seed. If Daniel and the rest of Desmond's brothers hadn't fought, perhaps they'd have lived as well. The need to put this girl down was nothing she could help. She'd be a message, something to draw out his fleeing enemies.

"Just…don't hurt the dog. I promised I would look after him." The girl had accepted her fate. Desmond was only the harbinger.

"Won't harm a hair."

She forced a nod. She was ready.

Desmond crouched next to her and put his claw against her cheek. "I'm so sorry, love."

He moved it across her throat.

# CHAPTER THIRTY-SIX

## Brooks

*Kensington, Philadelphia*

"I need a pick up."

Liz sounded confused through the phone. "What? Where the fuck you at?"

"Couple blocks from my place. They followed me, I had to bail."

"A'ight. Where we scoopin' you?"

Brooks climbed into the back of Macy's Honda, and she took off. Liz still held her shotgun. It seemed she was satisfying a hunger built up since the war. "You get my gun?"

"He pawned it. Sorry, Sarge."

"Fuck…fuckin' smack head."

Brooks had grown accustomed to failing the Sergeant, so this seemed fitting.

"We had a day. Had some words with our boy in the scarf. I don't think he likes the guys he's workin' for. He wasted one of 'em."

"What?"

"Took his head off, real shit. Then he gave me one in the jaw I didn't even see. Put me out again."

"What's next, then?"

Macy broke her silence. "They might be waiting for us at the cabin. Guy said steer clear. We're gonna head to my place and collect ourselves."

Brooks noticed Liz hadn't insulted the girl. He also noticed her voice was plain, deflated, unlike it had been at the cabin. *This chump with the scarf shake you that bad?*

Brooks sifted through the extensive record collection of Macy's father. He slid a Barbara Lewis vinyl out of its sleeve, puffed a film of dust, placed it on the turntable by the edges, and set the needle.

Liz shook her head with disdain. "Look at you…how cultured."

Brooks cranked the volume, drowning her out. He swayed to the rhythm the way his father showed him, bobbing to and fro as Barbara's voice melted the room. He made for the Sergeant, who shied from him before their hands met.

"I'll fuck you up." She couldn't keep from smiling.

He took her in his arms, and her feet moved with his. Then their chests touched, and they glided as one over the shag carpet of Macy's living room. "I didn't know you danced, Sarge."

She pulled her head back and met his eyes. "This your way of askin', mother fucker?"

The rhythm took them, sure as an ocean wave, and they were ear-to-ear once more. Brooks whispered to her, faint but true. "Leave the desert with me..."

For what seemed like a minute, Liz didn't respond. The music washed him of his visions—the face of the girl he shot, the sticky sensation of her blood on his fingers, the desert wind that scraped his cheeks. When Barbara was almost through, Liz whispered back, "We both know that ain't gonna happen."

From the kitchen, they heard shattering glass. Brooks broke from his partner and peeked around the partition to see Macy at the sink with her head bowed. He made a move to check on her when Liz dug a palm into his shoulder. "Nah…leave her be."

He flipped on the news as soon as he got the call. Dome lights shaded his block in blue and red. Strands of caution tape stretched across the entrance to the dope den. The reporter was halfway through a sentence. *"…Savagely mutilated in his own home, but the bloodshed didn't end there. A twenty-six year-old woman was abducted and taken to a house a few blocks away, where she was then murdered, her body left in the street."*

Brooks' stomach tightened and his legs felt weak. Not because Arthur and Layla were dead, but because he would have been laid up beside them if not for Macy's warning.

*"Police removed another body from* this *house…"*

They cut to Liz's place, and she shot up from her seat. Her shotgun clattered to the floor.

*"…where a twenty-four-year-old woman was found with her throat slashed. The weapon has yet to be recovered. Witnesses have been offering conflicting stories, but police are on the hunt for this woman."*

They popped up a picture of Liz. The photo from her military ID. She still looked alive.

*"Alexandra Elizabeth Campbell, the suspect of Sunday's roadside double murder, evaded police custody on Tuesday and remains at large. We urge anyone with information on her whereabouts to contact authorities. We will return here as more details unfold…"*

Liz's mouth hung open like a trap with a busted hinge. He had never seen her so pale.

# CHAPTER THIRTY-SEVEN

## Ben

*Montgomery County, Pennsylvania*

*"Thou know'st 'tis common. All that lives must die."* Ben winced and sprayed saliva through gaps in his teeth. *"Passing through nature to eternity."*

His third patch clung to his shirt as he peeled it away, tearing pieces of hair and skin, bursting capillaries along his rib cage. Death was close. Perhaps a week was an overestimation. He waited in his truck for the pain to subside, eyeing the granite cladding of Carter's manse.

He'd reread Carter's journal a few times to confirm the revelation. *The King's mother. Let's see you explain that Des, you cunt.*

Ben's plan had changed. He left Short Steve's unburned remains at the cabin and snapped one of the bear traps around his shin for authenticity. Desmond would weaken again, but this time it would work to Ben's advantage. He would scoop his friend without argument, and the two of them would shift it back to the lake so he could share his findings with the others. They would figure out what to do with Des, even if it meant slaying a few more wolves to weaken him further.

Inside Carter's, Des was anything but weak. He crouched next to a pitbull and massaged his head while the howlers joked and laughed, his smile as radiant as ever.

*What the fuck is this?* There was no doubt Steve was a wolf, and yet Des was unaffected by his passing. He flashed to his dream about the second red-eye. It didn't seem like the girl had been lying about their accidental involvement, but something wasn't clicking.

Des noticed him. "Oi oi! We've got a new lad. Meet Pedro."

The dog's tongue drooped low as he discharged frantic breaths.

Ben wasn't sure if he should bother asking. "Where'd *he* come from?"

"Gift from a fiend who's passed on, God rest her. How'd you do with the others?"

"Dead and burned."

"Brilliant!" He looked past Ben at the empty doorway. "Steve?"

"Left him at the cabin to watch over things. Can I talk to you for a second?"

They found a vacant room where the music from the bar was a hum. "What is it, mate? You look ill."

"Steve got wasted."

"Wut?"

"He's gone. Muscle girl slept him in the open."

Desmond chewed the news. It took all of fifteen seconds for him to cope with Steve's passing. "Bloke meant fuck all to me."

"Have you noticed the problem?"

"What? What are you on about?"

"I didn't burn him."

Des stared into him and leaned closer. "What d'you mean?'

"I mean…you might have been onto something coming down here."

It seemed the King had swallowed something jagged. "Maybe I've beaten it. The illness."

"I suppose that's a possibility," Ben said. "The most flattering and unrealistic one."

It took time before Desmond could drop his ego and accept the situation. "Come with me."

They found Eduardo at the bar. Des fastened fingers around his throat, and Eduardo grasped at his wrists to try to free himself. "Who the fuck *are* you, mate?"

He tried to answer but could only squeak. The howlers around him gathered.

"Steve went down. He's unburned, and I don't feel shite. So who the fuck turned you?" He loosened his grip to allow a response.

"Carter! Carter turned me, I swear!"

"You remember the girl? What I did to 'er head?" Eduardo's eyes bulged when Des fastened his grip again. "If I do the same to you, I'll feel ill?"

"Don't…please. I'll explain it."

Des released him as he hacked and spit. "You lie, I'll peel the skin from you and feed it to the dog."

Eduardo rubbed the redness from the pit of his neck before it healed. He looked to Ben, but he would find no salvation there. "Carter had a few guys he didn't turn, refugees from another line. He took them under his wing. I thought you knew about it."

*Maybe Carter wasn't buying Desmond's lies anymore either. Maybe he was thinking of jumping ship.*

"Who else came from the other line? Anyone still around?"

"Just Cat. The rest have been cooked."

"Where's the bird now?"

"Upstairs…back room."

Desmond dashed for the girl. Ben stepped into his path. "Des…don't you fuckin' dare. We're just gonna talk to her."

The King nodded, and they both made for the young girl's room.

Cat's face read like nausea more than fear. Ben decided he should do the talking. "I need to ask about how you and Steve came on this wolf business. He passed it to you through sex, right?"

She nodded, her eyes making frequent passes at the Wolf King behind him.

"And Steve? How'd *he* come by it?" The King's voice was sharp and succinct.

"We used to cut drugs for a smaller outfit nearby before Carter absorbed us. He kept us human to minimize liability. Carter had Steve and a few others digging stash points in the woods when Steve stumbles on some creep taking pictures of the house. He thinks it's a cop at first until the guy sprouts claws and attacks him." She swallowed, troubled by her own words. "The others surround him and take him out before he can finish Steve. They figured he must have been one of Carter's that went rogue until they showed him the body. Carter didn't know him. Never saw him before." She took a heavy breath. "Where's Steve now? He can tell it better than I can."

Ben had no time to sugarcoat. "He's gone. Some other wolves dropped him."

Though tears fell from the girl's face, her expression relaxed. There was relief behind her sadness.

Des scowled. "Why didn't Carter call me immediately?"

*Because you weren't top priority, Your Highness.*

Cat shrugged as a tear welled on her chin.

Ben had heard enough. "I believe her. No one's that good a fuckin' actress, Des. Look at her."

Desmond stared through the poor girl, provoking more tears. "Right. Okay. While we're all being Christly honest…" He stepped to Ben. There was blood on his breath. "Why didn't you burn Steve? If you thought he was one o' mine…why'd you leave him uncooked?"

*I should've left them all uncooked, you lying bastard.* "The girl dropped him in public and took off. It was burn him or catch her. I couldn't do both."

"You could've gone back for him." The Wolf King's nostrils flared.

Ben stood and stepped into the hall. He motioned for Des to follow.

"Christly honest?" Ben leaned in close. "Don't make me fucking laugh."

"What now?"

"Carter kept a journal…not to summon painful memories, but he says your mother passed from patching."

There was no change on the King's face. "Don't forget yourself, Ben."

"You'll have to forgive me. See, I'm dying slow because I put faith in a bullshitter. Your mother never read you any of those fables growing up? Boy Who Cried Wolf too on the nose?"

"You're a funny bloke." Desmond's face widened into his most punchable smirk. "But speak of my mother in that tone, I might lose my temper."

"Save your threats for the pups downstairs," Ben replied. "I know what you can do, and I don't give a shit. I'm half dead, anyway, and I might be the only clear head you've got right now."

Desmond's shoulders slackened. "It's true she died from the illness. Her body was too weak to birth us all. I reckon my father's seed poisoned her. Don't see how it connects to our troubles now."

Ben still wasn't buying it. He juggled options. He couldn't leave things unsettled at the lake. There were those there for whom he felt responsible. He stepped to Des again. "Who's the other King? You carried yourself like the one and only, but Cat saw two of 'em in her dreams, same as me…and you look a little uneasy. Is someone from your family alive?"

Des grimaced. "I saw them burn. My father first, then my brothers one by one. My home fell to cinders on the Mother Hill." His lips stretched taut in a venomous grin. "It rained near after…a jest from the Almighty." His gaze found the girl through the doorway, in a fit of shaking. "A miracle…from Christ on high…is the only way an O'Connell lived…"

It was a lump sum to take in. Des had never opened to him this way, and Ben fancied a guess as to why. A second red-eye knocked him down a peg. His ego wouldn't withstand such a blunder. "We should grab Steve's body and bring it here. Whoever this is, they'll come looking for him."

"The bird dropped him in public, did she not?"

Ben swallowed his tongue for half a second. "I can get him. Just give me some time."

"What? Break into the morgue? Nonsense. If this is truly a relative of mine…he has our scent. Should he have missed it, we've got proper bait right here." He looked at Cat. Both of them caught his meaning.

For a split second, Ben was back in his truck, contemplating killing an unconscious Wolf King. He should have followed his instincts then. "Hold on…"

Des lunged at the girl before Ben could finish his thought. She held an arm in front of her to block his advance, but it was on the ground pooling blood before her claws came out. She started a scream that was cut short when Des slashed open her throat. Blood pumped from the wound, and toneless air hissed from her destroyed windpipe. Des went for her heart next. It was here Ben's reflexes finally awakened. He moved to stop the Wolf King's onslaught, but he had already torn through her breast tissue and cracked through her chest plate. The entire attack lasted less than three seconds, but it looked like some psychopath had worked on her for days.

Ben thought of the dead girl from Bennington. Another soul snatched for nothing. Another young girl he'd been far too slow to save.

# CHAPTER THIRTY-EIGHT

## Macy

*Warminster, Pennsylvania*

Brooks posed in the mirror, wolf to man and back again, golden jewels in his head flashing on and off like hazard lights.

Liz spoke to Macy, loud enough for him to hear. "Look at him…they're both ugly, mother fucker." Even in mourning, she found the energy to bring him down. *Come on, Liz. Let him enjoy something.* Liz cringed as Macy unwound the braids from her hair.

"Sorry..." A bottle of bleach sat nearby, not yet used. The braids clung to Liz's scalp like rope. Macy's fingers cramped at the effort.

Brooks changed his face over and over again. Stage three was fascinating to him, but Liz was too grief-stricken and Macy too focused to find it amusing.

"Recon, then. What'd you find out about this asshole?" Liz had been ranting about all the ways she would kill Desmond, each method more graphic than the last.

The mechanic shared her findings. "I read a little about the drug runners from Carter's journals, but he wrote a lot more about his wolf situation. Traced it back to Derbyshire, England where he was linked to a family called O'Connell. I refined my research a bit, dug up some academic journals about the O'Connell family. They ran protection in Derby and slaughtered gangs who opposed them. Some versions have them shapeshifting and eating the flesh of fallen enemies, some have the patriarch going mad and burning his sons. In everything I found, I only came across one name…Daniel. Derby folk called him the Brigand. They say he held the family together, the true leader. Every account has him dying in the same fire that killed the rest. Some have him setting the fire. This Desmond that Carter mentioned…he might be an O'Connell, possibly the last living one, but the myths tell nothing about him."

"Cause there ain't nothing to tell…punk-ass bitch." Liz aimed her pupils at the Corporal. "Let's find our man with the red truck and squeeze him. Then we find Desmond and I pop his eyeballs with my thumbs." She held out her thumbs in case there was any confusion.

Brooks seemed content with Liz's plan. "How we gonna find him?"

"Carter's mail." Macy's response struck puzzled looks on both marines. "Carter had a bunch of his mail at the cabin. I saw it while I was looking through his journal. The address didn't match. That'll lead us to his house, and we can work from there."

Liz and Brooks nodded to each other. "You bring any of it with you…ow, fuck." Macy tugged at her braids again.

"I did not. We're gonna have to swing by the cabin and get it."

Brooks dipped his head. "Didn't you say the scarf guy—?"

"Fuck the scarf guy." Macy could feel impatience shaking from Liz's shoulders. "He tricked us. I'll lay him out with the rest."

Brooks returned to the mirror and swapped faces again, the grin of a child shining clearly in both.

Macy tugged, and Liz winced. She let out a grunt through clenched teeth.

## *Quakertown, Pennsylvania*

The cabin was quiet. Wind whispered through the woods. Liz crept onto the grounds with shotgun drawn. Macy and Brooks trailed behind. Her hood concealed her new hairdo—braids unwound and blonde as a Barbie. Macy thought it looked nice.

They came upon a fried corpse with a missing head. *The short one from before?* Its features were completely obscured by burns. His leg was snapped in one of Carter's bear traps. Macy was having trouble deciphering what the play was for the man with the scarf. Had the short man's death been an impulsive mistake, or was there a civil war brewing in Desmond's crew?

Inside, Carter's things had been ransacked again. Macy found a few letters and magazines, all bearing the same address.

Brooks dislodged a second shotgun from the wall and loaded shells into the receiver. "You want one?" He spoke to Macy.

She considered the opportunity. She'd fired a handgun with her father a few years back, but she had no experience with a mammoth of a weapon at her shoulder. The recoil would surely knock her over. "I don't think I'd be any good with it."

Liz must have figured otherwise. "Bring one anyway. I can show you how to kill shit if there's time."

There was something eerie in the cabin's atmosphere, something she hadn't noticed before. A foreign musk. Her lupine senses were infantile and disorganized, but Macy was certain the energy was off—that someone new had paid a visit.

## *Montgomery County, Pennsylvania*

She parked the Honda on the lonesome road that wound across Carter's property. The house was massive. Surrounded by woods on three sides, it seemed a fortress—a nest of evil looming in the boughs of red maple and hickory trees. Its front drive was a parking lot. Macy counted eleven cars, including the red truck. The scarfed man was inside. Through him, they'd find the King. Liz squeezed the butt of her shotgun, and veins bulged from the back of her hand.

"Guy's got friends, Sarge. Some scope to this." Macy noticed that Brooks didn't seem as angry about his dead comrades—the ragged girl and the big man who'd broken Liz's arm. He hadn't mentioned them once since the news. It was different with Liz. She blurted out what-ifs, ways she could have kept Serita safe. Sometimes she just repeated the girl's name until her voice trailed off. And then she would mutter other names. Juliana. Marcus. She might have been losing her wits.

Macy missed her father already, though she'd just dropped him off this morning. The rehab center didn't permit calls for the first week.

Liz squeezed her gun until Macy was sure she'd crack the stock. "You think you could disable those cars?"

Macy canvassed the lineup. Camry. Cobalt. El Camino. "I *know* I could disable those cars."

Liz cracked a hint of a smile. "Alright, killer."

"Alarms could be an issue. I can snip the fuse, but it'll go off until I do."

"Save those for last. Wait for us to get loud."

Brooks whispered apprehensively. "We gotta be careful, here. It's closing in on dark. You two'll turn."

"I don't feel the itch the way I did," Liz replied. "The wolf knows what I want. I'm gaining control." She turned to Macy. "You?"

Macy wasn't so sure. She could feel a hunger rising in her chest, the urge to clamber onto all-fours. She shoved this down, thinking of Sarah, willing the wolf to stay beneath the surface.

"Look at her fucking face," Liz barked. "She's fine."

"And are we sure we can kill 'em?" Brooks asked.

"I know they stay dead when you take their heads off, so let's go with that." She looked at Macy behind the wheel. "You got anything to add?"

Macy had plenty to add. She found the stronghold. If not for her, these two would be wandering the woods or dead. "Desmond…when we find him…before you 'pop his eyes'…can we ask about a cure?"

Liz locked on to the house again where their friend with the scarf awaited them. "Exfiltrate priority target for interrogation. Sure. We done that shit before."

# CHAPTER THIRTY-NINE

## Ben

*Montgomery County, Pennsylvania*

A fourth patch took over his eye. Ben stared at it in the mirror. A yellow grotesque, it was, bloody fur surrounding a yellow jewel like sludge. *I refuse to die in this gaudy cunt of a house.* Could his will to suppress the symptoms have faltered with Cat's death or was this thing progressing quicker with every patch?

The dead girl lay on the bed behind him. *"Watch the bird. Don't let anyone near this room."* Desmond's last instruction. The King had always been impulsive. He never shied from violence when it was necessary. But now things had changed. His deception accentuated all his other faults. *I refuse to die for a psychopath.*

Ben felt the burn of Cat's dead stare in the small of his back. Maybe it was a fifth patch. He wouldn't trouble himself to check. He figured he was as dead as this girl and the waitress from Bennington. He could hear Junior laughing.

With Desmond's secret busted open, Ben tried to piece together the dream that had tormented him for weeks. *Two red-eyes. Des and the mystery brother. A yellow decapitates one of them and becomes a red himself. Which one? And who is this yellow traitor?* Ben's organization was important to him. He never felt right about the life he'd chosen, laundering drug money, but he was damn good at it. He was organized. The life Des had given him had brought only chaos. After what Des had become, or perhaps what he'd always been, Ben wondered if he ought just to remove the King's head and save himself.

The idea was tempting, but even if he could somehow pull it off, would he follow the same brutal path? Was it the red eyes that gave Des such irrational bloodlust? *Just not Junior. Anyone but him. That kid as a red-eye might mean the end of the fuckin' world.* The thought sickened him. Perhaps his patches were a gift, and death, more of the same.

*"Are you scared?"* The echo of the dead girl's question bounced between his ears.

*No, but you were, and I did fuck all to protect you.* He stared into the gaping cavity between the girl's breasts, the chasm that spilled her life onto the sheets. He remembered something she'd said to him about the dream while they were listening to the torpid beast in Carter's shed. It shook him to the bone, though it seemed like a passing statement at the time.

*"I have this pain in my chest when I wake from it. A sharp burn…"*

# CHAPTER FORTY

## Liz

*Montgomery County, Pennsylvania*

They crouched in the weeds like the grunts they were, while the death throes of the sun disappeared behind the house. Brooks' eyes were distant. Liz wondered about his condition. "You still with me?"

"Yeah."

Liz could tell it was a half-truth.

"You remember the compound run from Kandahar?"

He thought for a moment. "Nuts to butts?"

"Nuts to butts."

They hugged the stone dressing of the house, Brooks' nuts to Liz's butt, shotgun propped over her left shoulder. In thirty feet, they came to a window. Liz pulled the screen, and the two of them climbed in, kittens on a cloud.

The house's laundry room was dark save for a crack of light that ran down the side and along the bottom of its door, slightly ajar. Liz went prone next to the crack and listened. She could hear the muffled sounds of conversation. On her knees, she pushed the door open slowly with the barrel of her weapon.

The hallway was deserted. Liz moved to the first lamp that lined the wall and turned it off. She did the same for three more as they moved closer to the sounds, checking corners the way they'd trained.

They came to a kitchen, where two men spoke over a meal. Liz could smell spices and the gamey scent of venison. The men spoke with hushed voices, like they were afraid someone would overhear.

"No peep from her since they went up there."

"Yeah, no shit."

"What do you mean?"

"I gotta spell it out for you?"

"Nah…come on."

On closer inspection, Liz could see the men were sorting drugs into plastic bags. The brown powder seemed so foreign to her. She had no impulse for it at all.

"Did you see him before he went up? You see his look? Guy almost ripped Eduardo's head off. You think Patchy could'a stopped him?"

"I ain't seen *him* either, now you mention it."

"He's probably dead, too. We're all probably fuckin' dead."

The grunts pressed on down the hall, shotguns on swivels. On Liz's left, another hall opened up, one she'd seen in a dream…a door with no knob, a woman's song. She felt Brooks bump up against her as she slowed down.

"Sarge?" he whispered.

Liz shook her head. Her vision cleared. The walls closed in.

At the end, the hall opened into a great room, where several men congregated around a piano. She couldn't see the scarfed man, but another caught her eye—English accent, wavy black hair, the stubble of a beard, sharp cheekbones, and a grin that pulled dimples deep into his face.

Beside him sat Pedro, chewing a bone, obedient as a watchdog.

# CHAPTER FORTY-ONE

## Macy

*Montgomery County, Pennsylvania*

The red truck went first. She'd scoped it before, got a read on its ins and outs. The man with the scarf didn't keep it locked. With her bolt cutters, she snipped the fuse box and moved onto the next, head low, light on her feet.

Next was a black Chevy. She jimmied the lock and cut the fuse wires. A rhythm took shape after that. *Sneak, pop and snip.* Only two had alarms, so she passed them over. She reached the tenth vehicle—another truck, this one more dilapidated than the rest. She jammed the metal sheet into the window well, and its alarm blared. *Way to go, Mace. All of two minutes before you sink the ship.* She snipped the fuse, and the lot was still again. It was just quiet enough to pick up approaching footsteps.

Quickly, she fell to her back and rolled under the truck into a puddle of oil. She fished her switchblade from her pocket and flipped it open. Her breathing was heavy and loud, though she fought with everything she had to keep it choked. A pair of boots stepped into view three feet from her head. She set eyes on the Achilles tendon and readied the blade.

Then she heard a *sound*.

The man in boots collapsed to his knees and onto his chest. His head had been removed. Blood pooled on the ground beneath his torn neck, and his body twitched to silent music. A second pair of shoes emerged beside the corpse. Macy was sure she'd been made. But the second pair disappeared, leaving her and her headless friend to bond on the pavement.

# CHAPTER FORTY-TWO

## Brooks

*Montgomery County, Pennsylvania*

"The fuck you doin' with my dog?" The end of Liz's shotgun was deadly still and fixed on the Brit's head.

He smiled, boyish dimples shining on his face. "You're sprightly for a dead bird."

Pedro sauntered over and tentatively sniffed at Liz's pant leg. He seemed to know he'd betrayed his owner.

Brooks switched between targets, keeping the Sergeant covered.

The scruffy Brit continued. "My brother sent *you*, then? *This* is his play? Two pillocks with shotguns?" The men surrounding him erupted with laughter. "Which one is it? I miss them all dearly. I'm dying to know."

"You Desmond?" Her finger tapped the trigger. Brooks was afraid she might let one go accidentally.

The man giggled and scanned the room. There was no fear in him. "They havin' a laugh?" Suddenly, a car alarm blared from the front drive. Before the Brit could react, it seemed like something struck him. He flinched in the direction of the noise.

Then it all blurred out. Muffled voices, faint images, and sand. Brooks was in the desert again. The Brit was an insurgent, his soldiers surrounding them. The house was a bunker. He and Liz had wandered in blindly to find themselves outgunned. More insurgents moved in behind them, and Brooks knew there was only one way out.

He opened fire.

# CHAPTER FORTY-THREE

## Ben

*Montgomery County, Pennsylvania*

The gunshots startled Ben from his thoughts. The second O'Connell had arrived. *But they're howlers. What the fuck do they need guns for?* He opened the bedroom door, and a claw swiped the side of his face, spraying blood onto the wall. He caught the second swipe at the wrist and met a yellow-eyed goon with dripping wet fangs. *Who the fuck are* you*?* Ben had never seen this man.

The goon tried to pull free, but Ben answered with a strike to the gut. Then he slashed at his throat with the other hand and sent the man's head through a window, into the evening air. He collected himself and scanned the hall.

The dead girl had led them here, as planned. They'd come to burn her. Ben conjured a new idea. He hooked an arm around Cat's waist and hoisted her over his shoulder. He wanted an appointment with Des' long lost relative, or whoever the hell this was. Not a fight, a discussion. With the girl's body in tow, he had just the thing to bait him.

Another stage three rushed to meet him in the hall. He set the girl against the wall. This one dodged Ben's slash and slammed him into another window, shattering it. He tossed Ben to the floor and stepped to him. Ben grabbed his leg at the knee and snapped it in the wrong direction. The howler screamed in pain as he fell to join Ben on the floorboards. They wrestled arms for a moment. Ben managed to grab him by the neck. He twisted and removed his head, bloody muscle and sinew tearing away from his torso like taffy. Ben's patches hadn't muddled his skills after all. *And Des thought* himself *a Wolf God.*

# CHAPTER FORTY-FOUR

## Liz

*Montgomery County, Pennsylvania*

Brooks was locked in a bloodlust. Man-wolves were taking slugs left and right. They were healing rapidly, and none were staying down. *The head, Brooks. The head. Idiot.* She was fixated on Brooks' tantrum and had forgotten how to shoot.

Pedro was gone. Liz hadn't seen him flee. She hoped against odds he hadn't caught crossfire.

The wolf that was probably Desmond changed his face. His eyes glowed crimson at the center of the room, and fur sprouted along his cheekbones. It was clear this wolf was different. His claws were longer and sharper than anything Liz had seen. The way the fur gripped his face seemed more natural, as if this was his true form. Liz lined her weapon between his eyes and pulled the trigger. Her pellets hit the distant wall and perforated a painting.

Desmond had disappeared, or so it seemed, until he resurfaced a foot from Brooks' face and brought down claws like guillotines. Both of Brooks' hands came away at the wrists. His shotgun clattered to the hardwood floor. His hands twitched as the nerves fought to keep hold of the gun, wrists squirting blood like geysers.

Liz didn't wait. She planted a dose of buckshot in the center of Desmond's chest and sent him through a set of double doors, onto the back lawn.

Brooks was on his knees, staring at the stumps where his hands had just been. More of Desmond's soldiers were finding their footing, but they were met with another wave of wolves that entered from the hall. A few more poured in from the open double doors. Liz pegged them as Desmond's until they attacked the others. She made for the wounded Corporal as the room became a hurricane of claws, with Liz and her handless accomplice at the eye.

# CHAPTER FORTY-FIVE

## Macy

*Montgomery County, Pennsylvania*

She counted ten blasts—a few bursts and some staggered shots. She may have killed her friends with the alarm, but she couldn't move to check on them. She could sketch the undercarriage of the truck from memory as the headless wolf emptied the rest of his blood beside her. To her right, she noticed a dirt bike leaning against a rust-brown shed. *Suzuki RM-Z250.* She considered mounting it and fleeing the scene, but she couldn't gauge its condition.

To her left, the front door of Carter's house burst open, and a man in a spiked jacket stumbled out. He dragged his left leg at first, but after a moment, walked normally. He released the lock to the shed, took a few steps back, and dropped to his knees.

From the black of the shed emerged a pathetic creature, similar to the sewer rat Brooks had described. Its hair drooped like a shaggy dog's after a bath. The kneeling man seemed to be crying. They shared an odd moment, staring like lost lovers reunited. The rat creature pounced, tearing away at his face and throat until only a fleshy pulp remained. Macy cupped her hand over her mouth to prevent a shriek from escaping as the creature hobbled for the woods.

*Why would he give himself to the beast that way?* He could have killed it with harsh language.

Macy decided she would never leave her spot. She noticed the sun had fully fallen and night had taken them almost unaware. The smell of oil was sharp, but familiar, and the shadow of the truck concealed her from all the hell that unraveled in the night.

She traced her finger over the truck's muffler as she started to turn.

# CHAPTER FORTY-SIX

## Ben

*Montgomery County, Pennsylvania*

The dead girl smelled of lilacs and wild berries, her flesh—angel soft. Blood from the gaping cavity where her heart had been dripped onto Ben's shirt. When he heard the voices behind him, he fell prone in the foliage. The girl's body formed a fleshy canopy over his head.

He spotted four men leaving Carter's house, one with bad scarring on his face and arms. They had two unconscious wolves in their possession—the bruiser from the cabin, along with the black kid, minus two hands. Ben changed his face and pricked up his ears.

The men spoke with English accents. The scarred one held up a finger to his mates and sniffed the night. "You missed one." Ben lurched forward, prepared to strike.

Another stepped from the group and answered. "We burned everyone who went down. All of *ours*, anyway."

The scarred man closed his eyes and sniffed again. "No…there's another."

He waved them along, and they disappeared into the woods. The scars were probably burns. The second red-eye. Des' brother returned from the grave to wreak havoc. *But for what purpose? Why the bad blood?* Des was missing, and with him, the answers Ben sought.

He muscled his way to his feet with Cat draped over his shoulder like a sack. He had his bait, and the scarred man had the scent. Now, it was a waiting game.

# CHAPTER FORTY-SEVEN

## Desmond

*Montgomery County, Pennsylvania*

He reeked of shit. He'd wriggled his way into a drainage ditch after dropping two of the unfamiliar wolves. His head was a throbbing blur. *Bested by a handless maggot and his brute of a girlfriend.* His father would have laughed himself drunk.

The men emerged through spots in his vision—four of them, carrying two more. He was tempted to call out, but he thought better of it when he saw the scars. *Fuck me bloody.* He fought with everything he had not to loose a guffaw. He squinted to get a better look, certain he was hallucinating. The burn marks were plain to see, but that didn't narrow it down. It was his left eye. He bore a scar that their father had given him with an iron when he was a pup, and the pigment in the iris had faded gray. *Ryan the bloody Runt. I must be mad as a bag of ferrets.*

Des had it pegged for Daniel. Daniel was the angry one. *He would hold a grudge long enough to cross a sea and separate me from my bollocks... though he'd have to grow another head first. But Ryan? Ryan pissed his pants like a Mary and cried for mum. Ryan couldn't bring down a doe with three hooves.*

He watched as his little brother led his mates into the shadows, still convinced he was dreaming. *Alright, guv. Thrilled to see you again. I'll kill you thoroughly next time.*

He fished out his phone and sent a message to New York.

# CHAPTER FORTY-EIGHT

## John Becker, Jr.

*Brooklyn, New York*

Ringo was a brawler on the chess board. He wielded his bishops like pawns and his queen like a rook. John glazed over the sheen of the redwood at the trap he'd set for his dimwitted opponent. He moved his queen into place. "Checkmate."

Ringo straightened in his chair and threw his hands up. "What…?"

"You're stuffed, big boy. Let it end."

He *was* a big boy. The muscles of his forearms bulged like tree stumps and his massive chest boomed with every breath. The oaf was as stubborn as he was broad. He wouldn't go quietly. With plump fingers, he mapped out possibilities across the board and sported a sour face when he found a dead end. "Fuck."

John was fit to burst while Ringo moved to reset the pieces. "Oi…hold it. What's right is right, yeah?"

Ringo sighed like an old nag. "Game's over. Allow me my dignity, at least."

"It's naught to do with you." John gripped a redwood pawn, its finish smooth and delicate in his hand. He swiped the piece toward Ringo's king, knocking it to the board with a *click*.

Ringo was entertaining Laura with his tongue when John burst in with the news. “Sweetheart…” He motioned to the door with his thumb. “Shift it.” She hopped to, Ringo the more disappointed of the couple.

“Becker, come on, I’ve made waves with this one.”

“I can see. Pull your trousers up and listen.” Ringo pulled them up and clipped his belt. “There comes a time in the life of a pup when he must face down the devil and spit. My father’s mantra. Truer now than ever.”

The vacant stare in the dog’s eyes was numbing. “You and your sayings, I can never follow.”

“Follow my finger, then.” He erected an index finger and opened the message he’d received from Desmond. An SOS. The King was in trouble, and Becker had been called upon to mend things.

Ringo’s eyes widened when he finished reading.

“Round up half the boys…the better half. Leave the rest to watch things here.”

“We takin’ the vans?”

“Yes, Ringo. Yes, we are.”

“Why both Harrys?” Travis fiddled with the knickknacks on his desk, nearly spilling his coffee and frying his computer.

“Young Harry’s strong, still has spring, and he won’t go nowhere without his old man, so I’m takin’ both.”

“Leaving me with scraps.”

John propped both hands against the desk and leaned in. "You needn't change a thing. They keep moving powder and pills. They start to patch, they go to the furnace. Don't be daft."

"Okay…" Travis finally folded his hands and offered John his full attention. "What if you don't come back?"

"Don't talk nonsense."

"Nothing personal…but say Desmond offers you a better deal? I gotta run this place myself? Some of the boys, I don't know if I trust."

"You think I'd leave you in the wind?"

He shrugged his chunky shoulders.

John rushed to him and pressed a claw to his throat from behind. A trickle of blood dribbled over his finger. "You make me doubt you, Travis."

"Easy…" Now the man started to shake, every breath a tremble.

John flipped out his phone and rang Young Harry. "Swing by the office, yeah? It's urgent."

Travis spit whatever words he could to save himself. "I might have overstepped—"

"Shhh. Save it, guv. I ain't the one to choose your fate."

When Harry arrived, he seemed unaffected by the scene. He closed the office door calmly.

"Oi, Harry. You know the books, yeah? The ins and outs?"

He motioned to Travis with a tip of his chin. "Better than this twat."

"That's a lie." Travis grew more desperate with each drop of blood.

"Shut it, fat man." John looked back to Harry. "Can you run the ship in my absence?"

"No bother."

Before Travis could blurt another syllable in his defense, John scooped his throat from him. It didn't take long for his life's blood to drain onto his desktop.

John shook it from his hands. "I'll only be a few days, I think. Have the boys fetch a mop."

They rumbled from New York at dawn—two white vans filled with bloodthirsty howlers, all at John's command. He rode shotgun with Ringo at the wheel, sucking his lips periodically to keep saliva from dribbling to his chin. He'd been waiting for the call since Desmond and his lackey left for Pennsylvania. Part of him knew it would come. A simple burn job wouldn't have drawn the King so far South. This was a special affair.

The scent of his father's charred bones still lingered fresh in his snout. The flames of his pyre had been his catalyst. He was a pup borne into the world through the smoke of legend. *The Becker name hasn't burned with you, Dad. I'll see to that.*

John Becker Sr. had sharpened his son for rule. He'd been turned by the King directly and dedicated himself for fifteen years before the sickness took him. He was royalty in Desmond's eyes, despite any petty quarrels between them—a lupine prince in a howler monarchy. Now his only son had been called upon in desperation, thrust into his own fire of sorts. Should he emerge unburned, he would claim his princely crown as reward.

"What are you smilin' about?" Ringo would never understand. He was so far removed from the King's bloodline, Desmond probably wouldn't feel it if he fell.

John scanned the iridescent horizon. "The sun rises for *me*, mate." Its beauty stretched for miles, ushering in a new age. "A changing of the guard and nature takes heed."

# CHAPTER FORTY-NINE

## Macy

*Montgomery County, Pennsylvania*

Hunger pangs doubled her over as she crawled from the brush, the morning air biting her skin where her clothes had torn. She couldn't bring herself to murder another deer. Not for food. Not for sport. She remembered holding the severed head by the antler—the way it stared.

*I killed them.* The raucous noise of the alarm still buzzed in her ear. *I blew their cover and sent them to their graves.* She named the trees as she passed them to blot out her negligence. *American Larch. Eastern Hemlock. Scots Pine.*

If Liz had somehow made it and Brooks hadn't, Liz would be a loose cannon, impractical and dangerous. If the opposite were true, Brooks would falter, unmotivated to continue. If both had died, Macy was out of friends, and she'd be hunted by Desmond's pack without a means of defense. A twig snapped beneath her foot and shot pain to her knee.

She found the Honda in the shade where she'd left it, and on its hood, grinning, sat the scarfed man without his scarf. His neck was rotten with scabby fur. His eye had gone yellow and a bloody patch of hair occupied a mass of his cheek, like he was caught halfway between man and roadkill. He looked the way Carter had described himself in his later entries—the dark stage. Perhaps this meant he was weak, but weak or no, this was the end of the line. She prayed it would be quick.

"Young lady…" The closer she stepped, the viler his face became. "Behold, the results of ignoring sound advice."

"Go ahead and do it." She dropped her arms to her hips. "I'm not gonna fight you."

His good eye assessed her ravaged apparel. "Sounds like depression talkin'. No need for that. You see my eye?" He pointed to the yellow jewel that threw off the symmetry of his face. "I've got every reason in the world to be down. And yet…I'm a pig in shit. You know why?"

*I don't even know your name.*

"'Cause I've got an out. And so do you, sister, if you'll have it." A breeze rolled through from the southwest, carrying leaves in frantic spirals. "My boss turned rabid. Not to mention, he lied to me. So, I'm back on the market."

"How does that help *me*?"

"For one, I ain't gonna put you down. You got a change of clothes?"

"In the car."

"Well, have at it. Don't let me stop ya."

She knew she shouldn't trust this man, but he'd let her slide before. There was something paternal about him. She saw the same in her own father—an overcompensation you'd find on a divorced man during his custody time. He spoke with undeniable verity. Her wellbeing concerned him. Even so, she didn't let herself get too comfortable as she shed her rags.

The man faced the road when he spoke, respecting her privacy. "I knew my speech wasn't sticking. I saw it in you. Your friend with the shotgun, she's a hot head, but she would've backed off. Not you. You got some determination that she doesn't. Can't fight that with a little showmanship and a warning."

"We might have given it up if you didn't kill her friends."

He cocked his head to look but stopped himself. "That wasn't me. My boss—eh, fuck it—Desmond…he's a lot like your friend. Acts before he thinks. I didn't know he was gonna do that." Regret spiced his words.

"It doesn't matter anyway. She's dead." It pained Macy to say it aloud.

"She isn't…"

"What?"

"Other guys came and took her…her and her man. He didn't have hands. Not sure what happened *there*."

"Other guys?"

He exhaled. "You finished?"

"Yeah."

He turned and crossed arms on the Honda's roof. "Some shit you should probably know if we're gonna go at this together. Bunch of King wolves got burned over in England…Desmond's family—"

"Yeah, I know." Her new friend seemed perplexed. "I read what I could find on the Derbyshire wolves."

"Hmm…well, I think one of his brothers survived, and now he's here, and he's pissed off. I'm lookin' to hear the story from the source…see if maybe he can fix my problem." He pointed to his eye again to clarify. "While we're at that, we can find your friends."

Macy considered the man's words. If he could be believed, it was an answer to her prayers and an opportunity for redemption. "What's the move?"

"Bait."

Her face curled, confused. "Me?"

"No." He popped the trunk and showed Macy the dead girl. "Her name was Cat. Des did *that* to her."

"Why?"

"Same plan I got. Still, though…" He waved his hand over the bloody gap in the girl's chest. "We could've found another way."

"Not sure I follow."

"She wasn't Desmond's. She was part of another line."

"How'd that happen?"

"Complicated. Anyway, he knows she's down. He'll be comin' back to see what's what."

"And when he does…we talk to him."

"If he's the talkin' type."

"If he isn't…?" She locked eyes with him, and they both knew the score.

The man's smile lit up. *"And though she be but little, she is fierce."*

There was something nauseating in the dead girl's gaze. Her last thoughts read clear in that stare.

"There's a clearing a little ways in with a creek. That'd be a better spot, I think."

Macy nodded.

He scooped the girl from the trunk and slammed it shut.

# CHAPTER FIFTY

## John Becker, Jr.

*Montgomery County, Pennsylvania*

Their front tire rolled over a corpse. John could hear the vertebral crunch. "Oi, you bodged him!" Through his window, he could see a pair of legs. "Back it up a bit."

Ringo crunched the body in reverse and snapped whatever bones he may have missed on the first pass. John stepped into the morning fog as the second van rumbled to a stop behind them. He recognized the dead howler— one of Carter's pack. He never fancied him, so sparking him was no burden. The body went up like a beacon and woke the world.

He turned to Ringo. "Roll up slow. Respect the graves, yeah?" The vans crept forward at a snail's pace, while John traced the battle lines. Some of the dead had already been burned. Perhaps they were the enemy. If so, their master was walking pain free.

When the vans settled in, John's boys piled out and sparked fires in steady increments. The lighter fluid flowed, and the flesh sloughed away in heaping mounds. The morning reeked of fire and death.

John came upon a busted shed and slipped on a soggy set of entrails. "Cock it! Ringo! Look at this plonker." The man's face was a pulpy red ruin. Ringo moved forward with a can, his hand over his nose. "Soak him good. Get rid of his stink." The oaf obeyed his Prince.

John scraped a claw along the frame of the shed's door. Whatever had devoured the faceless man broke free from here. With the condition of the shed, a gust of wind could have done just as well.

The rat emerged from the tall grass, drool dribbling a trail in its wake. It was the perfect portrait of pestilence, a hunchbacked deformity with a cancerous gait. Its claws brushed the concrete as it advanced, and its yellow eyes had lost their luster, two bulbs with burned out filaments.

John smiled, despite the inherent sadness in the air. "You went quick. I expected a bit more the way you grandstanded in my club." The rat didn't respond. It stared at John with sunken eyes, struggling for every breath. "You remember what I told ya, then? A promise is a promise. Ringo?"

The oaf stepped forward with the scent of seared flesh strong in his musk.

John removed his windbreaker. "Hold my jacket."

"I can take care of it. I'll just…"

"Hold."

Ringo held.

John paced as the rat arched its shoulders. "You know who he looks like? That alien puppet from TV."

"Alf?"

"That's it! It's fuckin' Alf! Uncanny."

Perhaps the rat's feelings had been wounded. It lunged for John, galloping toward him in a blitz. John dropped to his stomach when it leapt. As it passed overhead, he delivered a backward claw to its midsection that tore open its abdomen and spilled guts into the yard. Its growl became a pathetic whimper.

"Like the cat said…" He removed the rat's head with one swipe. *"We're all mad here."*

Ringo bathed him, and John sparked the match. The carcass

cooked well before they snuffed the flames, and the smell whet John's appetite. For how ugly and grotesque Desmond's protégé had become, he smelled of crisp bacon on his way out.

"When we're through here, I'm fixing breakfast."

"Becker," Abrams called to him from Carter's foyer.

"What? One of 'em come back to life?"

"I've got a pair of hands..."

John waved his own mitts at the boy. "So have I."

"Without a body, I mean. They're a bit curious."

The hands *were* curious. Their fingers snaked around the grips of a shotgun, and they'd been precisely torn from their wrists. John kicked at them with the tip of his boot. "What's a howler need with that?" A gun was dead weight for a man-turned-wolf.

"Right. I thought o' that." Abrams was a sharp one. "Another thing…none of the bodies match..."

John surveyed the other bodies in the great room, a mess of gore and broken furniture. "Keep 'em. We'll sort it later. Like a lost pair of gloves, these fuckin' things."

John left his boys to burning and took a stroll through the backyard. He found the drainage ditch and followed it for a hundred meters. There, beneath an awning of foliage, wet with dew and piss, sat his King. "You smell a tick worse than last we spoke."

Desmond smiled, teeth shining through shade. "Cheeky prick."

John helped the King to his feet.

He flipped Desmond's bacon as it sizzled and spit. "Your mate's crossed over." John thought it better to deliver the news now, before all of Desmond's strength returned to him.

"Ben?"

"The one you come South with. Patchy McGoo."

Desmond bowed his head. John couldn't figure what he'd seen in the patching man, but he wouldn't interfere with a man's grief.

"So what happened here? Looks like fuckin' bedlam. Nearly ran out o' juice."

"My brother is back." His tone was meek. He stared at the floor like a mental patient.

John turned to face him, the bacon still sizzling in the pan. "Daniel?"

Des shook his head. "Think smaller."

Now John was certain this was a jest. "Piss off. *Ryan*?"

The King stayed quiet.

"My *dad* torched him…"

Des tapped fingers on the table, accusatory.

John stared down at the bacon. "I'm embarrassed."

"Your dad did fine. My brother surprised me. Of all the fuckin' O'Connells could've made it out of that mess, I would've lost money on the Runt."

John and Ryan had played together as boys, before Des gave John the gift. Ryan was from wolf and John was from man, but they managed just fine. John remembered the day the boys snuck into Derby to hold court with Bloody Mary Porter. *Top notch brass, that one.*

Desmond's coup had left a bad taste in John's mouth. He learned that day just how far a man would go to seize power. But then, Desmond wasn't a man.

It was a long time before he could respect Desmond again, but as he grew, he understood. The King saw his pack as a cancer for Derbyshire, even tried to end his own life. When fate let him live, he found purpose. They'd migrated to the States near after with the few wolves worth the salt and started anew. Then, ten years ago, on John's fifteenth birthday, Desmond finally turned him. It was here he'd become John's God.

Ryan the Runt was back to reap revenge. He wouldn't have it from John Becker Sr. *His* ashes had already fed the gods. He'd tried claiming it from Desmond and blundered. John knew he was likely the next target, though he wouldn't have had the kid burned if it were *his* decision. Regardless, their friendship was stale, no matter how John tried to recall the taste. If the burned-up phantom wanted a dance, he could try and have it, but it would cost him his head.

Desmond was King. Desmond was God. Ryan was an angry memory better suppressed.

He shoveled the King's bacon onto a plate.

# CHAPTER FIFTY-ONE

## Macy

*Montgomery County, Pennsylvania*

The dead girl watched through filmy eyes as the man washed his face in the creek. Macy straddled a rock and gripped her stomach, fighting hunger and her own stubbornness. "What do you want me to call you?"

He cleared water from his eyes with a twist of his palms. "Ben…"

Macy winced as the cramps in her stomach thrummed.

"You okay?"

"Yeah. Just didn't eat last night."

He pivoted on the balls of his feet. "You fuckin' nuts? Why not?"

"Couldn't do it."

"What are ya, vegan?"

"No. It's the killing I'm struggling with."

"Jesus. You better shake that, kid. This thing's appetite won't be ignored. You'll die..."

"Yeah…I'm kinda getting that." The thrum in her stomach was causing a slur in her speech.

"I'll fetch you somethin'. Stay put." He stood from the creek bed and extended a set of claws.

"What if he comes when you're gone?"

"Talk to him. Tell him the deal." With that, he took to the woods, leaving Macy and the dead girl to discuss diplomacy. Macy was getting tired of having the dead for company.

Ben seemed like a straight shooter, but everyone seemed that way, she supposed, right before they gutted you or sold you out. She wanted to stow her paranoia, but the corpse had her doubting Ben's abilities to protect her.

She stared at the dead girl. Cat was her name. Cat's eyes seemed to be set on some hidden evil nesting beyond the creek. *What's your story?* The dead kept their secrets shackled in a dungeon devoid of light.

Before long, her thoughts inevitably turned to Sarah. The wolf was able to stifle the panic attacks, but it couldn't keep Sarah's lifeless purple face from emerging. She wondered if her mother still carried it, too. If she'd been able to find peace by distancing herself.

Guilt struck her, then, for selling the Ninja—the last thing Sarah had left her. *My best memory of you, gone for a few thousand bucks.* She closed her eyes and felt the bristling wind of the open road.

A twig snapped behind her. She fired the muscles in her core but couldn't turn. A tongue slid up her shoulder, leaving a streak of saliva.

"...Pedro?"

The dog stepped forward, panting and stretching hind legs.

He licked at her face, and his tags clattered, amplified in the surrounding silence.

Then Macy caught a scent. The same strange musk she remembered from the cabin when they went back for Carter's mail.

"Found him trottin' along the highway." It wasn't Ben. This voice was soothing like a light wind that tickled the hairs on Macy's back. "Worry in his eyes, I think...like he's lost his home."

An English accent. The voice wasn't threatening, nor intimidating, but there was a confidence hidden deep, a power unparalleled.

Macy turned and faced him. His hair was cropped short, one eye an intoxicating red, the other a faded gray, and his scars were repulsive.

Pieces of his lips had burned away, and his eyebrows came together in four or five fragments. A "King Wolf" was a misnomer, but Macy wouldn't be the one to tell him.

"I've answered your call. Where's my brother?"

Macy controlled her breathing to steady her heart rate. "I don't know your brother."

"I thought you'd be bigger…" Ben had returned. A rabbit swung lifeless in his hand. "The scare you put to Des. I've never seen him that way."

"Where's he run off?"

"That, I don't know. I'm through bein' his piss boy." He tossed the rabbit to Macy, and she chewed the tender meat. "Why wasn't last night a happy family reunion? Heard a sad story about all Desmond's people dying in a fire."

"That how he tells it? Like one of his Greek tragedies?" The scarred man let out a hiss that might have been a laugh to a serpent. He motioned to Cat. "Who's she?"

"One of yours. Des killed her to draw you out."

"Then she died in vain. I've been on that house for some time."

Ben twirled the tip of his boot in the water. Macy could see he had admired the girl. If he had been bitter before, he was furious now. "Why aren't you sick?"

"Discipline. Something Desmond never knew."

"Meaning?"

"My brother strayed from the magic that made us. It's weakened him." He paused to study the tangled fur sprouting from Ben's face. "It's weakened the ones he made."

Ben chewed his lip while Macy chewed the rabbit.

"What d'you want with me?" Scars asked.

"You've got her friends." He pointed to Macy. "And maybe you can answer some questions for *me*."

"I'll get the same in return?"

Ben pursed his lips and nodded. "I'm an open book."

"That your motor by the road?"

"Hers. I'd use my truck, but someone snipped the fuse box." With that, he glared at Macy. She buried her face deeper into the rabbit's belly.

Scars stepped toward Cat, and Ben shuffled aside with his guard up. He produced a flask from his jacket and doused Cat's body. He struck a match and cooked the girl with a flick of his wrist. "If any of Desmond's howlers follow us…I'll have to do the both of ya."

"Where are the rest of your boys?"

Scars didn't answer.

Cat's flames struck an orange glow in Ben's freakish eye. "Not that it matters now, but…she might'a had a chance if you'd taken her under your wing."

Again, Scars didn't respond. When Cat was cooked through, he kicked her body into the creek, and steam sizzled for the treetops.

Ben sniffed the air. "You came alone?"

"I've nothing to fear from the two of you... nor from Desmond."

"Awful reckless." Ben was sorting options with his eyebrows.

"Desmond's ego drives him. Been that way since Derby. They called me Ryan the Runt, but…" His words trailed off, and his eyes found the dirt. "He's not my equal."

"You sure about that? I've seen the man operate. No wolf moves that way."

"None *you've* seen..."

Ben's eye glistened in the morning fog.

The back seat of the Honda was an alien enclosure. Macy could feel the wheel in her hands as she curled fingers and gripped the air. Pedro slept with his head in her lap. Ryan commandeered her vehicle and cycled through her presets on the radio. He settled on Duran Duran. Ben lounged in the passenger seat with a foot on the dash, staring distant with his functioning eye.

A light rain pattered the windshield. It seemed Ryan was afraid to drive faster than fifty. "When did the patching start?"

His words seemed to startle Ben. "Few days ago. I wish it would take me already. I choose death over this fuckin' itch." He picked at the corruption on his cheek.

"It should be apparent to you now."

"What?"

"Desmond didn't do you any favors."

Ben smiled as a bead of blood trickled to his chin. "Why are the wolves he turned here patching faster than the Derbyshire wolves?"

Ryan raised a brow. "The Derby boys are patching as well?"

"Seems like they've held it off longer, but yeah. Carter went that way."

Ryan thought for a moment. "You lot are far from the shaman's reach. The one who made us, his corpse was at Mam Tor, where my family lived. He's ashes now, but his magic remains in us. Desmond all but abandoned our ways, turning wolves without rituals. His are malformed."

Ben popped the glove box, found a napkin, and dabbed at his face until it soaked red. "Any way to stop it? I read…I read some about your mother."

Ryan stared up the road. "The shaman's black magic brought a human child from a wolf's womb. My father. He had five children by a human woman. That's as far as it was ever meant to go." Macy heard a longing in his voice. His past was bitter to him. "Birthing five of us corrupted her body. She died from the patching soon after I was born." His voice lowered as he held back a whimper. "I haven't seen the illness on anyone else until my brother decided to make more of you lot here."

Ben brooded as the rain tapped a symphony on the windshield. "So, I'm fucked."

*We're fucked*, Macy thought, but remained silent.

"I was able to delay my mother's passing by giving her my blood. Might do the same for you."

Ben let out a sigh. "I'll take it. It's better than Des' offer. Hugs and…fuckin' empty promises."

The two were silent for a time while Ben compressed his cheek with the bloody rag. Macy bumped something with her foot. She peeked into the well between seats and found Liz's lockbox. Liz hadn't given it a glance since they'd picked it up, but she was curious about its contents. She figured it was filled with drug paraphernalia, but wondered if perhaps there was more to the marine than she realized.

It was a simple padlock with a three-digit code. A key would open it, but Macy hadn't seen one when she scooped it from the floorboards. She pulled open the seat panel and plucked a few skinny hex keys from the dark of the trunk. She went in through the keyhole underneath, and the lock came open with some fiddling.

Inside, Macy found a spoon with residue, a needle, a cotton ball, a small bag filled with brown powder, a dog tag with the name *Raymond S. Campbell*, another with Liz's name, five cassette tapes, a tape player and a pair of headphones. She shoved the dope fixings aside. They'd been untouched for days, as the wolf seemed to have cured Liz's habit.

She pushed the headphones into her ears and played the first tape. A woman sang a sort of lullaby. Her voice was transcendent. It carried Macy from the Honda, onto a sprawling plateau. She'd heard the voice before…in her shower.

There was sadness in Liz as she sang the words, but it was tragically beautiful. Macy sampled every tape. Each held soothing songs she recalled from childhood.

*Be still and sleep, my love,*
*Be still and rest those tired eyes.*
*Be still and sleep, my love,*
*The world awaits you when you rise.*
*I will be near, my love,*
*To come and greet you with a smile.*
*Be still and sleep, no need to weep, my precious child.*

She replaced the box's contents where she'd found them with tears in her eyes. Pedro slept soundly in her lap, drool collecting at the pits of his mouth.

"That girl…?" Ben said abruptly. "Said her man turned her through sex. And he was turned by some creeping paparazzi." He glanced at Ryan. "Yours, I'm guessing?"

Ryan considered his question. "One of my younger wolves. Bloody idiot. Nearly spoiled my whole—" He opened his mouth to continue but caught himself. Quietly, he muttered, "He's passed now, I won't speak ill of him."

*A young girl dead because one of your wolves was careless*, Macy thought, disgusted.

The wipers swabbed the droplets for half-seconds before new ones filled the gap. Ben stared at Ryan's puckered face for a stretch of silence. "Did Des do it?"

"Do what?"

"The fire... was it him?"

Ryan pressed his toe to the gas, leaving Ben's words hanging thick in the air.

"Son of a bitch."

Macy rolled her window down and touched her face to the bristling wind. She missed it. The open air turned her cheeks to putty on the Ninja's back. It shook her pain to dust. Perhaps that's what Ryan needed—a bike ride across an open sprawl.

*Burned by your own brother.* The thought of it sickened her. She hadn't seen Desmond at the house but wondered if that type of evil could read on a face.

Ryan parked the Honda about a mile into the woods. When the three of them stepped out, he covered it over with a camouflaged tarp cloaked in vegetation. He led them to a water drainage grate, crouched and pulled it open. "After you."

Ben smirked at the sewer entrance. "You fuckin' kidding me?" After some light arguing, Ben relented. He scooped Pedro over a shoulder, and the group descended the twenty to thirty-foot ladder, greeted by the sound of flowing water at the bottom. They stepped off into an old storm sewer with passages disappearing in four directions. One of them had been lined with oil lamps fixed to the cement with rivets. They followed this path for about a hundred feet before it opened into a cement clearing with a few dark alcoves. The smell of cooking found them and whet Macy's appetite. Two men played cards at a table, while another stockier man cooked on a portable grill.

Ben's lower jaw hung open. "Nothin' to fear, huh?"

The scent of game was overwhelming.

"Captain's on deck," said the cook.

As Macy's eyes adjusted, she could see hallways branching from the clearing like honeycombs. The combined effort of candles, oil lamps and sconces spread an orange glow. For a man who carried the memory of being burned by his own kin, he certainly wasn't averse to fire. Pedro panted at the sight of the meat but remained at Macy's side.

Ben wasn't as reserved. "What in the fuck you got going here, friend?" He scanned the glowing room.

Ryan diverted to Macy. "You still hungry?"

"Yeah."

He motioned to the man behind the stove. "Freddy…toss her a flank, yeah?"

Freddy stabbed one of the flanks he'd been cooling on a plate and tossed it to Macy. She fetched it from the air and sunk her teeth in. "Thanks."

"Your mates are a short way down that hall." He pointed at one of the alcoves. "I'll take you to them."

Macy nodded, slightly worried about following a stranger down a dark corridor. She chewed as Ryan led the way. They passed through a hall and down a flight of stairs where three cells waited. On closer inspection, Macy could see that they'd been fashioned from sewer grates. They'd been lit with overhanging lamps, dim in comparison to the flames of the clearing they'd just left.

The cells were empty, save for the last, where Liz leaned against the wall and Brooks lay in a cot with a blanket draped over him. She perked up when she saw the group.

"Jesus. Fucking finally. Smells like piss in here."

Ryan sniffed the air. "Wasn't sure I could trust you."

"But you are *now*?"

"Saw you and your mate sneaking into Carter's." Ryan unlatched the grate and pulled it aside. "Made me curious."

Liz nodded at the grate. "I could'a busted through that whenever I wanted."

"I know," Ryan said.

Liz frowned, which only deepened when she noticed Ben. “He with *you* now?”

Ben scowled. “I ain’t with anybody. I’m freelance, sweetheart.”

“Sound like a fuckin’ traitor to me.” She struggled to her feet. Pedro trotted in and licked at her knees. She knelt to scratch his head. “I don’t even wanna ask.”

Macy finished the flank, blood coating the webbing of her fingers. “Is Cameron okay?” The Corporal lay docile and unresponsive.

Liz looked to him with a sullen sadness. “He wouldn’t let me get close.”

Macy stepped toward him. The venison had given her a surge of energy.

Liz surveyed the burned man. “What’s your beef with Desmond?”

Ryan seemed unable to process the question. Ben answered for him. “There’s a growing list of wolves that prick needs to answer to…guy’s runnin’ out of friends.”

“I blasted him, but I didn’t get his head. Thought your crew might’a got him.” Liz looked to Ryan, hopeful.

Ryan found his tongue. “He killed two and disappeared.”

Liz released a sigh.

Macy lifted Brooks’ blanket and gasped. The stumps at his wrists had grown hair that spread to his elbows. Blood dribbled from his lips, and his teeth were stained red.

He had tried to nibble the patches away.

# CHAPTER FIFTY-TWO

## Desmond

*Montgomery County, Pennsylvania*

The King dangled the severed hand by the fingers and sniffed at the coagulated wrists in an upstairs office at Carter's manse. They'd been cut cleanly. He was rather deft with his violence. *Reckless*, he thought, regarding his brother's strategy. *Blitzkrieg tactics in a war of deception.*

He massaged the palms with his thumbs. The flesh was soft and malleable like a babe's. *Thank you, young one.* He'd be eternally grateful to the foolish invaders; they'd left him a trail straight to the Runt's throat.

"Got a thing for hands, then?" Junior paced at the King's back.

"Only when they serve a purpose." He held it for the kid to see. "This is a map."

"You, uh…?" He peeked over Desmond's shoulder. "…reading palms now?"

"Tracking."

"Oi, that's rich. You'll do Daniel homage."

The King's thoughts leapt to his younger brother. Wagner's second son, the most faithful to the shaman's mumbo jumbo and the most powerful wolf Des had ever seen. "Let's be thankful that's not the case." *I may never be that good.* Daniel had been a phenom, an ace at tracking and brutal in combat. "But I'll find the Runt. It starts here."

The hand glistened in the lamplight.

"Who *was* he?"

"Irrelevant. Who was Ferdinand, but a catalyst? Or Helen of Troy? A means to an end."

Junior nodded, though Desmond knew he didn't understand. "Why the shotguns?"

"Puzzling tactic from the Runt. Perhaps the time he spent in the bloody barn got 'im thinkin' like a mule." Their father often kept Ryan in the barn on the family grounds. His hatred for the Runt was boundless. He blamed Ryan for their mother's death. Des knew they all played a part, birthing five boys from a man-wolf was too much for her, but his father would not accept it.

Junior picked up the second hand and turned it over in his grip. "We set out tonight or wait 'til morning?"

This was the same hellion that caused bedlam as a boy in Derby. "You and my brother share a vice."

"What d'you mean?"

He placed the hand on his desk, and a thin bead of blood rolled across the mahogany. "Hitting an O'Connell requires a calculated approach." He knew this all too well.

"Right…I know…but we may allow the Runt too large a head start."

"He's after me, mate. He won't leave 'til it's sorted."

"*You* wouldn't... but how well d'you know this prodigal? He ain't the same toss I chased skirt with. Not after all this time."

"He's got Wagner's blood. Time won't muck with that." The King found it increasingly difficult to hide his frustration with the brat.

Junior tossed the hand, and it landed with the other. "I'm at your disposal, then."

"We get settled here first."

Becker's yellow eyes beamed like a child's.

"Then we'll go for a hunt."

# STAGE 3

"Let your plans be dark and impenetrable as night, and when you move, fall like a thunderbolt."

- Sun Tzu, *The Art of War*

# CHAPTER FIFTY-THREE

## Liz

*Montgomery County, Pennsylvania*

Stage three came to her much like a dope high. Her senses sharpened, colors shined brighter, food tasted better. But, unlike a dope high, she lacked the heavy feeling in her extremities. Quite the opposite, in fact. Her reflexes were almost instant. She could snatch flies from the air and release them unharmed.

With heroin, she'd lost control over time. With the wolf, she'd gained it. She could change in a flash, only her face now. She assessed her yellow eyes, pointed ears and dripping fangs in her pocket mirror. *I get it, Brooks.* It was all she could do not to smile.

This was the peak of her condition. True control over every fiber.

In a nook aglow with lamplight, Ryan tested her new skills, sharpened them further with a sparring match. "Take my head." The scars twisted his fragmented grin.

Liz planted heels beneath her. *All right, little wolf.* She changed her face and spread her stance. *Make it easy for me.*

She lunged, but Ryan wasn't there. He pinned her arm behind her back and popped her shoulder out of joint. Liz howled in agony as the man-wolves in attendance howled with laughter. Ryan tossed her to the floor where she realigned herself.

"A soldier on America's battlefield. I expected death by now."

*Not a soldier. A marine, asshole.* Liz knew it was an act. He was boiling her nerves so she might leap quicker, but she'd learned that anger didn't suit her. When Liz got angry, Liz got stupid. It was anger that drove her into a howler nest with a shotgun.

She struggled to her feet. She could see Macy in the crowd with a fretful mist about her eyes. Ben stood beside her, arms folded, patching face as displeasing as ever. Her thoughts fell to Brooks withering away in a cell. He'd been writhing there, nonsensical, refusing to be moved.

Ryan's remaining three howlers were restless. She couldn't strike him where he was, he was far too swift. She needed to strike where he *would* be. He shuffled left on her first pass. Her right shoulder throbbed with the reminder. He would shuffle left again. Liz knew his kind—cunning, but soft. She pivoted and lunged.

Ryan stood behind her again with her right shoulder in his grip. He idled so close to her ear, the heat of his breath whistled down the canal. This time, he released her intact. Her memories of basic training seemed distant, but she felt the same instincts awakening in hand-to-hand combat. She'd never faced someone like Ryan, however. The Wolf God analyzed her, brushing the scars on his cheek. "You'll do." He said nothing more, simply returned to his nook—a hideaway protected by curtains and a locked gate.

Liz sauntered to Macy and Ben.

Ben's scabs cracked when he smiled, and pus welled at the openings. "You almost had him on the last one. Saw him stumble."

"You didn't see shit," Liz blurted.

Ben and Ryan spent countless hours alone in Ryan's quarters. Liz figured the two had fallen in love. Ben denied his involvement in Serita's death until he was dry in the mouth, but Liz still didn't buy it. She knew no one could flip that quickly. He was loyal to Desmond and would return to him as soon as Ryan's hospitality ran its course. The only reason Liz tolerated him was because Macy had taken a shine to him. At that moment, the girl gave Liz a pleading look, which she responded to with a snort.

"I'm getting something to eat."

Liz passed Freddy's portable grill to find the cook, Doyle and Charlie smacking craps against the sewer wall. They chalked out a table and played for strips of jerky. Doyle was a grunt like she and Brooks. He fought the Taliban with the Brits in the years following 9/11. Liz asked him about his kill count, but he wouldn't disclose. She chose to respect his silence. She could see the desert plain as day in his face. Charlie was a baker's son from Derbyshire, a plain-looking man in his late twenties with the hairless face of a child. Spent most of the nineties with Doyle, spraying graffiti. "Writers in Derby were the county's pulse," he'd said. "We had an ear on everyone's shite." They'd gotten mixed up in Derby's gang activity and eventually crossed paths with Ryan's family.

Freddy was a different story. An older man, mid-forties, with gray in his temples and his nest of a beard. He wasn't a cook, in truth, but a ship's captain. He knew the O'Connell family through their protection racket. The wolves had kept his shop safe from local gangs. He'd helped Ryan cross the Atlantic.

"Liz the Wiz. Come to snatch all our bloody strips again?" Doyle's accent was sexy, as was the scar that split his face across the center.

"Keep rollin' like you do, I'll keep leaving full." She patted her stomach.

Charlie clinked the dice against the wall and read seven. He moaned and tossed claws in the air. Freddy laughed at his misfortune.

When the dice were passed to Doyle, he juggled them between fingers. "You'll never nick him, you know."

"What?"

"Ryan. It's a losing game. Even more than this, here." He rolled the dice and hit a four. "Four's on."

“So what, he’s playin’ me?” Liz asked, puzzled.

“You’ll get sharper, no doubt. You come within feet of the King, you’ll peel another wolf’s cap no problem. But that’s the best you can hope for. Don’t expect to make contact. That’s just the way of it.”

He rolled again and hit six.

Liz continued, “I might surprise you.”

Doyle smiled, and his teeth glistened—unusual sheen for a Brit. “This ain’t a movie, luv. No desperados in this game. There’s pure wolves, and then there’s us. We’ll spend our lives tryin’ to touch that throne, and we’ll have wasted our time.” He winked at Charlie who looked to his feet and grinned.

Doyle rolled. Six again.

“What’s the dream about then?” The infamous dream they all shared first came to her when she spent the night at Macy’s place, when she hit Stage Two. Two red-eyes. A yellow-eye snipping one of their heads. Already, she’d grown bored of it. She expected some semblance of it just about every sleep.

“I reckon that’s the subconscious tryin’ to convince us of the impossible. It’s not a new dream, Wiz. Been ‘round since Derbyshire.” Doyle claimed to have been at Stage Three for six years. Liz asked him if he was worried about patching when he came to the States, but he’d never leave his friend. He was confident Ryan’s adherence to the shaman’s magic would keep the wolves he turned healthy.

His dice smacked the wall—six.

Doyle fucked Liz like an animal. They’d retired to his nook complete with blankets and assorted bedding. His claws dug into her hips as he thrusted. She embedded hers in his back, and blood trickled to her wrists. Her reflexes weren't all that had improved with Stage Three.

*"You'll never nick him, you know."*

She burrowed deeper, and he let loose a howl as he spent himself inside her.

*How's that for a nick, little boy?*

He rolled to his back and caught his breath while the divots from her nails closed. "You're a proper minx, ain't ya?"

*And you're a disappointment. First fuck I've had in a month and that's all you got?*

It took several heavy breaths before he could speak again. "What's the story with your boy in the cell? You an item?"

She stood from the bedding and slipped into her underwear.

Doyle propped himself on an elbow. "I say something wrong?"

She pulled a sweatshirt over her naked breasts and left him to stew.

The hair had spread to Brooks' shoulders. He lay in his cot facing the wall, muttering incoherencies through clattering teeth.

As good as Liz felt, it was hard to enjoy it when this was ultimately her fate. A part of her wished she could have stayed in her hovel on Kensington Avenue, let the junk put her out gently.

"Scars is alright, I decided." The cell repeated Liz' words back to her. "He's pushin' me…like the Sheikh used to."

Brooks took a deep breath that raised his ribs and released a sigh that deflated him.

"You'd slap the shit out of him, though." She giggled to herself. "He's lucky you're laid up." Liz remembered pissing Brooks off in sparring. She brought the devil out of him when they went toe-to-toe, and eventually he started winning.

"You remember what the Sheikh used to say?" Gunnery Sergeant Robert Hartwell, nicknamed 'The Sheikh' for the cloth that covered his bald head in the heat. "You get three fuck-ups." She erected three fingers. "Three and then you turn it around. So…you shot the girl. Fuck her, anyway." Her ring finger went down, locked in place by her thumb. "You wolfed me up." She pointed to the pit of her elbow as if he could see through the back of his head and dropped her second finger. "And you got your hands snipped." She folded her index finger and made a fist. "Now you fix it."

Brooks' breaths took on a hypnotic rhythm.

"But if you check out now…that makes you an asshole. You understand? The hajis didn't kill you, some pretty boy with claws ain't gonna do it. Fuck that."

She could hear Pedro's tags clinking down the hallway.

"Now, you turn it around."

The dog entered the cell with Macy on his tail. He'd taken a particular liking to her. Liz remained indifferent. The girl had played her part when called. She had her own set of issues Liz found relatable, but Liz had no room for new friends, especially with old ones rotting away.

She scratched Pedro's head. The howler scent was familiar to him now.

Macy stared at Brooks while he whimpered. "Ben's trying, you know."

"What's he tryin'? Dicks?"

Macy never seemed to crack a smile at Liz's jokes. If she wasn't brooding, she was lost in thought, and humor didn't land. "Desmond was the only choice he had. He's adjusting."

"He's a two-faced motherfucker. I don't know why you let him work you. Even if he didn't kill Serita, even if he didn't know…you jump ship once, you get in the habit of it." Liz had decided to side with Macy in her search for a cure after seeing what this thing had done to her Corporal. She owed Desmond a slow decapitation.

Macy chewed her lip.

"You talk to your dad?"

"No signal down here. They don't take calls for another few days anyway."

Liz remembered her father crying over the phone, but he had always found the bottle again. She brought her hand to her empty clavicle. "Lemme borrow your keys."

"You going somewhere?"

"Nah." She stood. "Wanna grab my shit."

Macy hesitated.

"It's still there, right?" She would kill her where she stood if it wasn't.

"Yeah."

Liz pulled the tarp from the Honda's roof with cicadas buzzing havoc around her. They sent Charlie to make sure she didn't run. Ryan's wolves played nice but had no trust in their new guests. She found the box wedged in the footwell of the back seat. The combination was just as she'd left it. She thumbed in the code and popped it open. The tags were there, the dope was there, the fixings were there, and the tapes were there, but the tapes were out of order.

Macy's hesitation dimed her out before the tapes did. She was every bit the nosey little rat Liz had seen through her peephole.

# CHAPTER FIFTY-FOUR

## Ben

*Montgomery County, Pennsylvania*

The IV ran from Ryan's arm to his, and the crimson bead flowed through at a snail's pace. Ryan fiddled with it, keeping it taut. His attention was elsewhere, lost amidst avenues of stress and apprehension.

The transfusion took place at the center of Ryan's quarters, another recess off the main sewer. He had a small shrine on the wall complete with candles and artifacts. One bore a silver crucifix, another a set of car keys. *"The heavens themselves blaze forth the death of princes."*

Ryan managed a smile with his ruined face. "You know Shakespeare."

*Better than I'd like to.* "Lotta sleepless nights."

Ryan evaluated his tributes. He'd told Ben that he had taken his time after the burning, building a crew he could trust. Eventually, word crossed the water about wolves running drugs in Pennsylvania. He set sail two months ago with ten wolves. He'd lost seven since. "The shrines are useless. Fallen souls latch to me like ink…been luggin' a mess of them since Derbyshire."

Ben thought about Desmond. He would never bother to carry the soul of a fallen howler. When his wolves checked out up North, he burned them and went on with business.

"The others can come to reflect." Ryan studied the IV as his blood chugged through. "The two in the corner, there, were yours." His smile shook Ben to the bone. "The one whose head you sent through a window, he was nineteen. His mother waits for 'im in Derby. Suppose it falls to me to tell her his fate."

Ben arched his back. Even if he couldn't strike Ryan, he might still be able to run. He remembered Cat. The speed with which Desmond took her life was something he'd never witnessed. If Ryan was as fast as that, this shrine would be Ben's tomb.

"The other, I brought up…promising pup, but too eager."

"I'm not supposed to defend myself?"

"'Course you are."

"Why this, then?" Ben held up his arm. "I've seen you move. Why didn't you split me when we first met?"

The faded gray iris of the Wolf God's left eye expanded. "Whatever the boys were, their fates were slated. I've got a hold on blood magic, but fate is something that outwits us all."

Desmond changed man to wolf without a moment's hesitation, folding them into his pack. Ryan seemed troubled by every wolf he made, guilt still festering from his mother's death. On the same note, Des didn't nurture his wolves the way Ryan did. He left them to fend for themselves. That was what hardened them, sharpened their instincts in the field.

"Some of Desmond's wolves are stronger than I am. If I took out your best two, you're in trouble."

Ryan removed the IV.

"That's it?"

A trickle of red found Ryan's wrist before the wound closed.

Ben plucked the needle from his own arm. "The kid downstairs, you givin' *him* some?"

His silence answered 'no.'

"His buddy's gonna be pissed. The girl. She'll cause a stink if she finds out." Ben remembered the poor kid shaking behind his shotgun, sweat beads rolling off his brow. *What are you doing, Benjamin? You're a tumor, delaying the inevitable. The kid might have a chance.*

"Why didn't Des just kill him? To leave him like that…" Ryan stroked a thumb over his cheek scars. Ben wondered how well he really knew his brother, if they'd been close before the burning.

"Back in the day, did you know a wolf called Becker?"

Ryan's thumb froze in place. "He wasn't a wolf when I knew him. He helped Des set the barn ablaze with me inside."

"Junior?"

"His father. But I *did* know the boy. We were children together."

"His dad is fertilizer. The kid burned him himself."

Ryan's head snapped to him. "Where'd you hear this?"

"We passed through New York on our way down. Anyway, with Carter's crew wasted, Des will've called him for backup."

"You spoke to Junior yourself?" Ryan prodded now, his interest spiking at the mention of the brat. Ben wondered about their history overseas.

"We spoke. I pray I never have to suffer him again."

Ryan considered for a moment. "I need you and your lot when I hit Carter's again."

Ben perked up in his chair. "Please let me have Junior. I'll happily let the patches take me if I get to end that little fuck."

"He's yours. I need to put Des to rest…reckon I'm the only one who can."

Ben wondered how he would feel about Desmond's demise. A year ago, it would have set him adrift, but now that it was truly a prospect, it seemed past due. He let the moment linger. The plan had been laid, and there wasn't much more that needed saying. He glanced at Ryan's scars. He'd asked the kid why they hadn't healed like any other wound.

Apparently, the ritual that made his father involved fire, so Ryan figured fire didn't play by their rules. It may have also accounted for the burning of the fallen. Perhaps the fire snuffed whatever magic bound them to their maker.

Without another word, Ryan left Ben to bond with the flickering shrines of fallen howlers he never knew.

# CHAPTER FIFTY-FIVE

## Macy

*Montgomery County, Pennsylvania*

Ben found her in the area she'd claimed as she tossed a stick with Pedro, seventies soft listening on a portable radio. He didn't wait to spill his news. "We're hitting Carter's again. Ryan wants to snuff Des and his boys. He needs us for extra muscle."

Macy's heart began to pound. She knew she couldn't duck violence forever, but she was certain she'd be dead weight. "You okay with it?"

The dying man considered her question. He chuckled. "There's a lot Des needs to atone for. I won't stand in the way of judgement." He scratched the dog and sat down beside Macy. "I wonder about myself too... however this shakes out, Des and I will sort our differences in hell."

Macy wondered if Ryan had actually given Ben some of his blood, like he'd offered in the car. His condition looked about the same. Was that a good or bad sign?

"You get anything else out of him?" she asked.

"I did most of the talking…" He picked up Pedro's stick and chucked it at the far wall. The dog stumbled for it, slipping on a puddle of rainwater. "But I got a little. There was a family of shamans who owned the land that's now Derbyshire. Practiced some strange voodoo, Satanic shit." The dog returned the stick, and Ben chucked it again. "Industrial age came in, and suddenly their land shrunk tenfold. Then the gangs dirtied it up worse. This shaman, Mundi, who made Ryan's family, his magic was linked to the land. The soil, the birds, the wolves who prowled his hills. The other shamans were willing to let the land go, but Mundi went rogue and made a weapon. He performed a ritual that birthed a human baby from the womb of a wolf, got this whole party started. Des, Ryan…they were all sons of that baby. They were meant to clean up the gangs and degenerates and reclaim the shaman land, but…" Again the dog returned, and again Ben heaved the stick into the dark. "All they did was add another gang to the mix."

The more details that came to light, the more baffled Macy was. The odds of this mess reaching someone as ordinary as her were astronomical. "What about the burning?"

Ben scratched the mass of fur that had taken his cheek. "I wasn't gonna press him about that."

"Yeah." Now Macy grabbed the stick and threw it.

"Look, this is gonna get bad. Maybe you ought to take off."

He had a point. She wouldn't be able to live with herself if her shortcomings got someone killed. Sarah came to mind, even in this pit. *What choice do you have?* "No…I can't run anymore. Better I just face it when it comes."

Ben nodded and scratched his leg. "Well…I ain't in my best shape."

Macy looked him over and laughed aloud. He joined her, the dog tilting his head, waiting for another toss.

"Anyway…I'll look out for you if things go south. Your friend, uh…" He almost laughed again at the thought. "She's no fan of mine, but she'll look out for you, too."

"Yeah." Liz jabbed and belittled when she could, but Macy knew the Sergeant's true nature. Brooks had told her back in the cabin when

Liz was unconscious from the riot slug he'd hit her with. *It's a put-on. What happened to her overseas, she carries it. Pushes people away so she's got less to lose.* Macy wrestled the stick from Pedro's mouth.

"Scourge, huh?" Ben noticed her shirt.

She rubbed a thumb over the faded lettering. "I'm obsessed. I don't know what it is, but…" She thought of her method to quell her panic attacks. "They center me, you know?"

"Hmm."

She looked over at him. A bead of blood rolled along his cheek. "You like them?"

"Nah." He smeared the blood with the back of his hand. "That stuff missed my generation. I have a girl though, about your age. She's real into them."

It didn't surprise her at all that Ben was a father. She pegged it when they'd first met. "You remind me of *my* old man."

"He must be one strapping son of a bitch."

She looked at his patch and laughed again. "Yeah, that's something he would say."

Pedro was tired. He curled in a ball at Macy's feet.

"Well, I hope he's good to you." There was pain in his voice.

A silence stretched before Macy responded, "I'm hungry."

Liz throttled past Freddy's grill like a freight train, her features emerging through a screen of smoke. A chill quivered up Macy's spine when she caught the fiendish resolve in the marine's eyes. She braced herself in the seconds she had before Liz's claws pinched her throat closed and her back met the wall with a *thud*. Charlie gawked as Liz crimped the flow of blood to Macy's brain.

"You like the tapes?" Liz's mouth was in kissing range. A pucker from Macy and their lips would touch.

"Liz..."

"Shut up. That your game? Hmm? Pry in people's lives?"

She had no answer.

"Well, here, now you know me." She pressed harder, and Macy felt the cement behind her cracking.

Stars powdered her vision, and the room around her vanished in a flood of vertigo. She couldn't figure why, but a Scourge song came to her then. "Cadaver in the Jean Lafitte," track three on *Knee Deep in Bayou Sweat*. It rattled through Macy's skull, a benevolent tune that awakened her crumbling bones.

She remembered now.

Sarah played her the song in her bedroom. It was the first she'd heard them. It changed her, ignited a passion she'd never known. Before that, she hadn't known her sister well. They were five years apart in age and belonged to different circles. That was the moment. The beginning of a thread that would bind them long after Sarah's death.

She pried Liz's fingers from her throat and changed her face.

The marine's eyes bulged. "What the fuck?"

She used Liz's confusion as an opening, wrapping her arms around her waist and bringing her to the ground. Her fist came sailing down. With her eyelids pinched shut, she felt her knuckles smacking Liz's jaw. On and on and on she pounded. She would mash Liz's face to pulp.

After her tenth or perhaps eleventh connection, a pair of hands lifted her away. *Ryan?* Her fists whizzed through air long after she was taken from the room and thrown into a cell.

Her cage measured eight feet by nine. She was a doll a child would open on Christmas—an emo doll with an insatiable lust for speed and grease under the nails. She'd tried to break the grate, but the metal was too thick. Pedro chewed on his foot outside the bars.

Liz hunkered against the wall in the adjacent cell, legs propped in figure-four. Perhaps Ryan had expected them to settle their differences here.

With the sudden onset of Stage Three, Macy had overcome the feeling of intimidation. *Why so soon?* She didn't think her will was anything special.

Regardless, Macy spoke whether Liz would listen or not. "You have a nice voice."

A light smacking noise was Liz's response. She chewed a strip of jerky, kneading it between molars.

"I haven't heard songs like that since I was young, but I recognized some lyrics."

The jerky was Liz's world.

"I saw your dad's dog tags. I don't think the songs are for him, though."

A symphony unfolded between her teeth. A maestro waved arms and conducted the rending of meat.

"Your mom?"

Pedro reached a paw through the bars. Liz snuck a brief smile at him and chewed louder.

"That's who you were watching from the bench."

If Macy was right, Liz wasn't showing it. Her eyes locked on the dog.

Despite her company, Macy felt alone. She wondered how Ryan

would react if they couldn't repair their squabble. Would he throw them out? Leave them to be hunted by Desmond? Would he kill them both?

"You're nobody. How the fuck did you advance so fast?" Liz spoke with the serenity of a priest through a confessional screen.

"No idea. Maybe you brought it out of me somehow."

"Hmm." Liz was silent for a while. "Can you see him from where you're at?"

Macy pressed her face to the bars but couldn't see into Brooks' cell beside her. "Not quite. I hear him breathing, though."

Liz finally swallowed. "Somethin' funny about your friend Ben." Macy wouldn't quite call him a friend, but she listened anyway. "He hasn't gotten any worse since we got here."

"He wasn't wounded like Cameron. Maybe it's a slower process for him." *Let it go, Liz. We may be doomed already.*

"Yeah…stinks in here."

An hour later, the door at the end of the hallway clinked open. Ryan stepped through and marched to their cells. He scowled at Liz, but she wouldn't face him. "When I let you live... was it a mistake? Doyle said I was foolish, but I saw something else." He slammed a fist on her cell gate and drew her attention. "Was I wrong?"

Macy's heart pounded, but Liz's voice was a crib-side mother's. "I ain't the one you should watch."

"I'm struggling, you see." Ryan stepped within an inch of the grate. "I know you came on this accidentally, so I feel a bit responsible. But you aren't one of mine. I can't afford a thorn in my shoe."

Liz chuckled. "Don't waste time with threats. I been dead a long time. Part of me's buried in the desert, the other half on Kensington Avenue. Go pay your respects when you find the time."

Ryan pulled the grate from its setting and approached her. Before

Macy could blink, the King had Liz by the throat, suspended against the back wall of her cell.

Macy erupted. “Wait!”

Ryan didn’t look, but he didn’t take the marine's head either.

“You kill her, you’ll have to kill Brooks…and me. My death will rub Ben wrong, so you’ll have to kill him, too. There goes half your muscle. Desmond and his crew will eat you alive.”

Now Ryan shifted a glowing red eye to her.

“This thing with us…we put it to bed while we were down here. We can help.”

After a moment, Ryan set Liz on her feet and shifted his focus to Macy. “You impressed me. You hit your peak through sheer willpower.”

Macy stood surprised. Praise from a wolf god who’d barely acknowledged her existence.

“You’re Desmond’s wolves, but you needn’t be reckless like the killers in his pack. If you can’t learn the way we operate, you’ll wash with the next storm.”

He opened Macy’s cell and left them there. Liz massaged her throat as it healed. She looked to Macy and thanked her with a tip of the chin. The marine claimed to have died overseas, but Macy could see a spark of life in her yet.

# CHAPTER FIFTY-SIX

## Desmond

*Montgomery County, Pennsylvania*

The King's fingers blackened as he swabbed the ashen silhouette. Ben's final resting place. *Cheated of a warrior's death. When I've no more use for the brat, he'll pay in spades.*

He remembered when the brat's father pledged himself in Derbyshire. Desmond's father made a fool of him, but Becker Sr. had become more of a brother to Desmond than any of the litter.

Loyalty was his most precious gift. Des had seen the same in Ben at the beginning. He thought of their last exchange, when he'd killed the girl and lost his friend in a single strike. He'd seen it in Ben's eyes on the night of the raid. There was a vacancy there, a gap where trust used to live.

He wouldn't have traded Ben for ten Juniors. To meet his end at the brat's hand was a bitter notion. Des knew Ben would haunt him through every ring of hell to pay him back.

Following the scent from the severed hands had been a much more tedious chore than expected. They'd been combing the woods for days and seen no sign of the Runt or his pack. He could have been back in Derby, though Des didn't believe his brother would retreat.

Inside, Junior lounged on Eduardo's highchair, massaging his chin with thumb and forefinger. *Archduke John Becker Junior.* The thought filled Desmond's cheeks with the acid taste of vomit.

When the King reached the base, Junior shifted his weight. "She's warm for ya, Des." He descended the wooden stairs, noisy creaks abounding.

*If I needed a throne, I'd whittle one from your bones.*

He smacked the King's shoulder. "Another sweep o' the woods, then?"

With Ben's demise, Des had to reflect on his own decisions. He was baffled as to how he'd let such an incompetent reach such a lofty position. "Reckon I might go myself. You have a sit." He motioned upward to the laughable construction.

"I thought *I* was the jester." Finally, Junior dropped his playful demeanor. "Come, now. The Runt's got friends, dunn'e?"

"Not a problem. What *will* be is if one of you follows and gets dropped. I won't suffer the illness again. I won't give the Runt an edge."

"You think I'd let that gay boy get 'is mitts on me?" Junior got defensive, the way his dad did when his skills were called into question. "You think my father raised a twat?"

*He raised a bloody idiot, an untethered dog.* "No. I think you'd give it your best go…"

The kid's face folded in two.

"Your old man was a warrior. He raised one, I suppose, but you're not my blood. This 'Howler Prince' business…you cooked it in your nut." *And you killed my only friend in the States, you barmy cunt.*

Junior computed some silent equation. "I pulled you from a fookin' ditch. Blood or no, I'm owed a debt."

"You're not. And our blood's a different shade. The shaman blessed Wagner and his kin. He never accounted for you lot."

Junior stared at the King's feet. He'd met his idol and been denied an autograph. "Let me prove you wrong."

He tapped Junior on the cheek. "If the Runt slips me, strike at his head."

Something stirred in the boy's gut. "I know where to strike." Now Junior stared Desmond down like prey.

*Make a move, you up-jumped hellion. We'll end this here and now.*

When the brat studied the crimson glow in his King's eyes, he relented, shoulders deflating like pierced balloons. It seemed he'd remembered himself.

Des pushed past him, and the hunt was underway.

Rays of midday sun warmed him through the trees as he set off with the severed hand in his grip. He could almost feel it shake, remnants of the frightened hen to which it belonged. The scent wove through the woods like a living thing.

On this trek to find his brother, he thought of home. As boys, he chased Ryan and the others on the moors, through Blue John Cavern, Treak Cliff and The Devil's Arse. They'd run as wolves, unbound by their human complications. He'd have frozen that time if he could. He felt the stubble on his face, peppered with the grays of age and guilt. He thought of his brothers' last day, when the fire had taken them. The heavens rained down after—a moment too late, it would seem. When the flames died, it was all bones and echoes.

Ryan deserved his reckoning, though he wouldn't have it. He should have counted his blessings after surviving the fire. He was lucky to catch Desmond venturing South. Attacking him up North would have been fatal on the first attempt.

With the claw of his thumb, Desmond scratched away a dried blood droplet from a dampened leaf. He waved it under his nose, and the boy's scent doubled. It drew him to a clearing, cushioned by a creek, where more droplets thickened the trail.

Around him, the Mother Hill emerged like an evil crag, the O'Connell mansion fallen to cinders near its peak. Ryan waited for him, surrounded by the cursed memories of his childhood. The Runt looked a nightmare, a mutilated phantom that would frighten children. He made his way across the burned grass and stopped a mere six feet from his big brother. The faded iris of his left eye stared cold while the wind dusted them with ash. Then the Runt opened ruined lips. "When you speak to him next, tell old Becker he's shit at torching children."

Desmond focused on his surroundings. "Is this a trick?"

"Been watching you blunder about the woods," Ryan replied. "Waiting for you to come alone."

"I don't mean…" Desmond pointed. "I still see the smoke."

Ryan searched for his brother's meaning. "What are you on about?"

Mam Tor faded in and out of Desmond's vision. "Can't you see it?" He pressed two fingers to his temple to clear his head.

Ryan's mismatched eyes sharpened. "Christ, have you gone daft like Father?" His tone was meek. The Runt was genuinely concerned. "Don't tell me you've been praying to a corpse, Desmond."

Now the Wolf King stared at his brother's scars. His response was a laugh—a long, guttural laugh that rattled the mirage. Ryan laughed with him. They were children again, and Des had snuck a fart in his father's armoire.

Beside the eyesore that was the fallen manse, Mam Tor was still as beautiful as he remembered. Ryan had chosen a decent place to fall. Des was content finishing things here.

"You've a beard now."

*And you can't grow any hair on that prune you pass off as a face.* "It's all I've changed, really, since last we spoke." Desmond remembered the barn on the O'Connell grounds, charred black and crumbled to its foundations. Ryan had run there after Daniel fell. Des thought it to be the Runt's grave. "You've come for me, then?"

Ryan's gaze found the dirt. "Aye..." He'd exhausted his laughter early. Now it was all scowls. "But it ain't like you think."

"What d'you mean?"

Ryan touched his face. Des could see years of anguish in the Runt's eyes, but there was also maturity. An aura of self-reflection that surpassed his father or even Daniel. "I've forgiven you."

"Ha!" The outburst jumped from Des before his manners could stop it.

"I reckon I sound half mad, but I have. I hope it can give you a bit of comfort. I know you've suffered."

"You know fuck all about me, Runt." Mam Tor and its fog were fading. The sun had found them again.

Ryan smiled, that pious little curl of his lips that boiled Desmond's blood. "I know you won't admit it, but if it lets you rest easy, it needed saying."

The little bastard was right. He'd never know the weight he'd lifted with his forgiveness. He was also right that Des would never give him the satisfaction. "So why come across the water for me, then, now you've become the patron saint of bloody bygones?"

Again, the Runt brushed his ruined cheek. It seemed like a nervous tic. "It's true I need to put you down, Des, but not from anger." He waited for a response, but Des was silent. "You still got clouds in your head after all this time? Our existence is a desecration. Mundi made us to clean the filth from Derbyshire, and we only muddied it worse."

Desmond laughed again, this time unconcerned with manners. "Mate…" He found his brother's stare. "I burned the lot of ya. You want us gone, spark yourself and finish the job."

Ryan's tone turned sour. "I intend to. But I'll not let you continue with this farce. You can't rebuild what we had. Derby bled enough from our nonsense. Now you want to bleed the States as well?" He shook his head. "Let's see ourselves out, brother."

Des found himself wonderfully amused by the Runt's lecture. "You lie worse than father. You've his blood flowin' in ya whether you'd like it or not." The Runt's face curled like he'd caught a foul scent. He hated the fact that he'd come from Wagner O'Connell's seed. The man had treated him like scum, as he was the last born before their mother passed—kept him in the barn, burned his eye with an iron, beat him mornings. Des had certainly felt sympathy for the boy. He wasn't soulless, despite what his brothers may have thought. Yet now it seemed the Runt had joined Daniel in being holier-than-thou. A lost wolf who'd forgotten his nature. "Come and have your vengeance, then, you soft, scarred-up wanker. I know it lives in ya. You expect Daniel to do it for you?"

Before he could finish his question, the kid was on him. He ripped a claw across Desmond's abdomen. Des pressed a hand to his gut to keep his entrails from spilling into the mud. *Ryan the fuckin' Runt, you've been busy.*

Des spat blood and bit down hard. Ryan went for his head this time, but Des caught his wrist with his free hand and thrust a knee into his brother's gut. Ryan fell onto his back and the mud made a soft slurping sound when he landed.

Around them, the landscape perforated. Mam Tor was a filthy memory. Desmond's stomach had begun to heal, but some of his entrails had spilled through his fingers.

Before he could push them back in, the Runt was on him again. He remembered the fight he'd had with Daniel in the courtyard of the O'Connell estate. His brother's speed was unmatched—unmatched until this day, when the Runt plunged a claw into Desmond's chest and took hold of his heart.

His breaths froze in this sun-soaked clearing, no longer Mam Tor at all. A squeeze from the Runt, and it would be his grave.

*Finish it…what's keepin' ya?*

Ryan held the King's heart in his stunted fist, gentle as the head of a newborn. Some struggle had found him. Twelve years and the Runt still lacked their father's killer resolve. He removed his hand.

Desmond's chest sealed up.

*Christ, you're Daniel come again.* Des slashed Ryan's right arm off above the elbow and kicked him onto his back again.

Ryan rolled for the arm and pressed it back together.

Before the Runt's arm could mend, Des gathered his entrails and took to the woods at top speed, praying the Becker brat had a favor left in him.

# CHAPTER FIFTY-SEVEN

## Macy

*Montgomery County, Pennsylvania*

She sprouted claws and retracted them again. She remembered the way Brooks had flaunted Stage Three and could relate to it now.

"Keep switchin' on and off like that, you might hurt yourself." Ben was always plain with his words. "Enjoy it, though. You won't like what comes next."

Her smile was tugged flat as she thought of Brooks.

"Relax..." He patted her on the shoulders. "You're strong. Not a dope fiend or an…aging has-been. You'll hold it off a good stretch."

She tried her best to swallow the hopeful news like honey. "How long before the dream starts?"

Ben's brow curled upward. "Right away." He shifted weight, puzzled. "You haven't had it?"

"I don't think so." *Hmm. Am I somehow different from the others? Why?* "You think there's any truth to it? A yellow killing a red?"

"I'm starting to bank on it." He scanned the corridor for eavesdroppers and lowered his voice. "I'm thinkin' I probably owe it to everyone to get rid of Desmond, but I don't know. Might save my life if the dream's not just some voodoo bullshit."

She switched back to wolf and wondered if somehow vanquishing a Wolf King was the cure she'd sought.

•• ●● ••

"Faster. I couldn't feel the wind on that one."

Ben and Macy sparred in the main sewer junction. Macy sprang at him again and swiped open air.

"Closer, but still slow."

She tried again.

"Worse. Overthinking."

Again.

"Come on! I'm half dead!"

Again.

This time, Ben grabbed her arm and tossed her to the ground. "How the fuck you plan on dropping a Stage Three if a patching old man put you on your ass?"

She straightened her knees and brushed off the fabric on her thighs, surprised at Ben's change in demeanor when it came to combat. She wondered if he'd trained the wolves up North this way—if he'd been this tough with his daughter.

She tried again and missed by a mile.

"Right…let's take a break. I can't help you if you're afraid to shed blood."

Macy had violent thoughts that stemmed from her paranoia but was never able to bring them to action.

*Focus, Mace. Show him how you focus.*

She closed her eyes and found the open road. She could feel the bite of the wind—smell the oil and sizzling rubber.

She lunged.

Ben's claw closed around her throat and lifted her. The yellow jewels in his face beamed. He held her there, suspended in time as the room went dull. Then…a voice.

*Up this way. You have to go up.*

Her vision was a closing tunnel. …*Sarah?*

*Up. Up. Up.* A tree spread out around them. She could see her sister's hand outstretched to pull her to the next limb.

*I can't.*

Sarah's eyebrows furrowed. Her thighs pressed firmly to the trunk, and the shaking in her extended hand went still. *What choice do you have?* Beginning at her chin, a purple corruption took her face. Her eyes rolled over white and crab claws burst from the sockets. The flesh sloughed away until Macy reached for bone. *What choice do you have?*

Macy let go.

When she came to, the dust of the sewer stuck to her cheek. Ben's face broke the haze. He scooped her from the ground, and her balance returned to her. For a time, his face looked purple, but that, Macy knew, was the dying wheeze of the corrupted dream he'd choked into her.

She felt his gaze on her skin like the brush of phantom fingers. "What are you afraid of? What's holdin' you back?"

Macy almost choked again.

"Whatever it is, you've got to leave it."

She forced a nod. It might have been a lie. Could she keep Sarah from her thoughts long enough to do what needed done? Could she use her grief to her advantage?

These lingering thoughts made her wonder if she ought to just let the wolf take her.

# CHAPTER FIFTY-EIGHT

## John Becker, Jr.

*Montgomery County, Pennsylvania*

John was amused by the King's lack of awareness. *Too fixated on the Runt, are we?* He'd followed at a stone's throw and hadn't been made. He brought Ringo and his mates along. Together, they sidestepped the clearing where Des met his brother. *We'll let these two tango and tend to the fallout after.*

He held the other dead hand in his grip, necrosis piping rancid gas from the wrist. *Seems the King's forgotten me. Forgotten I'm a pup with an exceptional gift.* He followed the scent past the fraternal dispute. It wound through brush, descended, peaked at a rusted sewer grate with a newly-fastened latch.

He tilted his chin up at Ringo. "Find the run-off. Not a soul leaves living."

The oaf obliged him as he pulled open the grate.

# CHAPTER FIFTY-NINE

## Liz

*Montgomery County, Pennsylvania*

Macy wound Liz's hair into tight blonde braids. If a fight was coming, it would suit her to keep it close. Pedro sat beside her and nibbled a bone. She felt guilty. Brooks hadn't kept anything down in days. The man bound in muscle, who'd fought through hell for his country had now withered to a vomiting, patching sore.

Freddy seared more venison behind a sheet of smoke. The Sheikh taught her to respect the man in charge of your food. That man balances your life in his fingers.

Ryan's crew had been whittled down to scraps, but Freddy had the presence of ten men. His hulking physique, his commanding demeanor…Liz felt safe with him in the ranks.

The only threat to her safety made way to join her now. He sat across from her, the patch over his eye littered with scabs and other growths.

Ben chewed his meat, shooting sporadic glances at the dark corridor to the entrance grate. He seemed on edge, like he was expecting someone. He scraped his claw along his face while he chewed, shifting his position repeatedly. "Either of you seen Ryan today? He's not in his…office."

Liz offered the chump about as much attention as Pedro did. The dog would have made better conversation.

"No," Macy answered for the both of them.

Ben tried to read something in her face. Liz tried to keep from lunging across the table and choking him blue. She spoke up to settle herself. "Just came from Brooks' death bed."

Ben looked deeper. He found a place in her eyes where he hadn't been invited.

"Maybe you forgot about him. He had a shotty on your ugly mug. Would've blown it off except he's better than you."

Macy's hands froze. "Liz..."

"Shut up." She focused on the patching man. "You gonna go visit him? Thank him for sparing you?"

He lurched forward onto his elbows. "Look. I get it. We lack chemistry, you and I. But don't put that shit on me." He pointed to the dark corridor where Brooks was dying. "I have enough sins to be ashamed of. I'm not gonna take on someone else's."

Liz was elated. This was the first date she'd been hoping for. "I used to snuff slippery shits like you in Afghanistan. Smoke you out of your rat holes."

"You proud of that?"

"Never slept better after. Ain't nothin' I did to the hajis I couldn't sleep with."

"Well…" Ben turned his hand in the flame light. "I don't burn so fuckin' easy."

"You don't hide as well neither." The yellow orb in Ben's head reflected Liz's fury. "Maybe you think I'm some dumb bitch just wandered in from a smack den. A few weeks ago, you'd be right. But, you see…I'm Sergeant Campbell again, and Sergeant Campbell has a nose for sniffin' bullshit."

"Yeah?"

"Yeah. Whatever deal you got swingin' with scarface, I'm guessin' my friend didn't make the cut."

Now he smiled with half his mouth. Liz wasn't sure how he managed it. Perhaps the patches were giving him nerve damage. "I knew a guy up North…liked to make assumptions like that. I opened his throat for him."

"We ain't up North, pussy. Any time you wanna make a move, though…I'm wettin' my fuckin' panties for that."

Macy stopped again and sighed.

*Sorry, girl. I ain't much of a fuckin' diplomat.*

Ben sat back, relieving the pressure from his elbows. "Now we both sound like children." He exhaled. "You're wrong. Ryan and I have been hashin' out strategies. I know Des. I know how he can fall. If I'm you, I'm lookin' to make friends so I can help bring him down…for the kid." He motioned toward Brooks again.

"I'll figure the truth…one way or another. We'll settle our differences then."

"I know you don't like me. You don't do much for me either. But it might do us both good to find a common interest." He pointed up at Macy. "Watching her back."

"I don't need instructions from you, motherfucker. I know whose back I gotta watch."

Ben retracted his finger. "Fair enough." He glanced behind him, into the depths of the main sewer canal. "I'm gonna stretch my legs." He left them there, disappearing into the dark. Charlie stood from his game of cribbage with Doyle to keep tabs on Ben. They were still under supervision. Even Ryan's ugly boyfriend.

Macy tied off the end of another braid. "Well…kept the threats and insults to a minimum, so…progress."

"Fucking guy reminds me of every CO I ever had. Always holding a sack of secrets he just can't wait not to tell you."

Macy tossed a venison bone to Pedro. He snatched it from the air.

"You gonna follow through on your promise?"

Liz felt her head to ensure the braids were snug. "I'm tryin' to be nice."

"Not that one…"

She rolled back the reels to try and remember which promise Macy meant.

"You said you would show me how to kill."

She chuckled. "You know how. The way you were wailin' on me the other day…couple more hits and you're there."

Macy shook her head. "I don't think I could've finished you. I kill a deer by accident, and it follows me for weeks. How do I shake *that*?"

Liz thought the girl might have been testing her, but her expression was earnest. "Why you carry that knife around?"

She shrugged.

Liz remembered struggling with killing in the desert before Juliana died choking on shrapnel. After that, she knew the filth she'd been disposing.

Her thoughts about the desert were suddenly derailed by whistling and a sustained growl from Pedro.

The tune of *The Itsy-Bitsy Spider* echoed from the entrance tunnel. Freddy looked up from his grill. Doyle looked over from his cards. In a moment, a yellow glow entered the sewer. The whistler wore a grin that almost outshined his eyes. "The Runt's army. Enough to make the Spartans tremble." Three more sets of eyes joined the whistler's, and the lamplight seemed dim in comparison.

Liz knew the cold sweat feeling of an ambush. She popped to her feet while Macy was still blinking her eyes. Freddy and Doyle charged the whistler's group. Liz took Macy by the wrist, snapped Pedro to attention, and sprinted for the opposite tunnel.

# CHAPTER SIXTY

## Macy

*Montgomery County, Pennsylvania*

They followed the stream of storm water to an exit draped in foliage. Ben and Charlie waited just beyond it, drinking in the sunset beside the small creek of sewer runoff. They turned to greet the girls when Ben's face dropped.

"Company!" Liz barked. "Crew of yellow-eyes."

Before he could respond, a deep voice cut in from the trees to the east. "Oi, who the fuck are you lot?" An oaf of a man stepped from the brush. He sounded slow, like a man in need of special schooling.

The whistler's voice startled Macy from the sewer's outfall. "I thought I did you in..." He was addressing Ben, glaring at him like prey.

Ben shrugged. "Oops." He laughed in the whistler's face. "Here I was basking in your absence, Junior."

The oaf approached them, and Pedro attacked, sinking his teeth into the big man's Achilles tendon and shaking violently. The oaf changed his face to yellow eyes and dripping fangs. He tried to pull the dog free. Pedro held his grip, despite the force of the brute.

Liz rushed the man and buried her claw in his shoulder, but the ogre was much quicker than his appearance suggested. He spun out of her grasp, took hold of the dog, and chucked him toward the woods.

Macy screamed to her lungs' limit and dove for the big man's midsection. Liz jumped onto his back as his wayward claw struck Macy in the side, tearing her open at the ribs. He grabbed at Liz, opening wounds on her face and arms that closed almost instantly.

Macy grasped her own wound while it sealed itself. She glanced behind her and saw Junior tackling Ben, the two disappearing over the edge of a hill. Charlie lay unmoving, blood pooling from a hole in his chest.

Liz hollered from the back of her rampaging bull. "Do something, goddammit!"

Macy looked for an opening where she might sneak a claw into the big man, but they were moving too fast for her.

She wobbled in to slash at him again, but he fastened his mitts onto her shoulders with the strength of a thousand men. She swiped him from gut to breast. His grip loosened, but not enough for her to break free. Liz reached over his head and grabbed him by the lower jaw. She pulled with every ounce of strength and let out a deafening cry. Macy could hear the big man's vertebrae popping one by one as his grip on her loosened more and more.

When his head separated from his shoulders, Liz fell backward holding it by the jaw. The man's enormous body fell forward onto Macy, sending the air from her lungs in a painful rush.

Minutes of blindness and suffocation beneath the dead giant seemed like hours, but eventually, Liz pulled the hulking mass from her chest, and she could breathe again. Liz yanked her to her feet. "That's a good start."

Macy looked toward Charlie's body. "We gotta help Ben."

"Fuck that." Liz caught her by the elbow. "Desmond finds us, we're cooked." Pedro hobbled to join them. "Let's go."

They took to the woods, Macy anxious about the fate of her patching friend.

# CHAPTER SIXTY-ONE

## Ben

*Montgomery County, Pennsylvania*

He had to admire the speed at which Junior snatched Charlie's heart from his chest. It seemed Charlie expected a head strike. He blocked high, and Junior went low. The kid didn't wait to assess his kill. He made for Ben with equally impressive speed and tackled him over the edge of a hill.

They rolled to its base, every impact forcing the air from Ben's lungs. They landed with the kid on top. *My fucking luck.* Ben felt just about the weakest he'd ever felt, but he mustered the strength to kick the kid free and hop to his feet. He coughed blood into the dirt. Stage Four would no longer abide physical stress like this.

The brat looked at him, the same toddler's mischievous grin that seemed to be his permanent expression. "You're through, mate." He held a hand up, motioning to Ben's face. "You look like I dug up my dead dog. You gonna drag it out, or you gonna let me do you a favor?"

Somewhere on his journey, Ben had lost his soul.

He'd thought of finding Desmond and killing him—if perhaps fulfilling the dream would cure him of his illness. In this moment, staring down a psychotic piss ant, it was clear how he'd atone for his sins. He thought of the girls he'd seen Des mutilate, the empty look in his eyes. He thought of the girls he'd left at the sewer's outfall and wished them well. He wondered where Ryan had gone, if he'd crossed paths with his brother and lost. Either way, he figured fewer red-eyes in the world was ideal.

He thought of the wolves at the lake. He hoped they had the sense to pack things in and find better callings, but he'd sent a text anyway. *We're stuffed here. Des is gone. The lake is yours to claim or toss, but I know you'll use your head. Take care of yourself.*

Blood dribbled from his bottom lip as he stared down Junior. Stage Four was a swift beast. It was angry with him for slowing the process, and now it made up for lost time. He could feel the patches consuming his limbs, numbness surging to the tips of his fingers. *This* was his atonement. His seat in hell would be filled, and if he could drag Junior down with him, it would be all the better.

*"No reckoning made, but sent to my account with all my imperfections on my head."*

He lunged at the brat and was side-stepped with ease. It wasn't much of a fight after that. He hardly needed Junior's help falling onto his back. His lungs were two rotting bags of noxious gas.

When the kid knelt to end him, Ben noticed the sweetest gem that could have ever caught his eye. Beneath Junior's left ear, gripping the flesh of his neck like a leech, was a beautiful, dripping patch. Ben pointed to it and laughed the poison from his lungs.

Junior reached and felt it, pulling away a red hand. His childish grin was gone.

"Welcome to hell, you little shit." Ben figured he'd blown the last of his wind.

The moment was so sweet, he hardly felt it when Junior clawed into his chest and crushed his heart.

# CHAPTER SIXTY-TWO

## Desmond

*Montgomery County, Pennsylvania*

The King stumbled into Carter's manse, holding his guts like sausage links. He was miffed to find the place empty. He called for the brat in every direction but was answered by his own echo each time. He tripped on his way to the kitchen table and spread out on top with royal arms outstretched. *The Runt mullered me good.*

He hated the idea of tucking his own guts in, but it was either that or spill his life's blood. He struggled to his feet and over to the sink, where he washed his hands thoroughly. *Where the fuck did Carter keep his Brandy?*

He searched the cabinets until he found a half-finished bottle of Hermitage. *There you are, love.* He took it over ice, smooth and sating. He let the flavors linger, eyes pinched with images of a better time.

When he was good and ready, he cut himself where his wound had healed and tucked his guts into the open slash. The wound closed, and his body corrected itself. He still felt ill.

More bodies were down nearby. *Probably Junior's. Little throb's dead from the neck up.*

Des fixed himself a second beverage and claimed a leather seat in the great room to plan a second run at Ryan.

*If the brat and his boys have fallen, I'm left to find the bodies and torch them on my own. The Runt'll have me before I'm through. I doubt I'll top him in this state.*

He set his glass down, half-finished.

*New York, then. A shag, a nap and some reinforcements.*

He stood from his chair and marched for the brat's van.

# CHAPTER SIXTY-THREE

## John Becker, Jr.

*Montgomery County, Pennsylvania*

He pulled his claw from the bollock's heart and shook blood from it. When he turned to see about helping Ringo, he met a cold stare—half red, half gray.

"Hello, John." Ryan's voice was as soft as he remembered, but there was a somberness to it now. A raspy quiver that came with trauma.

"Ryan the Runt." He was baffled at the notion that Des had lost to his brother. When he'd seen them fighting as he passed, Des seemed to have the upper hand. "How 'bout I pluck out that ruby and hang it from me neck, you sodding rib eye?"

There would be no reconciling. John changed his face and charged.

Everywhere John swiped, he found air. The Runt was toying with him, and he felt an unwelcome, growing sense of trepidation. "Face me proper, you seared cunny!" He took a shot at the Runt's head and got a clout in the ribs for the effort. He didn't remember falling, but the Runt stood over him as the wet grass dampened his hind parts.

"Becker…enough. We can discuss matters like gentlemen."

*Bugger that.* John rallied his strength and made for Ryan's abdomen, but the Runt caught his arm. He heard a tear and a pop. Suddenly, John was free to swipe again, but he was swiping with a stump.

The Runt held his arm in front of him like a prize trout, and John's howl sent birds into skyward frenzies.

# CHAPTER SIXTY-FOUR

## Macy

*Montgomery County, Pennsylvania*

Room 201 at the Hopewell Inn smelled like stale sex, but dogs were welcome, and weekday rates were half off. Macy had hotwired an '08 4Runner to get them here. Pedro slept in a ball at the foot of Liz's bed while she showered. Macy listened to the running water and Liz's rendition of *Have You Ever Seen the Rain* by Creedance Clearwater Revival. *Damn, if she doesn't do it justice.* She bobbed her head, outstretched on her busted mattress, while she contemplated their options.

She'd hit a dead end in her search for a cure. It seemed the only promising angle came from this dream she'd yet to have herself. Liz and Ben had told her about a yellow-eye killing a red, changing his own eyes after. Had this happened before? Some imprint from a past event? Or was it a premonition? Ryan was the only red-eyed wolf she'd seen. She was sure the whistling demon in the sewer was Desmond until his face glowed yellow. She was taking a lot of folks at their word.

She thought of Ben. She hoped he'd taken his enemy's head and that he might find them here at their sex-stained respite. She felt safe with him, despite his ailment.

Liz entered the room wrapped in a towel. She dropped it to the floor, pulled on the clothes she'd been wearing all day, sat beside the dog, and scratched his head. "You feelin' salty about that ape we dropped?"

Macy looked over to find the marine was grinning. "Not really." She hadn't thought about the big man once since they checked in.

"There you are. I knew you were a cold bitch. Just gotta stretch your legs a bit."

"I didn't do much." Even Pedro had done more damage, tearing into the big man's heel.

"You did your part." She pulled her hand from the dog and pointed. "And that blank feeling you have now, hang onto it. It's all that prick deserves." It was clear Liz was trying for some sort of profound lesson, but it wasn't quite landing. Liz came from a different place. A place where killing was necessary—where the only way to overcome it was to do it until you were numb. Macy couldn't ever imagine herself there.

Liz popped an ice chip from the bucket into her mouth and decided to continue an earlier conversation. "My mom, she married a real piece of shit."

Macy started to respond but chose instead to listen. It might have been the only opportunity she had.

"I pissed hot for dope, and they sent me back stateside. I find out she moved." She rustled the fur on Pedro's stomach. "Went to see her at her new place, try and apologize, set things right…a cop picks me up. I found out later the piece of shit she married put a restraining order on me. I'm guessin' she agreed, 'cause I ain't heard from her since."

It was difficult for Macy to avoid hugging this rugged soldier who wasn't so rugged.

"I got no other family to speak of. I thought I might be able to pick up the life I had with my mom, like she might be the one who could forgive the things I did over there." She shook her head rhythmically back and forth.

If ever there was a time for Macy to open up about her own mother, this was it. *Tell her, Mace. Tell her how Sarah slipped the guardrail and plunged to the riverbed. Tell her how mom left you when you needed her most. The purple face your father had to identify. Spill it.*

But she couldn't. Not to Liz, not to anyone. Those words would forever be thoughts.

"So, is there any hope for me?" asked Macy.

Liz wandered back to war. "The ones I dropped in the desert, I knew I was only givin' them what they paid for. I saw what they did to my friends…to their *own* people. When you're firing from a helo, you get that disconnect. Like nothin' on the other side of that windshield is really livin'. In your case…gonna be more personal. No way around it."

Macy mulled over Liz's words. Liz tried to help, but there would be no reconciliation for what Macy would need to do. She wondered if there should be. "You gonna give her the tapes?"

Liz took a moment to think about the question. She nodded. "Someday. Right after I kick my stepdad in the balls."

Now they both laughed.

"What about you? What's your plan when they let your dad out?"

The answer had been a stitch in Macy's side for some time. "I'm steering clear until Desmond is seen to. And I need a cure for this thing. I can't let it kill me. I can't leave him behind."

Liz nodded.

"Speaking of…what's our move?" Macy asked.

"Don't look at me. *You're* the planner. I work better in the field."

Macy smiled, charmed by Liz's trust. "We have a few options. I was thinking we rest until morning, then we go by the sewer and get a read on the fallout. See if we can grab Brooks."

"Yeah." Liz spun onto her back and closed her eyes.

"I'll keep watch if you wanna get a couple hours."

She smiled with her eyes closed. "I slept in pop-ups in the desert, fifty yards from a haji camp…I'm never really asleep."

Macy settled in to find some rest of her own.

# CHAPTER SIXTY-FIVE

## John Becker, Jr.

*Montgomery County, Pennsylvania*

He was weak with nostalgia. To see the Runt again, he found himself immersed in childhood memories—ogling girls in Derby, lighting firecrackers near the cathedral.

Doyle had also made the voyage across the sea. Last Becker remembered, he was spray-painting walls in Castleton.

Ryan and Doyle had dragged him back to Carter's place after the squabble at the sewer. He cleared his throat of sputum. "Sing with me, Runt. You know it well." A song piped from his lips that conjured more memories.

> *"Quivering child stands alone in a mill,*
> *Sings a prayer to his God that would strengthen his will."*
> *"Through the flames of his sin he lay perfectly still,*
> *And the dark ones will drag him—"*

"Shut your crippled gob." This wasn't the jovial Doyle he remembered. This was some impudent stiff.

He turned to Ryan, who was seated on a bar stool dripping some somber reminiscence. Another memory struck him, then. Suddenly, the burned god that maimed him took on the face of the boy with mismatched eyes from his youth. He remembered Daniel, the Runt's protector, always frowning, taking heads but finding no joy in it. He missed them all. The O'Connell family, whom he'd considered his own. Tears lined his lashes, but he refused to let them fall.

He wobbled as his consciousness wavered. He brought a hand to his stump to find another patch seeping rotten fluids where the arm had been severed. *No…I haven't lost my balls.* He could see the lights flickering, though it may have been the patches taking his mind. "Des'll come back…he'll burn the lot o' ya." He nodded off and came to again. "…when he does…" He pointed to Ryan. "I'll take me good arm…and fuck you with it."

Doyle interjected. "You'd best mind your words, cunt. Those blokes in the sewer were mates of mine. Reckon we'll head up to New York next and pay it back."

Ryan held a hand in the air. "We could've done this easy."

Spit strands dangled from John's lips like gossamer. He avoided Ryan's gaze, battled overwhelming sadness.

Ryan swallowed heavily. "We were all brothers, John... yet you stood by while I burned."

"Just…state your terms. You O'Connells are likely to jabber us into old age."

The Wolf God seemed to be fighting tears himself. "I think of our lives as boys, and it sickens me. To know what it was ultimately worth."

John laughed. Now the strands of drool fell to his shirt.

"That said, I won't enjoy killin' ya."

"What's your price, Runt? Don't fiddle with me."

"I only ask that you put aside your bitterness…and join me against Desmond."

When John's eyes could stay open, it read clear he was facing death. His next move would determine his fate, and he was running out of sassy quips and subterfuge. "…I can be a feral twat. I know it. But I'm smart enough to know when I've been bested. I put my stock in the wrong god, and it cost me my wanking arm."

The smile Ryan cracked seemed forced. "We're not gods, mate. We're a glorified street gang that imploded from within. Lost to our purpose. Ash on Derby wind. I stayed 'round Castleton a good while after you lot cut and run." The Runt chewed his lip. "Things settled rather quickly…we weren't hardly missed."

John had revered this family for so long, it felt a sacrilege to accept Ryan's piss-poor eulogy. "Your father will be remembered…and Daniel. Des, even. Stitches in Derby lore. But the Runt? A stillbirth kept in the dark with the bloody livestock."

Ryan's face was weighted with something. He considered his words carefully. "Will you come North with us? Hunt Des and tame his crew as recompense?"

Oftentimes, the Runt's piety tickled him. "I'd sooner have ya torch me and spread my ashes on the Hill."

Ryan's face burned sorrow, but his eyes were cold. The dead icy stare of a killer.

# CHAPTER SIXTY-SIX

## Liz

*Montgomery County, Pennsylvania*

She leaned against her headboard, never noticing when exactly she'd fallen asleep. Her dream had the foul scent of something final. Bodies lined the blood-red hall. Serita, Juliana, even Layla. Their dead eyes followed her on her slippery march. Beyond the walls, her stepfather's voice boomed. *"I make you a ghost for real."*

Her mother's song was still absent. She'd forgotten the tune and the lyrics were lost to her. In place of the door stood Macy, her face a stone warning for what would come. Liz could not raise her rifle. Her eyes drifted downward to the blood-soaked boards. The M4 slipped from her fingers and clattered an echoing coda. *"Rest now."* Her mother's voice. A tingling vibration. A longing that surged underfoot. She took her place beside the fallen and awakened with a gasp.

She glanced over at the sleeping girl. Liz had watched Juliana die in her arms in the desert. She'd abandoned Serita and let Desmond take her. She wouldn't let Macy fall. No chance.

They waited in the brush near the storm sewer at dawn, examining the body of the giant they'd slain. Liz pointed to Charlie's charred corpse at the entrance. "You see that? They torched him."

Macy squinted to sharpen her view. "Good sign. Ryan's boys pulled it out."

She stood to approach the sewer when Liz grabbed her by the sleeve. "Easy. Always assume some bullshit." Liz pushed to her feet. "Stay behind me."

Liz approached the headless colossus with Macy on her tail. She scanned the tree line and the sewer, ready to pounce at the first sight of a wolf. She noted the big man's corpse. "We really plucked this motherfucker, huh?"

Macy made for the hill where Ben had been tackled. When Liz joined her, she could see a body at its base covered in blood from a gaping chest wound. Macy started down the hill, and Liz followed.

They knew it was Ben before they reached him. His good eye was glossed, staring past them, fixed on nothing. His chest was torn open, tattered tissue from his destroyed heart clinging to a bloody shirt. Liz could see the bend of a grin on his lips. Maybe the man had found some comfort in the end. Despite her distain, Liz was disturbed by his passing.

She looked to Macy whose eyes were moist. The girl marched for the sewer. "Let's go."

Liz didn't argue.

Inside, it was quiet. Freddy's burned corpse lay near the entrance corridor surrounded by three unburned members of Junior's crew. Liz figured the cook had slain all three. She nodded and bid him safe passage.

Ryan and Doyle were not among the dead. Nor was Junior. *Tread careful, bitch. You've got a god and a grunt on your ass.*

They crept toward the hall of cells.

It seemed a great deal longer to her now. In brief snapshots, she could see the hall from her dream, but her mother's voice was gone.

The dreary sewer rat that had once been Corporal Cameron Brooks, her friend and savior from the desert, stared back at her through rusted bars. Its eyes were sunken, limbs bent and frail. It bore none of Brooks' features.

It was sickening to see her friend this way. He'd struggled a long time with his demons. He deserved a cleaner end. She wanted to tell him again that she didn't blame him for the wolf problem. She didn't blame him for the discharge either. No one had forced the needle to her arm either time.

He'd saved her life in the desert more times than she could count, and she couldn't even save his once. It was the same with Juliana. *They're gone, and I'm here. The cycle repeats.*

The Brooks-rat sniffed the floor and returned to its cot to rest. Ryan had left him in the damp dark with the care you'd give a fungus.

Liz searched the Wolf God's quarters for a cell key. With the candles dull, the sanctuary had lost its luster. What had once been a circle of shrines had become a collection of dead wax.

She rifled through drawers, bedding and supplies. She found pictures of Carter's place. It seemed Carter had a group of slackers under his wing. They weren't careful in their comings and goings, and Ryan had become a regular paparazzi.

She found some older pictures, shots of Ryan's family—a stern looking group of young men with hound's eyes. They interested her just as little, but she could see why he wasn't ready to part with them.

She found a wooden crate in the corner of the nook. Inside, she found a key, along with a three-foot tube with needles caked in blood at each end. She examined it closely, unsurprised but still disappointed. Ryan's blood must've held it off for Ben. Meanwhile, Brooks lay comatose in a basement cell with nothing but his own poison slugging through his veins.

She dropped the tube. She would make use of every precious second and see that both Wolf Gods paid their due.

Brooks had found something resembling sleep through shivers and winces. He'd eaten none of the meat she'd left for him. She unlocked the cell, lifted the latch, and joined the Corporal on the floor, placing a hand on his side and riding the wave of his lungs. He didn't buck at her presence. Perhaps he remembered his Sarge's touch.

Liz looked up at Macy. "Give me a minute with him?"

The girl stepped away without argument.

She spent an eternity there, with her hand against his ribs, catching a subtle beat from a heart that may have still been his. *Carter be damned.* She'd piece together the bastard's ashes and kill him ten times over for the hell he'd put them through.

She prayed Brooks would check out on his own and save his Sarge from the burden, but he was too much a fighter for that. *"Leave the desert with me."* He'd twirled her across Macy's living room with such grace, she thought he was her father reborn. She'd left herself then. The hardened exterior she'd built for years slipped her skin. *"Leave the desert with me."* The sweet tones of Barbara Lewis carried them somewhere far. There was magic in the Corporal's hands, magic in his feet. The weight of her rifle was lost to her.

*"Leave..."* It sounded so simple. She'd never touch another needle, never take another life. She looked down. The thing he'd become didn't dance. It barely breathed. She knew then she could never leave, but she could help him on his way. She sang lightly—a tune she remembered from her mother.

*Be still and sleep, my love,*
*Be still and rest those tired eyes.*
*Be still and sleep, my love,*

*The world awaits you when you rise.*
*I will be near, my love,*
*To come and greet you with a smile.*
*Be still and sleep, no need to weep, my precious child.*

Liz leaned in close.

*I tried, brother…but the desert claims us all.*

She slipped Macy's switchblade under his chin quick and clean and delivered him with a single swipe. Her claw would have done the same, but she didn't want his death to have anything to do with the wolf. He didn't put up a fuss. He didn't flinch. He just went.

His blood pooled on the cell floor, and with it, Liz hoped, all the phantoms that had caused him such unrest.

Liz allowed a moment for Brooks' soul to pass on, but her anger came rushing back to her. Anger toward Ryan and his kind for leaving her friend to rot this way. Anger toward Desmond for putting him here.

She looked down at her hand, at the quarter-inch patch of rot that itched her something awful. She'd noticed it first in the shower at the motel the previous night. She wondered who would wield the blade when *her* time came.

She met Macy at the outfall and handed her the knife. "Had to borrow this…"

Macy's face curled when she saw the sticky blood on the blade and hilt. "Liz, I'm sorry…"

Liz looked away. "Save it."

For a stretch it was all sniffles from Macy and the wild song of the woodland critters. Liz thought of Brooks the way he ought to be remembered—smiling and dancing to old time classics.

They took in the violet hints of a sunrise. Liz figured she wouldn't interrupt it, as it may well have been her last.

Macy wiped her face. "Let's finish this fucker."

# STAGE 4

"All things are subject to decay and when fate summons, monarchs must obey."

- John Dryden

# CHAPTER SIXTY-SEVEN

## Macy

*Montgomery County, Pennsylvania*

She dragged the bodies from the 4Runner to Carter's pit—the giant, three of Junior's cronies, Brooks and Ben. His was the heaviest, though he was the smallest of them. She wanted to thank him for sowing the seeds of her plan with his own.

She went inside to grab Junior's corpse. They'd found him on a barstool with a surgical slit in his chest. On their sweep of the perimeter, Macy discovered fresh tire tracks leading away from the manse. It could have been Ryan, Doyle, Desmond or all of them, but the house was empty. A dreary silence trapped it like an old photograph.

Liz had gone to tend to the dog while Macy made a stop at the cabin. The pieces of her plan were set. If it worked, it would bring one or both of the red-eyes to them. The rest would be up to timing and fate.

She kicked Junior's body, and it rolled into the pit, resting beside Ben, a bunkmate for the hereafter.

She glanced at the creeping dawn and then down at her phone. The time was 5:32. Liz would return in a few hours, and then they'd wait. Perhaps a day. Perhaps two. If the bait failed, they'd travel North to find another lead.

*Patience, Mace. What choice do you have?*

# CHAPTER SIXTY-EIGHT

## Liz

*Montgomery County, Pennsylvania*

Her second patch festered beneath her right breast, between two ribs, about the size of a fist. Though she loathed him, she thought of Ben—what he must have felt when the patching started, when he knew the end was near.

Pedro stared from the motel bed with his usual clueless optimism. This pained her all the worse. She had to make arrangements for him.

He followed her outside to the Honda where she let him ride shotgun.

On her way to the driver's seat, Liz felt her knee buckle. She caught herself on the hood, with Pedro piping a low-toned growl inside. She pulled up her pant leg to find a third patch. Her knee had been taken over by fur seeping pus and blood. *The fuck? That's way too quick.* Ben had been patching for days, maybe weeks, and his weren't this severe until he was close to the end.

Liz had been comfortable with death since Afghanistan. Her habits had her feeling like a living corpse waiting to fall. Now, things were different. The wolf had given her a glimpse of herself free of vice. She'd forgotten how it felt to be hopeful, to value yourself and your ambitions. She didn't want to leave it.

She thought of her mother. *If she could have seen me, remembered who I am.*

Tears found the corners of her eyes. She wiped them and gunned the Honda toward home.

## *Kensington, Pennsylvania*

Pasquale was working Devo's corner when Liz descended on her squalid strip. He slid his bike tires to a halt at her feet. "I thought you was dead, girl. They sayin' you killed like thirty people."

"Who you callin' 'girl', motherfucker? I'll kill *you* in a minute."

"Chill. Shit." He reared his front tire and flipped the handlebars. "I knew they were lyin' anyway. You and Serita were like this, you know?" He crossed stained-yellow fingers.

"Yeah..." Liz thought of her time bunking and junking with Serita. It felt like a different life.

Pasquale smiled at the pavement the way he always did when a sly remark occurred to him. "You look kinda funny as a blondie, I ain't gonna lie."

She smacked the side of his thick dome.

"Ah...my bad, Liz. Shit."

"I'll fuckin' tell your mom you're slingin' again."

"Nah, nah...be cool." He spotted the dog and held his hand out for him to lick. "Damn! Pedro lookin' swole. What you feedin' him?"

"Bones of young dealers."

He smirked. When he finally looked her in the face, he squinted and leaned in over his handlebars. "You growin' a beard?"

She rubbed the side of her cheek—a fourth patch of hair. *Motherfucker.* Behind him, she caught a police prowler edging its way up the street. She tugged Pedro along and ducked into an alley.

"You remember a little Walther PPK passin' through here?"

The pawnshop reeked of antique dust and body odor. The man behind the counter had sweat stains on his white undershirt. "We don't move that kind'a thing here."

Liz scanned the shop, ensuring she was alone. "Look, I ain't a cop. The piece was mine. Some giant dickhead sold it without my permission."

He pursed his lips, reading the fiend before him. "Sorry to hear it…but we don't move that kind'a thing here." The man's face was unpleasant, each component misshapen in its own way. She struggled letting the Walther go, one of the few memories of her father, but the ones she held in her head would have to do.

She itched her neck, and blood welled beneath fingernails. She wouldn't last another day at this rate. In the Honda, she wrapped her patchy face with a torn piece of linen. When Pedro roused, he hardly recognized her. She felt every bit as weak as she did when smack worked her like the strings of a marionette.

It was over.

Alexandra Elizabeth Campbell was meant to die seven years past in the Afghan dunes. She crawled free of the crashed Viper, and her life had been a train wreck ever since. She refused to meet her end as a sewer rat with piss-yellow eyes. Instead, she would kill the red-eyed chump who took her Corporal or die in the effort, putting an end to this borrowed time she'd never asked for.

"How long's he got for someone to take him?" She'd worn the linen like a hijab so the vet wouldn't ask questions.

He rubbed fingers over Pedro's glands and shined a light into his eyes. "Depends on his condition. Right now, he's a little overweight, but we can take care of that. Long as he stays healthy, he'll stick around until someone picks him up."

"What's the longest you've seen?"

"Two years…give or take. We don't euthanize animals to save space. That's a last resort."

*Hear that, Brooks? I should have dropped you here.* "How much?"

"Fee is fifty." He found her eyes through the slit in her scarf. "We'll take good care of him."

Once paid in full, she had ten bucks to her name. She left without a backward glance, before Pedro knew what she'd done. *Be good, boy.* With him, she left her final ounce of purity. A kiss on the brow was a *goodbye* she simply couldn't stomach.

The Schuylkill River was at rest.

Brooks' phone shook in her clammy hand. She thumbed her mom's home number and waited an eternity before pressing 'send.' It rang twice before she heard a quaint, "Hello," from the other side. She knew her mother's voice in an instant and was unprepared.

A thick, syrupy silence followed, and it seemed for a moment that her mother had hung up. "…Alexandra?"

"I, uh…" Tears choked off whatever semblance of an apology she'd worked up. What began as a momentary hiccup devolved into a quivering sob, and suddenly, she was a little girl again. Sergeant Campbell didn't cry. This was someone else.

*Speak, you junkie. You won't have another chance.*

She tried her damnedest and managed nothing. The words were there, eight years of them, but they were locked in a cage, and Liz had swallowed the key.

"Baby girl…please…" Now Liz could hear sniffles from her mom's end.

*I'm sorry.* The thought would have to do.

When she was certain her effort was fruitless, she hung up and tossed the burner into the river.

# CHAPTER SIXTY-NINE

## Macy

*Montgomery County, Pennsylvania*

Liz returned with a mess of unholy patches gripping her skin like leprosy. The marine's condition brought Macy to tears. "Jesus Christ, Liz."

Liz smiled the best she could manage. "Yeah…I'm fucked up, girl."

Macy hugged her. Liz jumped at first, but after a moment she relaxed, letting herself weep tears she'd probably been holding back for years. They held each other there for as long as they could.

"Why's it taking you so quick?" Macy detached from her to allow an answer.

Liz considered with her eyes on the dirt below. "Brooks and I…we couldn't hold it off as long. Our will was strong from the Corps—" She coughed blood into her hand. "—bodies weak from our habits."

"Don't you speak about yourself in the past tense, you bitch." She wiped a few more tears away. "I won't allow it."

Liz snickered and brushed her ruined face.

Macy rested her hands on the marine's shoulders. "We can pull this off. If only one shows up…you can have him."

"No…" She wiped a dribble of red from her lip. "This ain't my show no more."

"Liz…I swear to God, I'll let him split me. You're taking him." She stared into the marine's bloodshot eyes until she got a nod.

# CHAPTER SEVENTY

## Desmond

*Brooklyn, New York*

Young Harry was a good lad. He hardly flinched at the news that his dimwit of a boss had gone rogue. He set up Desmond in a private room to rest. The nap had become a night's sleep, tucked beneath assorted blankets freshly washed of sweat and semen.

The illness bludgeoned him. He remembered his fall from the Shivering Mountain and wondered if he'd prefer that impact over this infernal ache. He'd seen Daniel in his dream. *Let him finish you. Put our cursed blood to rest.* His father was also there, kneeling before the shaman corpse. *You desecrate my name, bastard.*

Despite his ghosts, the sleep had helped. The ache relented. Not much, but enough. He would make the trip back, return with help to burn the dead and finish Ryan.

Young Harry brought his coffee for him, two sugars, no cream. He tipped his mug in gratitude and sipped. "Have a sit with me, yeah?"

The kid brushed the leather of the VIP dance chair and sat, bent forward, latching to the King's words.

"I always reckoned you had a better head than your bollock of a captain…"

Harry's face was stoic. He was immune to flattery. Focused.

"But you're untested. I'd like to see how you move in the field."

His back straightened. The lad was keen on proving himself.

"You got someone you can trust enough to leave things with?"

"My dad. He knows the books, the whole machine. Got enough muscle here to keep him safe."

Des sucked the sweetness from his Colombian dark roast. *Would've spared me an ache to bring this kid South from the start.* "Good. You and I are heading back. We'll burn the dead, I'll finish Ryan. If Becker's turned his cloak…we'll finish him as well. You got the stomach for it?"

The kid nodded without a half-second's hesitation.

"Reckon I'll stay sentient long enough to do what needs done, but we'll burn the dead quickly." He topped off his coffee and set his mug on the glass table. "You'll drive."

## *Montgomery County, Pennsylvania*

When they arrived at Carter's manse, his aches weighted him in a lump sum. Harry fetched two cans of petrol from his trunk and followed Des through the house. They swept every nook to ensure the place was empty, then proceeded to the pit out back where his aches hit their summit.

*The bloody hell is this?*

Piled in a mass grave lay a rat creature, Becker's oaf, three of his fallen mates, the brat himself and…

Next to Junior, with his heart torn from him, lay Ben. Last he'd seen his advisor, the man had gone completely torpid, put down by the brat on the front lawn. *Another lie from the little throb.* He stared at Ben's dead eye. *Where did you go, mate? Who was it delivered you?*

Harry's phone rang from his pocket. He flipped it open and

answered. His face whitened. "Des…"

The King snatched it and held it to his ear. "Yeah?"

"Someone's here…" Old Harry's voice rattled with fear. "Wolf with a red eye, scars on his face. Him and another bloke were havin' a word with the boys downstairs when they started tearing them apart. I'm tucked in a private booth. Hurry back—"

*Ships passing in the fucking night.*

As he wondered if the mass grave was Ryan's diversion, he heard a pop from the house. A bullet burst through Harry's shoulder and dropped him to a knee.

Des ducked to avoid more gunfire when a dirt bike bolted for the tree line. A girl rode its back, a small bird with tattoos. She held her middle finger in the air for Des to see.

The King laughed. *This one's got the bollocks of an ape.*

He changed his face and pursued the bike. The girl had underestimated his speed. He closed the distance between them as she entered the woods. It was one foolish play after another with this crew, but he admired their perseverance all the same.

When he could smell her sweat, mere feet from the catch, something snapped beneath him.

He looked down to see a trap biting into his flesh the way it had Steve at the cabin.

*Cunning,* he thought, as another girl emerged from the foliage and lunged for his head. He caught her from the air—the musclebound woman with the blonde braids, but shaggy now with patches—and chucked her into a tree trunk a few yards away. He heard her bones crunch on impact and the wind leave her as she hit the ground.

His head began to throb as he glanced through the tree line at Harry soaking the pit in petrol. *Torch them, you fucking halfwit.*

The bike throttled past him, threading trees like a suture. The small girl made for Harry in a rush, emptying rounds from her pistol while

Des pulled the teeth of the trap open and removed his leg from it.

He heard a twig snap to his left.

The brute had regained her footing. She was patching something awful, worse than Ben had been. She charged him again. He tossed the trap, glancing it off her thick head and causing a stumble.

Now, his pain dropped him. *Torch. The Fucking. Bodies.*

He could hear the bike skid against the grass. Tearing flesh.

No smoke. No cooking meat. Just fresh blood.

Frozen by his illness, he could hear his father again.

*Bravo, my troublesome whelp. What a legacy you'll leave.*

# CHAPTER SEVENTY-ONE

## Macy

*Montgomery County, Pennsylvania*

The Wolf King had been snared.

Macy spun the bike's tail, kicking a cloud of dust into the morning air. She could see Liz charging Desmond and getting tossed like a toddler.

Beyond them, the other man soaked the bodies in gas. She ripped the throttle and made for him. *Take him, Liz. I'll keep him sick for you.* She wove her way through trees and thickets until she cleared the woods. The man and the pit grew remarkably fast. She emptied rounds into him from Brooks' 45, causing him to fumble and drop the can. When she was near enough, she leapt from the bike and wrapped her arms around his waist. They both went down, the gravel and sod snuffing their breath. The Suzuki teetered and skidded to a stop a few yards beyond them.

The man beside her changed his face. This one's eyes were yellow, but Macy wouldn't take him lightly. He swiped at her, and she rolled, pushing herself to her feet before his next slash caught her in the side of the face, tearing her open. It would have been her throat if she hadn't ducked.

She hardly had time to heal before he was on her again. His strike came whizzing for her. She raised a hand on reflex, and his claw caught in the flesh of her palm, poking through bone and spraying her face with blood.

She pulled him close, spun him, and threw him toward the woods. Her palm healed as she darted after him. Before he could stand, she mounted him at the waist and started slashing at his face. He threw his arms up to block. She clawed away at them, mincing flesh and cartilage.

He thrust his hips with such power it tossed her from him. He had the strength advantage to match his speed.

Macy could hardly see the strike that opened her throat.

She squeezed her wound, pumping warm blood through her fingers, and sprinted to the nearest tree.

Sarah spoke to her as her throat closed. *Up, Mace. You have to go up. What choice do you have?*

With the man in close pursuit, she climbed. It felt oddly natural to her after all these years. She could see Sarah ahead, guiding her through the limbs, outstretching a helping hand when her shoe slipped. *That's it. One limb at a time. Right, then left. Left, then right.*

The man behind her had just about every combat angle in his favor, but this was *her* domain.

Sarah spoke again. *What choice do you have?* Her hand was within reach. Safety. Comfort of the familiar. Macy only needed to accept it, and she'd be free from the danger below.

*I'm sorry.* She withdrew her hand. Her sister's face curled. *I love you, Sarah.*

She hung with her left hand. With her right, she broke off a branch, turned, and plunged it into her pursuer's eye. The remaining jewel in his head went dull. He fell from the trunk, landing lifeless in the dirt below.

Liz's voice took over for Sarah's. *That blank feeling you have now, hang onto it. It's all that prick deserves.*

# CHAPTER SEVENTY-TWO

## Liz

*Montgomery County, Pennsylvania*

The trap Desmond threw had taken a piece of her head with it. She lost vision in her right eye and stumbled. She could see the Wolf King holding his own head, wincing like it pained him. He collapsed and writhed, swiped at open air as if battling ghosts.

She rushed him as he postured up. "Oh, fuck off, you." He delivered a backhanded slash that removed her hand at the wrist.

The pain was crippling, but she didn't wait. She screamed herself hoarse and fell on top of him, plunging her remaining claw into his chest.

He spun them and mounted her, but she held him close, using any strength she had to prevent his escape.

She could feel the desert heat. Smell the flames from the wrecked chopper. Her gear was crushing her lungs, cutting her inhales by half. She broke three ribs squeezing her way into the unwavering sun. Julianna lay shivering, despite it. A shard from the viper's hull protruded from her chest.

Liz moved to tend to her when she turned and spoke. "What the fuck are you doing?"

The Sergeant stood stunned. "What?"

"He's gonna kill you, you dumb bitch. Hold him up."

Liz put pressure on her ribs to relieve the discomfort. "Who do you mean?"

"Hold him up!"

She snapped back when Desmond pushed away from her, her claws still dug into his chest. The Wolf King met her gaze, ruby eyes twinkling with laughter. "Look at the state of us."

Liz laughed with him.

Over his shoulder, on a branch above, she saw a pair of yellow eyes. They didn't belong to a timid coward, afraid to hurt animals to fill her stomach.

They belonged to a cold-blooded killer.

With the stump that was once her left hand, she pushed Desmond upward, detaching from him.

The yellow-eyed killer struck like lightning, putting to bed the dream that had haunted the wolves for months.

# CHAPTER SEVENTY-THREE

## Macy

*Montgomery County, Pennsylvania*

Desmond's head left his neck, hitting the dirt with a resounding *thud*.

Something changed in her when she landed. She could see the world differently. Every subtlety, every critter tapping tree bark, every gust of wind brushing leaves for miles around. She could feel weakness fleeing her—physical, emotional, mental—relics from a previous era.

Sarah's image faded from her thoughts, obscured by mist. Her problems, her apprehensions, her episodes of anxious dread all burst to ash. *I've done it.* She didn't feel the guilt she'd expected, but instead, a surge of energy. Something like a victory. The Wolf King was irrelevant. This victory was within.

She allowed herself to breathe—to take in the nature surrounding her where she felt at home. Its song was a part of her now.

Macy gathered her wits and pulled the headless body off Liz. She sat down beside her, cradling the dying woman against her chest. Liz's breathing was a series of staggered wheezes, broken frequently by red coughs.

She managed words after a minute, though not many. "If you let me turn into a fuckin' sewer rat, I'll pluck those red eyes out of your head."

*Red eyes?* She must have misheard, or perhaps the Sergeant was delirious. Macy smiled through tears and opened her switchblade. "You were supposed to take him, Liz. Why didn't you take him?"

The Sergeant smiled back and coughed blood. There'd be no more words from her.

Macy wondered what she would do if it was Sarah in place of Liz, if she could have somehow ended her sister's suffering.

They watched the sun as it rose over Carter's house.

*To end your sister's suffering—a duty as much as a burden.*

She whispered faintly in the dying woman's ear, "Thank you."

She slipped the knife into Liz's heart as quickly as she could. The marine stopped moving, eyes distant, far from her troubles.

Macy wondered if a piece of her soul had left with Liz's, there in the wooded glade near the pit where the others rested, the trees in attendance whispering epitaphs.

She pulled Brooks and Ben from the pit and added both pieces of the fallen Wolf King. She burned the fleshy lot. Clothes melted away, skin seared to a midnight black, and flesh fell from bones. For a deity as renowned as he was, Desmond burned like any one of his followers. Soon, he was a pile of ash. She hoped his brothers would thank her from the grave.

She buried Liz, Brooks and Ben beneath an American Larch. Every shovel's worth of soil weighed hundreds of pounds. Her arms were fit to snap. Before long, only a loose stretch marked their final resting place. She'd remember the spot and visit it often. Though she'd never be able to properly thank them for what they'd done, Macy would hold them close forever.

For a victory, this was tart. She pounded the shovel onto the grave, and its head jettisoned outward, chipping away at the bark of an Eastern Hemlock.

She poured herself a gin and tonic at Carter's bar and sipped it slow. She wasn't marking time, but she guessed about an hour passed before Ryan's soft voice found her.

"May we join you?" Even with her senses sharpened, Ryan had crept up on her without revealing his presence. She had a lot to learn.

He circled the bar with Doyle on his tail. They fixed their own spirits and flanked her when they sat—Ryan to her left and Doyle to her right. For a while, no one spoke. Sipping and reflecting, a loaded silence. He scanned her red eyes and newfound aura. She let the piney taste of the juniper clutch her throat on the way down.

It was Macy who finally broke the silence when her glass was empty. "He went quick…didn't suffer. If anything, he looked to be enjoying himself."

Ryan seemed to find comfort in this detail. His posture settled. He stayed that way for what felt like minutes. Then he found her eyes again. "You did well." His praise was short, but Macy accepted it. She was happy to keep her head.

Macy filled them in on the particulars, a sum for Doyle to process, but he swallowed the news with a gulp of his brandy.

"That's too bad about Wiz. God rest her." He tipped his glass to her. "I underestimated you, wolf girl. I certainly won't mourn the royal cunt's passing." He shot a glance to Ryan. "Sorry."

"It's what we came a ways to do. You spared me the burden." Ryan seemed melancholic. Though his brother had wronged him, Desmond's death wasn't sitting well.

Macy considered their options. "What's the move, now?"

Ryan exhaled, setting elbows on the bar top. "I'm grateful for your work, here. And now you are…what you are, you won't have to worry about a cure any longer. I'm not sure what it is you've become. I came to rid the world of red-eyed beasts. Instead I've gained another."

Her gut grew heavy. *Another fight, then, before I'm free?*

He studied the apprehension on Macy's face. "Don't worry. You haven't done enough to deserve killing, but you've complicated things." He spun on his stool to face her directly. "Join us on our trek north. I've matters to settle there. Then we'll figure out what this means…" He pointed to her eyes. "And what should be done with you."

*What choice do you have?*

Macy nodded. "I have some things of my own to settle first."

Macy sat on the bench where it all began for her.

"The food here tastes like a sweaty pair of balls." Her father's voice had more flavor to it than she'd ever remembered, even through the phone.

"I'm sure you'd know."

"Ha…"

Speaking with him warmed her to the bone, despite the night's chill.

"What you been up to, girlie?"

*Taking the heads of Kings.* "Nothin' to report. Any word on when they'll cut you loose?"

"It's looking like a few weeks before they'll even consider it."

Macy was relieved. The longer he stayed tucked away from his problem, the better.

"This is fuckin' embarrassing."

"Look, if you're better when they let you out, it's worth it. No one's judging. I've had just about the strangest few weeks of my life."

Her father paused before continuing. She could hear a nurse yelling in the background. "You'll have to fill me in."

"Sometime. Sure."

Another pause from him. He was prepping a spot of painful honesty. "Look, I've been a shit dad for a little while. I know you're not one for excuses, so I'll spare ya. You needed me…especially these last couple years. I…I was supposed to be there…"

"Dad…"

"Nah, it's…I'm gonna be there. Soon as I'm out of Shawshank, I'm me again. I love you, you little turd."

She let his words linger. He'd never know how healing they were, how sweetly they'd eased her torment. "I guess it takes being lost to really find yourself."

"Damn straight…"

At a nearby house, a weeping woman would open her door to find a box of tapes, each with songs more soothing than the last.

Macy slipped the helmet over her head, and its visor darkened the night. Her muscle memory kicked in straight away. She was finally home.

*Meet the Ninja, Liz…the only thing keeps me sane.* A quick trip to Doylestown and she'd bought the bike back for more than a new one would've cost using the stacks she'd taken from Carter's. She'd never hear it from her, but she knew her friend would be proud.

She revved the engine, and it kicked up a bluster.

*What choice do you have?*

She held Sarah's face in her mind's eye. No longer was it purple, but a soft pink—the color it ought to be. It had a home there, next to Liz's and Cameron's and Ben's. The faces would stay with her to help her focus, not hinder it.

As Macy throttled toward Vermont with the Ninja tucked tightly between her legs, she stared ahead, wondering about her fate.

Her ruby eyes split the thick black dark.

# EPILOGUE

The red-eyed man stood at the precipice of his journey. An anomaly had arisen, perhaps altering his objective altogether. He pondered the girl's role in this—wondered if it was fate or an accident that had gifted her the power of his fallen family.

*Can you see it, Daniel?*

What would his older brother have made of this? Or his father, for that matter?

The girl ripped her throttle and took off into the night. He followed at a subtle distance. His friend snored beside him, near-ignorant of the monumental event that had unfolded in Pennsylvania.

*If the power can be transferred through death, what were any of us really worth?*

When he crossed the sea, he was sure his travels would end with his own demise, the extinction of his kind. With every swell of the North Atlantic, he thought of his death. How best could he make it painless? Where would his soul land when he entered the void?

As he watched the single taillight of the girl's bike taper toward Vermont, a thought brushed him like an icy evening chill. He wondered if perhaps his work was unfinished—if a deeper darkness awaited him before the end.

# ACKNOWLEDGMENTS

This book was a long deadly hunt through the woods. It began not as a book, but as a screenplay treatment that I was toying with back in 2014. It was rough, to say the least. Vulgar for vulgarity's sake. It screamed, "Look how edgy I can be!" It went through dozens of iterations over the years and, ironically, it took a pack to sharpen it to the novel you have in your hands. Or…on your screen. Or in your ears.

I'd first like to thank Kristen Gilligan, who took a huge chance on me, as well as an insane risk starting her own publishing company, Left Field Publishing. Without her, this book simply would not be. The work she put in and the connections she made were invaluable and I am eternally grateful to her dedication to the art and to the craft.

I want to thank Len Vlahos, author of many young adult novels like *The Scar Boys*, *Life in a Fishbowl* and *The Story of Oog*. He was one of the first readers of *The Crimson Traveler* back when it was called *Howlers* and offered advice and guidance for the journey this book would take.

I want to give an enormous shout out to my developmental editor, Jeff Hart. He's a surgeon. He pinpointed the things that were bothering me about the novel that I couldn't quite articulate and offered brilliant insight on how to fix them. I always say that first drafts are like hauling a chunk of marble up a flight of steps and rewriting is taking a chisel and carving the statue. Jeff Hart helped me carve this statue.

A heartfelt thank you to anyone who worked on this book and helped make it better. My copyeditor, Cameron Berry. My proofreader, Grace DiChristina. My beta readers, Deborah Almassy, Robert Almassy, Cynthia Almassy McGuigan and the late Carolyn McGill Almassy. Without you all, this would be a trashed file on my laptop and a lingering 'what if'.

I want to thank my father, Joe Strollo, who grew up in Kensington before the drugs infested the neighborhood. He later policed those same streets. His insights helped me keep aspects of the story authentic.

Finally, I want to thank my wonderful wife, Priya, for standing by me while this story had my brain in a vice. Her love and support helped me keep my sanity (except on full moons).

# ABOUT THE AUTHOR

Born and raised in Northeast Philadelphia, Matt graduated from Drexel University's School of Screenwriting and Playwriting. He was working for the Philadelphia School District when he began exploring his creative interests writing his own songs and playing drums and guitar in local bands. In 2015, Matt trained and coached for NBC's American Ninja Warrior and was a national finalist on the television show. He has since continued his career at the Philadelphia School District as a certified high school English as a Second Language teacher. Matt has been greatly influenced by a number of fantasy and horror authors including J.R.R. TOLKIEN, GEORGE R.R. MARTIN, PATRICK ROTHFUSS, WILLIAM PETER BLATTY, and STEPHEN KING. Matt lives in the suburbs of Philly with his wife.

# THE CRIMSON TRAVELER PLAYLIST

On Spotify

# SIGNATURE DRINKS

## THE CRIMSON TRAVELER

ALCOHOLIC

**A dark, smoky cocktail with a deep red hue—part blood moon, part dive-bar survival.**

The crimson color echoes the wolf imagery and blood motifs.
Mezcal adds a smoky, feral edge fitting the darker tone.
Bourbon grounds it in the American setting of Philadelphia and Pennsylvania.

### INGREDIENTS

1.5 oz bourbon
0.5 oz mezcal (for smoky "wolf" edge)
0.75 oz blood orange juice
0.5 oz pomegranate juice
0.25 oz maple syrup
2 dashes Angostura bitters

### INSTRUCTIONS

Fill shaker with ice.
Add all ingredients and shake hard.
Strain into a rocks glass with a large ice cube.
Garnish with a charred orange peel.

## PEDRO'S MOONLIGHT FIZZ

NON ALCOHOLIC

**Named after Liz's loyal pit bull Pedro, who repeatedly brings her back from the brink.**

Bright, sharp, and restorative. Tart, slightly wild, refreshing after heavy themes.

### INGREDIENTS

3 oz cranberry juice
2 oz fresh lime juice
1 oz honey or agave
2 oz ginger beer
Sparkling water to top

### INSTRUCTIONS

Stir cranberry, lime, and honey over ice.
Add ginger beer.
Top with sparkling water.
Garnish with lime wheel + rosemary sprig.

# DISCUSSION QUESTIONS

1. Liz begins the story as a former Marine living with addiction while trying to survive on the streets of Philadelphia. *What do you think the story suggests about how different parts of a person's identity—who they were and who they have become—continue to shape them?*

2. When Liz realizes that her body is healing from injuries that should have killed her, she has to decide whether to ignore what's happening or confront it. *What does this moment reveal about how people respond when reality suddenly stops making sense?*

3. Throughout the novel, ordinary people gradually discover that powerful forces are operating just beneath the surface of everyday life. *What might the story suggest about how much of the world's power structures remain hidden from those living within them?*

4. Throughout the story, Liz often relies on the instincts and training she developed in the Marine Corps. *How do past experiences, especially difficult or intense ones, continue to influence how people react to new challenges?*

5. Macy's memories of her sister's death continue to influence how she sees the world. *In what ways can grief shape how someone interprets danger, responsibility, or the choices they make?*

6. When Macy begins researching what might be happening to her, she finds rumors and stories that are difficult to believe but hard to ignore. *What does the story suggest about how people search for understanding when they encounter something they cannot easily explain?*

7. Liz and Macy both find themselves drawn into situations they did not choose and do not fully understand. *What does the story reveal about the different ways people respond when their lives suddenly move beyond their control?*

8. The wolves in the story live within a hierarchy that comes with both power and danger. *What larger ideas about power, loyalty, and belonging does this structure raise?*

9. Several characters in the novel carry deep guilt about past choices or actions. *What role does guilt appear to play in shaping how people see themselves and the direction their lives take?*

10. By the end of the book, the characters are only beginning to understand the larger world they've become part of. *What questions about identity, responsibility, or control does this new reality raise for them?*

# QUIZ

# WHICH WOLF ARE YOU?

1. **Someone betrays you. What do you do?**

   A. Cut them out of your life immediately.
   B. Wait. Watch. Revenge later.
   C. Confront them head-on.
   D. Try to understand why they did it.

2. **Your biggest strength is:**

   A. Leadership
   B. Intelligence
   C. Survival instinct
   D. Loyalty

3. **It's midnight and you're out alone. What feels most natural?**

   A. Running through the woods under the moon
   B. Watching everything from the shadows
   C. Hunting something, anything
   D. Protecting someone beside you

4. **Your friends would describe you as:**

   A. Intense
   B. Calculated
   C. Fearless
   D. Protective

5. **If you had to choose, which matters most?**

   A. Power
   B. Knowledge
   C. Freedom
   D. Family

6. **Your ideal environment:**

   A. A throne room or command center
   B. A hidden lair where you observe everything
   C. Open wilderness
   D. Somewhere safe with people you love

# ANSWERS!

## Your Wolf

**Mostly A:** THE ALPHA

You're a natural leader. People follow you even when you don't ask them to. You're decisive, commanding, and sometimes intimidating.

STRENGTH: Leadership
WEAKNESS: Control

**Mostly B:** THE SHADOW WOLF

You're a strategist. You see patterns others miss and prefer to operate quietly.

STRENGTH: Intelligence
WEAKNESS: Isolation

**Mostly C:** THE LONE WOLF

You're a wild spirit. Rules don't interest you much.

STRENGTH: Independence
WEAKNESS: Recklessness

**Mostly D:** THE GUARDIAN WOLF

You are loyal to the core.
You'd protect your pack at any cost.

STRENGTH: Loyalty
WEAKNESS: Self-sacrifice

# ABOUT THE PUBLISHER

LEFT FIELD PUBLISHING–where creativity meets collaboration. We're a forward-thinking publishing company created to combine the best attributes of traditional publishing with the best attributes of independent publishing. We exist to help authors bring their work to market in a cost-effective way while allowing them to retain control over their writing projects.

***Our vision is to reimagine what publishing can be—bold, collaborative, and purpose-driven—by amplifying genre-defying voices across fiction, non-fiction, YA and kids books. Because great books aren't defined by a category.***

**Visit us at www.Left-Field-Publishing.com.**

**Connect with us!**

Facebook: /leftfieldpublishing
Instagram: @leftfieldpublishing
TikTok: leftfieldpublishing
YouTube: @LeftFieldPublishing-m4g
LinkedIn: Left Field Publishing

EXPLORING UNCHARTED CREATIVITY
LEFT FIELD
PUBLISHING
EST 2024
LITTLETON . COLORADO

WEBSITE